The Secret Life of Nature

The Secret Life of Nature

*Living in Harmony
with the Hidden World of Nature Spirits,
from Fairies to Quarks*

PETER TOMPKINS

RUPA

Published by
Rupa Publications India Pvt. Ltd 2009
7/16, Ansari Road, Daryaganj
New Delhi 110002

Sales centres:
Allahabad Bengaluru Chennai
Hyderabad Jaipur Kathmandu
Kolkata Mumbai

ISBN: 978-81-291-1444-0

Fifth impression 2019

10 9 8 7 6 5

Contents

There slumbers in every human being faculties
by means of which he can acquire for himself
a knowledge of higher worlds.

Rudolf Steiner

Preface

Researching for *The Secret Life of Plants* in the 1970s, I accumulated some extraordinary material on nature spirits, but the book was already too long and—said my publisher—too "far out." Better not strain credulity.

Years passed, more material accumulated, and in the late 1980s I found a way to include a chapter in the appendix to *Secrets of the Soil*. That chapter, "Three Quarks for Muster Mark," in which I observed that theosophists as effective clairvoyants could match and even improve on the efforts of particle physicists, was to change my whole approach to the world of nature spirits and to Nature.

In that chapter I recount how, at the end of the last century, theosophists Annie Besant and Charles Leadbeater described in a book called *Occult Chemistry* the physical makeup of every then-known chemical element, including some isotopes not yet discovered. This extraordinary feat they claimed to have accomplished by means of intensive yoga training in India under expert guidance, which provided them with the faculty known in the extensive literature of Indian yoga as *siddhi*. This psychic power allows yogis to develop an inner organ of perception that enables them to attune their vision to microscopic levels.

The two theosophists' feat was carried out partly in Europe and partly in India. Charles Leadbeater, lying prone under the ministrations of a masseur, would psychically visualize the interior of the various atoms, while Annie Besant, sitting cross-legged on a rug with a pad in her lap, would sketch the inner makeup of all the then-known elements, one by one.

The impact on the world of the resulting extraordinary opus was minimal. When *Occult Chemistry* was first published in 1895, scientists rejected its amazing revelations as pure fantasy. Almost a century was to pass until the mid-1980s, when an English authority on particle physics, Dr. Stephen M. Phillips, browsing for rare books in Los Angeles, happened to run across a copy of an old theosophical book, Kingsland's *Physics of the Secret Doctrine;* it contained a few of the *Occult Chemistry* diagrams.

Back in England, Phillips, his curiosity aroused, found a copy of the third edition of *Occult Chemistry* and, as he puts it, "was hooked." Armed with the advantage of the most recent theories in particle physics, Phillips was quickly convinced by the accuracy of the diagrams with which Besant and Leadbeater had illustrated their book. With uncanny detail, they had described every element known in their time—from hydrogen to uranium, including several isotopes as yet unknown—each with its correct number of what today are named quarks, particles discovered well after the death of Besant and Leadbeater, and subquarks, the subject of today's intense inquiry. But more of this later.

Not until the end of the 1970s were particle physicists able to postulate the existence of six different kinds of quarks—to which they gave the facetious names of up, down, charm, strange, top, and bottom—along with their corresponding antiquarks. The theosophists had gone further, clearly depicting subquarks, the next smaller particles of matter so strenuously being researched by modern physicists with their supercolliding smashers of atoms.

Stephen Phillips's summary of the theosophists' feat posed a challenge to the world of physics when he declared, "The new patterns derived by application of the rules of theoretical physics tally perfectly with the diagrams which illustrate *Occult Chemistry.*"

My own deduction seemed equally provocative. If Besant and Leadbeater, using their yogic powers, could accurately describe matter down to its ultimate physical particles, what of their equally detailed descriptions of the Third Kingdom, the realm of nature spirits? If the two theosophists could describe unseeable quarks, why not pay attention to their equally detailed description of another whole world equally unseen by most of us but perfectly real to sensitives from Paracelsus to Blavatsky, from John Dee to Rudolf Steiner, depicted by every race on earth—a world of gnomes and nymphs, of sylphs and salamanders?

Such an approach might provide data as surprising as was accumulated in *The Secret Life of Plants,* perhaps even more so. Might not the mystery of plant growth—from the strange and beautiful specimens of the Amazon to the common buttercup or daisy—be better explained by the tender care of invisible nature spirits as described by clairvoyant theosophists than by the impersonal formulae of mathematics or the sourceless promptings of gene and DNA?

While Rudolf Steiner, the Austrian clairvoyant, perhaps the greatest philosopher of the century, developer of anthroposophy from theosophy, was declaring that the elements—from hydrogen all the way up the scale—could be consciously motivated by intelligence, Besant and Leadbeater were pursuing their ultimate physical atom into the "astral" land of fairy. Why not follow in their footsteps?

What had so far cooled my enthusiasm for fairy dowsing were the bowdlerized tales of the Brothers Grimm and the saccharine pedantry of the fairy world of Disney. Surely a truer, more brilliant, more vivifying world of nature spirits must be clamoring to be verified.

Twenty years ago when I first thought of researching that world, Sir George Trevelyan, British sponsor of that extraordinary educational device, an ambulant university, the Wreakin Trust, told me at Findhorn if I wished to know about fairies I must study the occult world of Rudolf Steiner. It has taken me so long because there are 490 books on or by Steiner in the Library of Congress.

To Steiner, it is only occult knowledge, virtually what was taught in the mystery schools of antiquity, that can lead to knowledge of the world from which our world is derived and can lead to the world of fairy. Nor is such knowledge obtainable by means of our ordinary faculties; it is only obtainable clairvoyantly or "outside" the body, by means "that lie hidden in the soul, like a seed in the earth." The resulting data, "the single, undivided property of all mankind," does not, says Steiner, admit of differing interpretations any more than does mathematics.

Then came the world of shamanism and more research. As occultism and shamanism are twin forks of one primordial wisdom heritage, I found the shamanic legacy on nature spirits agreeing almost completely with that of the occultist. The great German anthropologist Gerardo Reichel Dolmatoff, expert on South American Indians,

The Secret Life of Nature

has compiled a bibliography of almost a thousand books and papers written by professional academics on various facets of shamanism around the globe, dealing with such occult lore as out-of-body travel, forests teeming with spirits, and the healing power of plants. Were shamans not gifted with some supernaturally subtle clairvoyant view of nature, especially of the curative properties of particular plants among the scores of deadly poisonous ones, the forest would surely be strewn with the corpses of the experimenters. Shamans must be seeing something in some other dimension.

But whereas the integrity of the shamanic tradition, once laughed at as primitive fantasy, has been revalued in recent years and much of what it has to say about the spiritual dimension underlying and upholding the physical dimension is being taken seriously by specialists in fields from psychology to physics, the occult side of the primordial wisdom tradition, though in many ways more comprehensive than the shamanic and more understandable to a modern Western temperament, is deliberately ignored. Why?

It is ignored largely because of the false and unnecessary stigmas attached by an ignorant or ossified establishment to occult authors such as Leadbeater, Besant, Blavatsky, Steiner. These stigmas fester for the most part because the writings of these authors are simply too "far out." All were subjected to the standard vituperation of the Victorian era, as often as not salaciously sexual. Besant, a suffragette and political activist for women's rights, considered by Bernard Shaw the greatest orator of her time, was pilloried, not for her political ideas, but for having too explicitly explained to poor women the mechanics of contraception. Imprisoned in the Old Bailey as a pornographer, she was the first woman in Britain to defend herself in court and to obtain acquittal. But her daughter was torn from her by the Lord Chancellor on the grounds that as a freethinker she was unfit to be a mother. Leadbeater, anticipating Wilhelm Reich's revolutionary insight into sexual frustration and the compulsive violence, sadism, and war that it engenders, was ostracized, accused of "molesting" small boys when he suggested masturbation as a healthier relief than violence. Blavatsky's reputation was destroyed by a sting operation mounted by the British Society for

Psychic Research, which falsely accused her of lying and of faking the supernatural. Steiner had his extraordinarily aesthetic anthroposophical headquarters in Dornach, Switzerland—its details personally designed, carved, and hand-painted by Steiner under the guidance of spiritual insight—burned to the ground, they say, by a Catholic priest who was jealous of the brilliance of Steiner's exegesis of Christian doctrine.

What their opponents had against these pioneers of the occult was their effort to make comprehensible to the West the ancient wisdom of the East, an endeavor that threatened, and still threatens, to shatter established beliefs and the careers that rest upon them.

But now that the shamanic side of the nature spirit story is duly being accepted for its surprising integrity and coherence, is it not time to put aside residual skepticism about the occult tradition?

Although I approach the subject as a reporter, relaying extraordinary information described by clairvoyants—data that sometimes does indeed defy credulity—in the end I find their evidence so compelling and so rational that even though not myself clairvoyant, I now tend to subscribe to their conviction that to resolve the evils and problems of this world we must all learn to commune with the world of nature spirits and the angelic hierarchies from which they derive. To achieve this goal, Rudolf Steiner mapped out, by the early 1920s, the required steps for a modern initiation into the wisdom of the ancient mysteries, an initiation in essence identical with those found in the shamanic tradition. But even if one does not reach that exalted goal in this life, access to the information inevitably changes one's approach to living. It has changed mine radically.

Walking through the woods, I do not see the spirits, but I sense them all around me, and I no longer feel alone. My communion with plants, no longer metaphorical, is actual as I consciously breathe in life from their leaves and return the gift transmuted by my lungs, aware that sylph and undine have transmuted those leaves from sunlight. I feel *chez moi*, at home in the world, and apply the lessons imparted by Merlin to young King Arthur as taught me by my English master, T. H. White, when I was a boy at school: *Be* that pike! *Be* that hawk! *Be* that oak!

All of nature assumes a magical vesture. Like Aleister Crowley, I swim in nature like a fish in the sea, and nature swims in me like the sea in a fish! Even ticks, fleas, lice, and mosquitoes find an explanation when attributed to the plethora of noxious thoughts produced by humans. No longer do I rail at the inanities, inadequacies, and injustices of a totally corrupt politico-scientific establishment; I am more sanguine now, certain that they, too, will mend their ways. Instead of recoiling at the sight of some physically or spiritually distasteful person, I now rejoice that but for some angelic grace that person could be me and in some distant way is me. And it is sobering to realize that nothing one does, says, or thinks can escape the scrutiny of a vast and friendly audience—eyes wide, staring in wonder from the underbrush—only waiting to applaud the least sign of an upright, noble, or loving gesture.

Readers from all around the globe still write me that *The Secret Life of Plants* radically changed their way of looking at nature and their way of living. This book, I hope, may do the same, or more.

CHAPTER

I

Ingenious Hoax?

In 1920 Sir Arthur Conan Doyle, creator of that stereotype of fictional detectives, Sherlock Holmes, got himself involved in a real-life detective story, perhaps the least stereotypic of the century and the most puzzling to him: the world of fairy. Incidents surrounding this inquiry represented to him "either the most elaborate and ingenious hoax ever played upon the public, or else . . . an event in human history which may in the future appear to have been epochmaking in its character."

A convinced spiritualist and writer on spiritualism, Doyle, then in his sixties, at the height of his popularity as novelist and playwright, had become involved in this particular quest as the result of a story he had agreed to write for the *Strand Magazine,* an illustrated English monthly, dealing with the subject of human beings in different parts of England, Scotland, Wales, and Ireland who claimed to be able to see and describe the "little people." These were insubstantial creatures of a fairy world about whom Doyle had accumulated "a surprising number of cases."

The article was to be a straight piece of reporting. "The evidence," wrote Doyle, "was so complete and detailed, with such good names attached to it, that it was difficult to believe that it was false."

As justification for wandering into so fey a world of fancy, Doyle pointed out that in the rational world of physics we see objects only within the very limited band of frequencies that make up our color spectrum, whereas infinite vibrations, unseen by most humans, exist on either side of them. "If we could conceive a race of beings constructed in material which threw out shorter or longer vibrations," wrote Doyle, "they would be invisible unless we could tune ourselves up, or tune them down."

As Doyle put it, "If high-tension electricity can be converted by a mechanical contrivance into a lower tension, keyed to other uses, then it is hard to see why something analogous might not occur with the vibrations of ether and the waves of light."

With this statement Doyle's contemporaries, Thomas Edison and Nikola Tesla, magnates of the electrical, would hardly have disagreed: both were actively working on devices to communicate with, and, if possible, photograph spirits of the departed and spirits of the fairy world.

Basic to theosophical reasoning was the contention, founded on millennia of Eastern wisdom and protracted occult investigation, that one's physical body consists of matter in seven different states: solid, liquid, gaseous, and four subtler "etheric" grades, all interpenetrating. Furthermore, one's immortal self was seen as employing seven distinct bodies made up of progressively finer wavelengths, also interpenetrating, which allow the individual to operate on several planes of existence: physical, etheric, astral, mental, and higher.

What had shattered Doyle's philosophic complacency was a letter he received June 21, 1920, containing two of the most extraordinary photographs he had ever seen. One depicted a young English girl delicately touching hands with a dancing gnome; the other showed the face of a younger girl observing a group of what appeared to be wood elves dancing in a ring.

At first sight the prints appeared to Doyle to be some clever photographic trick, with every indication of being out-and-out fakes, "a scandalous hoax" that Doyle, donning his Holmesian fore-and-aft, determined to shatter.

The woman who had sent Doyle the photos said she had obtained them from her cousin, Edward L. Gardner, president of the Blavatsky Lodge, a leading branch of the Theosophical Society in England. Gardner, whom she described as "a solid person, with a reputation for sanity and character," had used the photos to illustrate a theosophical lecture on the "etheric and astral levels of life."[1]

---

1. The Theosophical Society, founded in New York in 1875 under the auspices of Helena P. Blavatsky, was dedicated to "the study and elucidation of occultism, to vindicate the preeminent importance of Eastern religions, and to explore the hidden mysteries of nature and the powers hidden inside the physical human."

Doyle promptly wrote to Gardner explaining his interest, emphasizing how essential it was for the facts to be given the public. He suggested that an independent investigation be launched before it was too late. Could he (Doyle) examine the original negatives from which the prints had been made?

Gardner wrote back that he was willing to be of assistance in any way possible, that he had obtained the original plates and had already submitted them for careful professional examination to "two first class photographic experts, one in Harrow and one in London."

The first had declared the plates to be perfectly genuine and unfaked but inexplicable. The second, who had already been instrumental in exposing several "psychic" fakes, had also been entirely satisfied they were unfaked negative plates.

Gardner explained that when he had cycled over to Harrow to see the first photographer, a Mr. Snelling at 26 The Bridge, Wealdsone, the photographer had exclaimed in amazement: "This is the most extraordinary thing I've ever seen! Single exposure! Figures have moved. Why, it's a genuine photograph! Wherever did it come from?"

Gardner added that Mr. Snelling was an expert who for over thirty years had worked with a large photographic firm, Illingsworth, where he had turned out "beautiful work in natural and artificial studio studies."

Snelling, described by Gardner as an untidy little man with unruly hair and large staring eyes whose fingers were habitually stained with photographic chemicals, also corroborated: the two negatives were entirely genuine, unfaked photographs of single exposures taken outdoors. He pointed out that it would be very easy for him to detect any double exposure, and he laughed at the idea that any expert in England could deceive him with a faked photograph. While revealing movement in the fairy figures, the negatives, said Snelling, showed no trace whatever of studio work involving card or paper models, dark backgrounds, painted figures, or any other attempt at subterfuge. "In my opinion both are straight, untouched pictures."

The letter spurred Doyle to go to London to meet Edward Gardner, a handsome man some ten years his junior, sporting a colorful bow tie, whom he characterized as "quiet, well balanced, and reserved, not in the least a wild visionary type."

Gardner, impressed by Doyle's size and military manner, showed him the two negative plates plus some extraordinary enlargements of the photos that Doyle found "superlatively beautiful. . . . The exquisite grace of the flying fairy baffled description."

Doyle promptly took the plates to the Kodak Company offices in Kingsway, where he saw a Mr. West and another expert of the company. After careful examination, both could find no evidence of trickery or superimposition.

The possibility that photographs of fairies could actually have been taken in the north of England "under circumstances which seemed to put fraud out of the question" appeared to Doyle to be no less momentous than Columbus's reputed discovery of a New World.

It was clear to Doyle that if the photographs and the manner in which they were obtained could be made to hold their own against criticism, they were bound to excite considerable attention. "It would be no exaggeration to say that they will mark an epoch in human thought."

At lunch at his club, the Athenaeum, Doyle showed the prints to his friend and well-known physicist, Sir Oliver Lodge, whose opinion in psychic matters he respected. As a member of the British Society for Psychical Research together with Sir William Crookes, inventor of a tube for demonstrating cathode rays, forerunner of the television screen, Lodge and other leading scientists had become interested in phenomena of what was termed the "etheric world."

The four levels of etheric matter, finer than solid, liquid, and gaseous, were labeled by theosophist Charles Leadbeater as E_1, E_2, E_3, and E_4, the last being the most subtle.

"I can still see his [Lodge's] astonished and interested face," wrote Doyle, "as he gazed at the pictures in the hall of the Athenaeum Club."

As a first step toward possible authentication of the photographs, it was agreed that Gardner visit the girls' parents in Yorkshire, Mr. and Mrs. Eddie Wright, on whose property the exposures were reputed to have been made.

In mid-July of 1921, Gardner duly took a train to Bradford, a large industrial center in a valley of the Aire at the foothills of the English Pennines, traveling with what he called "an open mind."

It was a lovely summer afternoon when Gardner reached the town of Bradford, where he took a tram to the village of Cottingley, a picturesque Old World spot half concealed in a break in the upland. On the outskirts of the village, Gardner found the Wright cottage at 31 Lynwood Terrace. Mrs. Wright, a cheerful woman in her forties, known as Polly, greeted Gardner and introduced him to her daughter Elsie, a pretty girl of sixteen, tall, slim, with a wealth of auburn hair clasped in a narrow gold band.

Pending the return of Mr. Wright from work, mother and daughter entertained Gardner with the story of how the photographs had been taken.

Three years earlier, in July of 1917, just as Elsie was turning thirteen, her ten-year-old cousin, Frances Griffiths, had come on a visit from South Africa. Together the girls spent much of their time in the glen at the back of the cottage where Elsie claimed to have seen and played with, ever since she was a child, all sorts of fairies, elves, gnomes, and other denizens of the woods.

Mrs. Wright admitted that she had taken little notice of what the children had told her about fairies, attributing the stories to mere fancy or imagination, but one Saturday at lunch Elsie had asked if she could borrow her father's camera to prove that the fairies really existed.

At this point in Mrs. Wright's narrative, Mr. Wright came home from his job as manager of a small nearby estate. Described by Gardner as "a hearty Yorkshire type, of forthright speech and character with a sense of humor and cheerful disposition," Mr. Wright sat down to tea and laughingly explained that at first he had refused to let the girls have the camera, a Midge quarter-plate given to him by a relative, because he "didn't want the girls spoiling my plates." But the girls had been so persistent he finally put a single plate in the box camera and showed Elsie how to trigger a snapshot.

In less than an hour the girls had returned and begged him to develop the plate because they "had taken a photograph."

Mr. Wright explained that he took the plate to the scullery cupboard where he did his developing, and with Elsie wedged beside him put the plate into a dish, fully expecting only a blur. Instead he was startled to see, almost at once, dark figures that he took to be swans.

When Elsie saw them she called out to Frances, "The fairies are on the plate!"

Frances, outside the door, skipped up and down and squealed with delight.

A sun print developed by Mr. Wright caused him no little amazement, and though nothing he could say would induce the children to give any other explanation than that they had indeed photographed fairies, Wright remained convinced that the figures appearing on the print must have been made of paper or some such substance.

Wright assured Gardner that he had been to the glen to search for scraps of paper and that he and his wife had ransacked the girls' bedroom when they were out but could find no evidence of trickery. A month later Elsie had taken another picture, which showed a fairy about ten inches tall leaping up close to Frances's face.

Gardner, seeking a chance to cross-examine Elsie, asked if she would show him the site where the photographs had been taken.

Behind the cottage, its cultivated garden bordered a glen of wild foliage where a small stream known as "the beck" tumbled through a little valley on its way to the river Aire, less than a mile away. As Elsie led the way, she informed Gardner she had no power of any sort over the action of the fairies, that the only way to "'tice" them was to sit passively with her mind quietly tuned in their direction. If faint stirrings or movements in the distance heralded their presence, she would beckon to the fairies to indicate they were welcome. Elsie added that if there was not too much rustling in the woods it was possible to hear the faint and high sound of pipes.

Gardner found a spot that was unquestionably the same as in one of the photographs and noticed several large toadstools on the bank of the stream, two of which he picked to take home.

Elsie pointed out where she had knelt to take the picture of her friend Frances surrounded by a group of dancing fairies, reminding Gardner that she had seen and played with fairy creatures ever since she could remember.

Back at the cottage, Gardner tested Elsie's drawing ability and noticed that whereas she could easily sketch a landscape, the fairy figures she attempted in imitation of the ones she claimed to have seen were "uninspired, and bore no possible resemblance to those in the photograph."

When he suggested to Elsie's father that Sir Arthur Conan Doyle might want to make use of the photographs, Wright demurred, and when offered money he firmly declined, saying that if the photographs turned out to be genuine, they shouldn't be spoiled by lucre.

With some difficulty Gardner got Wright to agree to their being published, but only on condition that the family's name and that of the village be disguised.

In his report to Doyle, Gardner said he was impressed that the most probable motives for fraud, money and notoriety, were obviously absent. He said he was impressed by the sincerity and candor of the Wrights' testimony, which he considered unquestionably honest. He was satisfied that if there were any dishonorable or counterfeit intent behind the photographs, it was without their knowledge.

Satisfied on this crucial point, Doyle and Gardner agreed to publish the photographs with a story that appeared in the Christmas 1922 issue of *Strand Magazine*.

Realizing that an event such as "fairy photographs" would cause a small furor and that they would need additional supportive evidence as incontrovertible as possible, Gardner suggested that Elsie and Frances each be provided with a camera and two dozen plates with which to take more pictures.

Frances, who was then living in Scarborough, a traditional resort for the working classes on the northeast coast of England, was invited to spend part of her summer holidays at Cottingley with Elsie.

Gardner acquired two good Cameo cameras of the folding type that used single plates and had the factory at Illingsworth provide him with two dozen quarter-plates marked in such a way that only the factory manager and his technicians could recognize them when exposed.

On a second trip to Cottingley, Gardner gave the girls the cameras and showed them the simplest way to use them, advising them to go into the glen only on fine sunny days to "'tice" the fairies. He also suggested the most obvious and easy precautions concerning lighting and distance.

Gardner reported to Doyle that he found Frances to be mediumistic, explaining that by this he meant her "etheric" body contained "more loosely knit ectoplasm" than usual, "ectoplasm which the nature spirits could have used to densify their own normal bodies sufficiently to come into the field of the camera's range."[2]

Gardner said both girls were "good clairvoyants, quite unspoilt because unaware of it." He said they also had the advantage of being able to see only the "subtler physical region but nothing beyond, their extra sensory perception being strictly limited; hence there was very little confusion or distortion in the focus of their clairvoyance."

Gardener did not stay at Cottingley to try to witness any further fairy photography, explaining that he felt his presence might prevent anything appearing on the plates.

"The fact is," he admitted, "that the fairy life will not come out from the shrubs and plants unless the human visitor is of a sympathetic quality. Such a visitor needs to be not merely sympathetic in mentality, for that is of little use; he must have a warm emotional sympathy, child-like in its innocence and simplicity."

The girls encouragingly told Gardner they thought that within a couple of months he could get used to the fairies or, rather, they to him, but he modestly told them he doubted he could cultivate the necessary quality even in that length of time, which, in any case, he could not spare.

During August of 1921 it rained almost continuously throughout England. The girls, who knew the fairies would not appear in overcast weather, were able to get up to the glen for only an hour or so when the sun peeped out brightly, enabling them to take two shots, followed by one more.

The three plates were posted to Gardner with a candid disclaimer: "Afraid they are not very good, but two are fairly clear."

---

2. Ectoplasm is described by Webster as an external layer of protoplasm, the latter being regarded as "the only form of matter in which the phenomena of life are manifested." By occultists, ectoplasm is considered to be a temporarily extrudable component of the human body—amorphous, cloudlike, fleecy, vaporous, gray-white—densified into tangible form by the special and unconsciously exercised psychic abilities of certain rare people.

When developed, one clear photograph showed a fairy poised on a bush offering Elsie a flower. The other showed a fairy gaily leaping up in front of Frances's face. Elsie reported that the leaping fairy had jumped up several times in front of Frances but that when she took the snap it had jumped so near that Frances tossed her head back "to nearly spoil it all."

Of the third picture, Elsie explained that it had been a chance shot, taken among the grasses at the fringe of a pool near the beck where the girls had spotted movement in the grass. Hoping for the best, they had taken the snapshot of a "tallish figure."

This third photograph proved most interesting. It showed a dense mixture of grasses and harebells with intertwined fairy figures and faces, and Gardner recognized that its features could be extremely valuable for testing. It also showed a fairy bower, or arch of flowers, something rarely reported in the annals of fairy watching. Professed fairy watchers told Gardner the photo appeared to have caught the fairies indulging in a "fairy bath." This they described as a special co-coonlike restorative vessel used after lengthy spells of dull and misty weather.

Gardner immediately took the negatives back to the Illingsworth manager, who, upon careful examination, declared them to be from the plates delivered to Gardner. The manager added that he could not commit himself as to the authenticity of what had appeared on the first two plates, but about the third he was emphatic: "An impossibility to fake."

Extra-sized enlargements were made from the plates and subjected to rigorous analysis for any sign of paper, canvas, paint, or anything that could have been used to represent fairy figures. An exhaustive search was made with high magnification to see if any supporting thread could be distinguished to account for the leaping fairy. Nothing was found amiss.

With this new evidence, Gardner wrote again to Doyle: "It is not easy to convey the sense of integrity I felt at the end of the investigation: to share it properly one would have to meet the parents and the children as I did. Here I can only register my own personal conversion to the acceptance of the five photographs as genuine in every sense of the word. It took a great deal of time and concentrated attention to convince me, but I can claim that the inquiry was thorough."

Following publication of the article in the *Strand,* so many inquiries were made by an aroused public that the *Daily News & Westminster Gazette* commissioned one of its best reporters to search the county "to discover the truth in order to break the fraud."

Being a Yorkshireman himself, the reporter had the good sense to start out from Bradford. By following up each rumor he soon tracked down the Wright family in Cottingley, where he interviewed mother, father, and daughter, each separately. He then visited the glen sites to verify them against the photographs. He visited all photo labs in the district and consulted many other possible sources of information. Friends of the Wright family were particularly closely questioned. All to no avail. The reporter could find nothing even vaguely suspicious. Having found no flaws, he concluded his story: "In the end I very nearly believed in fairies."

2

Fate of the World

Interest generated by the fairy article was so great that Doyle and Gardner decided to institute an even more thorough search for answers. They wanted to see if they could establish just how the fairies could appear on a photographic plate, how it was that fairies existed in the glen, and how so extraordinary a phenomenon could be reconciled with modern physics.

Gardner's first move was to contact a friend with the gift of clairvoyance who claimed to be able to see fairies. Far from being a crackpot, the friend was a World War I officer in the British Tank Corps, Major Geoffrey Hodson, whom Doyle considered to be "an honorable gentleman with neither the will to deceive nor any conceivable object in doing so."

It occurred to Gardner that Hodson might be able to check on the statements about fairies made by the Cottingley girls and, with luck, obtain a further set of photographs.

Like Gardner, Hodson was a member of the Theosophical Society, a student of Buddhism, a practitioner of yoga, and a man who at first had regarded fairies as merely the products of the imagination. He had come to view them worthy of consideration thanks to an unexpected occult experience that had obliged him to change not only his views, but the tenor of his life. Hodson's first encounter with the world of fairy had come about in an unusual way. Seeking employment after the war, Hodson had settled in the industrial cotton-spinning town of Preston in Lancashire to organize a boys' club for the rehabilitation of youths discharged from correctional institutions.

Before buying a house in Preston, Hodson and his wife had rented rooms in an old manor house with a pleasant open fireplace in its large, comfortable drawing room. There, as Hodson recounted the story, his black-and-white fox terrier, Peter, would sit and stare into the fire, especially in winter. One day, for no apparent reason, Peter abandoned the fire in favor of a far corner of the room, where he sat staring fixedly into space. When the dog repeated this odd behavior for several consecutive evenings, Hodson decided to find an explanation. Sitting by Peter, "he quickened his clairvoyant faculty by the practice of Yoga."

The result was as unexpected to Hodson as it was to become formative of his future life. He described seeing a large, lavender-colored, luminous ovoid filled with small figures "in the traditional forms of brownies, elves, fairies, and the like."

Gradually, says Hodson, the ovoid opened outward to liberate the little creatures who "flew all about the room, some to settle on the picture rail, others on the architrave of the door, whilst one—who resembled the traditional brownies—strutted up and down the hearth rug to which Peter had returned."

Sensing a possible significance and even spiritual guidance in this strange adventure into fairyland, Hodson at once began to examine the little folk with more detailed care. As the visitations were repeated on a number of evenings, Hodson dictated his observations to his wife. The result was a considerably large manuscript, which opened a whole new world for the Hodsons. What had started as a purely personal pursuit of occult knowledge soon became responsible for completely changing the Hodsons' lives.

Captivated by their discovery, the Hodsons spent most of their spare time in the spring and summer of 1919 in the fields and woodlands of Lancashire. By motorcycle and sidecar they traveled through mountain and moorland, making detailed notes of the various types of fairies and nature spirits discovered in the countryside. Their dog, Peter, would accompany them on these expeditions, sitting quietly to watch the investigations.

It was thus that Hodson came to the attention of Gardner, who soon found a way to dragoon the tank major into assisting in the investigation of the Cottingley fairies. With great good humor, as Gardner put it, Hodson agreed to sacrifice his scanty August holiday in 1921 to go to Cottingley.

The weather that summer was bad on the whole, but it cleared enough on occasions for Hodson and the girls to walk in the glen or sit by the beck as Hodson took notes on what he and the girls could see. The whole glen, according to Hodson, was swarming with many forms of elemental life, including wood elves, gnomes, and goblins, with even the rarer undines floating on the stream.

Hodson would pick out a psychic object, point in its direction, and ask the girls for a description. He says that within the limits of their powers the girls' descriptions were correct but that their powers of clairvoyance were more limited than his.

On August 12, as all three sat on a fallen tree in a beech grove near Cottingley, Hodson observed the girls as they watched two tiny wood elves racing toward them. The elves, as Elsie described them, wore a tight one-piece skin, shiny as if wet; their hands and feet were disproportionately large, their legs thin, ears large and pointed, mouths wide and toothless. Pulling up short, the elves stared at the humans with evident amusement but no fear. Then, as Frances approached them, they withdrew, as if in alarm.

In a field Hodson and the girls spotted figures the size of gnomes, making weird faces and grotesque contortions. To Elsie these forms appeared singly, one dissolving into another. To Hodson's more powerful clairvoyance, the whole group was visible at once.

Hodson noted in his booklet, "Elsie sees a beautiful fairy quite near; it is nude, with golden hair, and is kneeling in the grass, looking this way with hands on knees, smiling at us. It has a very beautiful face, and is concentrating its gaze on me. This figure came within five feet of us, and after being described, faded away."

Hodson noted a group of female figures playing a game somewhat resembling the children's game of oranges-and-lemons, dancing in a ring "like the grand chain in Lancers." The result of the game appeared to be the formation of a vortex "which streamed upwards to an apparent distance of four or five feet above the ground; and in those parts of the field where the grass was thicker and darker there appeared to be a correspondingly extra activity among the fairy creatures."

In the beck itself, near a large rock, by a slight fall of the water, Hodson spotted a water sprite, entirely nude, which he described as of dazzling rosy whiteness, with a beautiful face and long hair, which it appeared to be passing through its fingers.

Two days later, August 14, at nine o'clock of a moonlit evening, the girls led Hodson to a field densely populated with brownies, fairies, elves, and gnomes. Hodson says Frances could see tiny fairies dancing in a circle, expanding their bodies to a height of eighteen inches, whereas Elsie could see fairies dancing in a vertical circle, floating slowly up and down before coming to rest on the grass. Hodson could see couples a foot high, females and males, clothed in etheric matter, ghostlike, dancing in a slow, waltzlike motion.

At ten o'clock the following evening, in a field lit by a small photographic lamp, Elsie described a group of goblins the size of brownies, differing from the wood elves, looking more like gnomes. Meanwhile, Hodson became involved with a band of fairies under a female director whose arrival in the field caused a bright radiance to shine around her, visible to the girls sixty yards away. Of the leader he noted, "She is very autocratic and definite in her orders, holding unquestioned command. They spread themselves out into a gradually widening circle around her, and, as they do so, a sort of glow spreads out over the grass. They are actually vivifying and stimulating the growth in the field."

Three days later, August 18, their last day of observation, Hodson recorded that in the glen Frances saw a fairy as big as herself, clothed in flesh-colored tights and a garment scalloped around her hips, with a lovely face whose expression seemed to invite Frances into fairyland. Another, with body clothed in iridescent shimmering golden light, hovering among the leaves and branches of a willow, smiled and placed a finger on her lips.

Hodson says that during his visit to Cottingley he became convinced of the bona fides of the girls as well as of the authenticity of the photographs they had taken. "I spent two weeks with them and their family, and became assured of the genuineness of their clairvoyance, of the presence of fairies, exactly like those photographed in the glen at Cottingley, and of the complete honesty of all parties concerned."

But when it came to taking more photographs, the girls were not so successful. Anxious to obtain more negatives, Gardner had provided the girls with plenty of fresh plates, but the girls had to admit, sadly, that although the nature spirits would "come out" and approach them, they retreated almost at once with a sort of gesture of dislike. As a reason for this failure, Hodson concluded that the nature spirits were no longer able to use Frances's aura to strengthen their own forms and thus failed to appear on the plates.

In a letter to Doyle, Gardner surmised that Frances's attainment of puberty—she was now fourteen—could be the reason for her failure to obtain new photographs. "Sufficiently dense material of a suitable nature was not to be had," wrote Gardner, "or rather, was unacceptable."

According to Gardner, in order to produce a visible photograph, the "associated aura" of the two girls was needed. Neither girl was apparently powerful enough to produce the required effect by herself. Gardner explained that it had evidently been a very delightful sensation for the nature spirits to take Frances's auric material, or ectoplasm, in order to densify their own bodies. "The fairies," said Gardner, "had probably done this often, before the camera was used at all. The tangible and concrete clarity of shape and outline obtained was evidently an enjoyable experience, resembling a stimulating bath. It was while using her aura that the forms came within the optical field of the camera, as they were then much denser than their normal structure."

Gardner believed that had anyone been near the girls at the time they successfully photographed the fairies, they, too, might have been able to see them dancing. Gardner further explained that the clairvoyance of both Elsie and Frances was altogether another matter from Frances's mediumistic qualities, and their viewing the fairies was due to the use of what he termed their "etheric eyes." He described the word *etheric* as denoting "a field of electromagnetic activity in which many bio-chemical transformations take place."

According to Gardner the girls could thus continue to see the fairies even when photography was no longer possible. "Everyone," said Gardner, "possesses these etheric eyes; they resemble concave disks behind and around the eyeball, something like a saucer-shade behind an electric bulb. The etheric discs endow the physical eyes with vitality and fire, but normally do not function independently. When etheric sight is exercised, about another octave of light, more or less, becomes consciously objective: this independent activity of the etheric eyes when it occurs may be under some control or none."

As for the objective existence of the fairy beings seen by the girls, Gardner insisted that "all that can be photographed must of necessity be physical. Nothing of a subtler order could, in the nature of things, affect the sensitive plate."

Gardner maintained that "spirit" photographs, such as those produced via mediums at seances where "extra" persons appear on the plate, necessarily imply a certain degree of materialization before the "form" can come within the range even of the most sensitive of films. However, he pointed out, well within our physical octave are degrees of density that elude ordinary vision. "Just as there are many stars in the heavens recorded by the camera that no human eye has ever seen directly, so there is a vast array of living creatures whose bodies are of that rare tenuity and subtlety from our point of view that they lie beyond the range of our normal senses. Many children and many sensitives see them: hence our fairy lore—all founded on actual and now demonstrated fact."

Gardner said fairies use bodies of a density that he would describe in nontechnical language as of a lighter-than-gaseous nature, but he added that it would be entirely wrong to consider them insubstantial. "In their own way they are as real as we are, and perform functions in connection with plant life of an important and fascinating character."

As a result of the Cottingley investigation, many clairvoyants attested to both Gardner and Doyle that they had seen all sorts of nature spirits tending to plants and vegetables, that grass and trees could everywhere be seen pulsing to the touch of tiny workers "whose magnetic bodies act as the matrix in which miracles of growth and color become possible."

Of the fairies photographed at Cottingley and of the nature spirits described by Hodson, Doyle wrote, "It is hard for the mind to grasp what the ultimate results may be if we have actually proved the existence upon the surface of this planet of a population which may be as numerous as the human race, which pursues its own strange life in its own strange way, and which is only separated from ourselves by some difference of vibrations."

Posing the question as to what connection this fairy lore might have with the general scheme of psychic philosophy, Doyle answered that though the connection might be slight and indirect, it would certainly widen our conception of the possible, shake us out of time-rutted lines of thought, and help us regain an elasticity of mind more open to new philosophies. "The fairy question is infinitely small and unimportant," said Doyle, "compared to the question of our own fate and that of the whole human race."

To Doyle there seemed to be but one eventual outcome. Assured by Hodson that "the angelic hosts are our fellow citizens on this planet and eagerly await our recognition" and that they "would not only respond, but hold sensible communion with us," Doyle was prepared to give full support to Hodson's contention that cooperation between the angelic beings and humans should and would play an important part in the development of a new race on earth.

Gardner echoed the sentiment: "As we cease to ignore the activities of the Devas and nature-spirits, and recognize their partial dependence on the human mentality and the amazing response forthcoming when recognition is given, we shall find many of our difficulties and problems solved for us and the world far more wonderful than anything we have yet conceived."

3

The Biggest Fairy Story

The first I heard of the Cottingley fairies was at Findhorn in 1973. E. L. Gardner had died in 1970, a centenarian, but I was directed to his son Leslie, then in his sixties, whom I found in a flower-surrounded cottage in the village of Hastings-on-Thames northeast of London.

From Leslie Gardner's cheerful greeting it was immediately clear that he believed implicitly in the authenticity of the photos taken by Elsie and Frances, and he promptly produced the original glass plates bequeathed to him by his father. A correspondence followed in which Gardner was meticulously helpful, providing me with further information, data that I planned to incorporate into *The Secret Life of Plants* along with interviews with Ogylvie Crombie, Dorothy McLean, and others who could describe the world of nature spirits from personal sensitive insight. When, to Gardner's distress, this material was excluded by the publisher, partly because of length and partly because it stretched the imagination, I received a long reprimand from Gardner with which he terminated our exchange.

Curious to tap Geoffrey Hodson's encyclopedic knowledge about nature spirits as well as to validate his insight into the astronomic and geodetic expertise of the ancient Aztecs and the Maya, about which I was writing another book, I traveled to New Zealand for a remarkable interview with Hodson, then living in Auckland. There was no question in his mind about the authenticity of the photographs taken by the girls at Cottingley.

And there the whole episode might have ended, fading peacefully into the mist of time, had not an enterprising English television producer, Lynn Lewis, alerted to the old fairy story by an obituary article on E. L. Gardner, gone in search of the Cottingley girls. Elsie, by then in her seventies, was tracked down to the Yorkshire Midlands, living comfortably in a semidetached house with a front garden, in excellent health, but reluctant to reopen the story about the fairies. While still in her twenties she had left Cottingley for America to marry a Scottish engineer, Frank Hill, with whom she had then lived in India for a quarter century before returning to England to retire.

She said she did not wish to revive the subject, afraid it might lead people to dabble further into occult phenomena, especially into such unhealthy aspects as spiritualism, Ouija boards, and amateur seances. "As for the photographs," Elsie added, "let's say they are pictures of figments of our imagination, Frances's and mine, and leave it at that."

Elsie's remarks prompted Stewart Sanderson, president of the British Folklore Society—a spirited group of amateurs more interested in recording stories about fairy folk than in supporting a belief in fairies—to conclude, quite arbitrarily, that Elsie had given Lewis enough clues to deduce that the photos had been faked. Sanderson, a professor of English at Leeds University, then launched an establishmental attempt to debunk the whole affair by digging up a copy of a wartime advertisement with an illustration of fairies that he claimed suspiciously resembled the fairy in the first Cottingley photo.

In his 1973 presidential address to the folklore society, Sanderson pointed out that in 1916, the year before the snaps were taken, Elsie had been employed in a photographer's studio in Bradford where she had acquired sufficient skill to do simple retouching and that as a schoolgirl she had shown considerable talent in drawing and painting fairies.

Next it was Frances's turn to face the media. She, too, had married, in her case a soldier, Sidney Way, who, like her father, had risen to warrant officer in the course of many postings in England and abroad, including a long spell in Egypt. They too had retired to the Midlands.

Interviewed by a reporter from the magazine *Woman*, Frances, then in her late sixties, the mother of two children, made no attempt to deny the authenticity of the fairies: "They were part of our everyday life. We didn't go looking for them, as if on a great adventure. We knew they were there and if the light was right and the weather was right it was just a matter of taking pictures of them as you'd take a view. . . ."

This slight ambiguity between Elsie's and Frances's versions sparked another producer at YTV (Yorkshire Television) into putting together a twenty-minute updating of the Cottingley fairy story, arranging for a day's filming of both women back in the original Yorkshire village, the first time in over half a century the two girls would be together again at Cottingley.

To take care of the now matronly ladies, the producer recruited the services of an enterprising journalist, Joe Cooper, who arrived in the village September 10, 1976, to act as chaperone and comment on camera about the proceedings.

Cooper described Frances, just then a year shy of seventy, as a formidable character with an impressive air of authority acquired as a matron at Epsom College, a school for boys. Arriving from a nearby hotel, Frances addressed Cooper, as he put it, "forthrightly and with flashes of humor, speaking with a faint Midland accent."

Shortly thereafter Elsie, by then in her midseventies but looking ten years younger, arrived wearing what Cooper described as "fashionable slacks and a black Gatsby Billycock hat on her blonded gray curls." Hers was a Scots accent, legacy of thirty years in India with her Scottish husband.

Cooper described the telecast's interviewer, Austin Mitchell—later a Labour Member of Parliament—as standing in front of the Cottingley cottage and saying, "It was here, almost sixty years ago, that Elsie Wright and her cousin Frances used to play in the beck . . . a stream down there, just behind their house. And it was there they claim they not only saw the fairies . . . but also photographed them in July 1917."

Down by the beck, Frances led the group toward the waterfall, the cameramen heavily handicapped in the slippery terrain, while Elsie and Cooper moved along higher ground until Elsie found a spot where one of the photos had been taken.

"Round about here the gnomes used to come out," she said to Cooper as Cooper shouted for the crew.

Asked to describe how the picture of a materializing gnome could have been taken, Elsie answered, "When it became clear, Frances pressed the trigger on the box camera. The gnome began to look very clear."

Mitchell: "Do gnomes come and go?"

Elsie: "Yes."

Mitchell: "I mean, why didn't you sort of make a grab for it?"

Elsie: "You couldn't. . . . It's like grabbing for a . . . for a ghost, or something."

At the end of the TV shooting, Mitchell's conclusion, in support of the orthodox establishmental approach, was that the whole thing had been "a sort of unconscious trickery, ossified down the years into gentle old ladies thinking they're telling the truth."

Among the crew and the production team, the general verdict was that somehow there must have been trickery but that nobody would ever know. Elsie and Frances, it was charitably assumed, had terminally arrived at a state of chronic self-delusion.

A woman from the village who had watched the proceedings summed up the villagers' opinion: "Oh, it was a joke. . . . Nobody in Cottingley believed the fairies real."

When broadcast, the opening shots of the YTV program showed a grinning Mitchell looking over cutouts of fairies produced by YTV technicians. But journalist Cooper's faith was not shaken. He remarked that "minds all over the West Riding [area of England] began to ponder on how Elsie might have acquired wire, tools, time, expertise and the privacy for such a deception."

Cooper admitted the Cottingley fairies had "an 'improved' look about them, but insisted that did not mean fairies weren't real. Retaining his faith in Elsie and Frances, Cooper wrote to Elsie in August of 1978, saying he was certain fairies had been seen on many occasions and that in company with Yeats and others he believed them to be all around us, "as are television, heat, light, and delta and gamma rays."

To back up his views, Cooper tape-recorded the remarks of a very sober professional forester, Ronnie Bennett, who worked in the woods near Cottingley and whose testimony added substance to the girls' story. "As far as Nature's concerned," said Bennett, "I think I'm as close to it as many'll ever get. . . . I have places in this wood where I've seen Cottingley fairies. . . . What I saw was very similar to the photographs you sent me. . . . I was astounded when I opened it and . . . there's one lady there and there's this fairy. . . . I was nowhere near as close as that. . . . There weren't many seconds . . . I didn't make conversation . . . and I didn't see one, I saw three. . . . And I didn't sleep for three nights after I'd seen what I'd seen."

The following year a young Barnsley playwright, Geoffrey Case, as. convinced as Cooper that fairies had been seen and photographed by Elsie and Frances, was commissioned by the BBC to write a children's play based on the Cottingley affair. The play, produced by Anne Head—to whom Frances had passed on her description of fairies seen in South Africa—was filmed at Cottingley in the summer of 1978, and its first showing took place on BBC2 Wednesday, October 20, 1978.

This too-supportive program prompted a strong reaction from the publicists of orthodoxy not only in England but also in the United States. America was home to. such official debunkers for the establishment as Randi the Magician and defamer Martin Gardner, both members of the Committee for the Scientific Investigation of the Claims of the Paranormal. Considering themselves and those who commission them the only ones authorized and qualified to determine what constitutes real science, they pulled out their short knives as they gave Elsie and Frances the horse laugh.

Gardner, famed or ill-famed for lampooning Atlantis, Orgonomy, Dianetics, reincarnation, ESP, dowsing, the Great Pyramid, and any subject indicated by his mentors as unacceptable, had attacked the dowsing rod and the pendulum as "doodlebugs," labeling their practitioners as scambags. He ridiculed Ignatius Donnelly's coherent and scholarly defense of the Atlantis myth, then garbled the brilliant mathematical deductions about the Great Pyramid produced by pyramidologists John Taylor and Charles Piazzi Smith, efforts he arbitrarily and incorrectly labeled "pathetic pseudo-science."

As late as 1970, when I published *Secrets of the Great Pyramid*, the subject was still virtually taboo thanks to Professor F.A.P. Barnard. As president of Columbia College in New York and president of the American Association for the Advancement of Science, Barnard had labeled the Great Pyramid "a stupendous monument of folly," attacking its builders for the "stupidly idiotic task of heaping up a pile of massive rock a million-and-a-half yards in volume." In Barnard's opinion the.

pyramids "originated before anything like intellectual culture existed; have been constructed without thought of scientific method, and have owed their earliest forms to accident and caprice."

So virulent was orthodoxy in defense of its indefensible citadel, mocking the theory that the ancient Egyptians could have had an advanced knowledge of geometry, geodesy, and astronomy, that just a few years before my book appeared an eminent engineer in Baltimore stated in the booklet *Designing and Building the Great Pyramid:* "There is no evidence in the Great Pyramid that they [the ancient Egyptians] had any conception of true north or knew that a north-south line was perpendicular to an east-west line."

Randi the Magician, known as "hit man" for the American committee, attacked Doyle's story about the Cottingley fairies as "one of the most fatuous and enduring hoaxes ever perpetrated on the species." He took issue with Doyle, denying his belief—shared by his eminent scientific friends Sir Oliver Lodge and William Crookes—that the evidence for survival after death is "overwhelming." And he attacked Doyle's fairy investigation, saying, "The case features all the classic faults of such investigations: gullibility, half-truths, hyperbole, outright lies, selective reporting, the need to believe, and generous amounts of plain stupidity are mixed with the most outrageous logic and false expertise to be found anywhere in the field."

That the committee was grossly prejudiced was made clear by one of its own disaffected members, Dr. Dennis Rawlins, editor of the *Zetetic Inquirer,* who resigned and attacked the committee as "a group of would-be debunkers who bungled their major investigations, falsified the results, covered up their errors, and gave the boot to a colleague who threatened to tell the truth."

Cooper, in an attempt to present a more balanced view of the Cottingley fairies, produced three more articles in early 1980 for the magazine *The Unexplained* in which he said he was "inclined towards belief that the Cottingley fairies had actually been photographed." He concluded his argument by saying, "The critics—Lewis of *Nationwide,* Austin Mitchell of YTV, Randi, and Stewart Sanderson and Katherine Briggs of the Folklore Society—all these are fair-minded individuals interested in balancing probability on the available evidence. The extremely delicate balance did seem to have shifted in favor of the ladies' honesty during the 1970s, but, obviously, many points could still bear being elucidated by further research."

Elsie and Frances both expressed themselves satisfied with Cooper's write-up, for which they each received from him forty pounds as compensation for the information they had supplied. It was then that Cooper was commissioned to write a book on telepathy for the publishing company Constable, and the idea germinated of writing a book with Elsie on the fairies.

Elsie showed interest and while discussing the project with Cooper remarked blandly of the first photo: "If we hadn't seen the fairies, I don't think I'd believe this photograph. That leaping fairy jumped up five times. . . . The photo's blurred because Frances was throwing her head back."

Cooper: "Do you remember the first time you saw fairies?"
Elsie: "No."
Cooper: "Who saw them first?"
Elsie: "I think we both saw them together."
Cooper: "You weren't surprised at all?"
Elsie: "No. I don't think so. No . . . The fairies were wonderful, and I try to forget all about them. . . . You get tired of talking about them down the years. But they seem to be pulling me back—pulling me back to ideas . . . that we're all one, and if we don't come together there won't be any of us left."

Encouraged by Elsie's attitude and anxious for more material, Cooper went down to see Frances at Ramsgate where she lived in what he described as splendor in an apartment of the Georgian building she owned. He says he encountered a woman with a sharp mind and waspish humor, who, unlike Elsie, did not seek media attention. By then a widow, Frances was riddled with arthritis "but still active in social and civic affairs, bemoaning the lack of intellectual and amusing company, sustained by visits from her children and grandchildren."

Cooper asked Frances to tell him exactly what had happened all those years ago at the beck.

"Well . . ." said Frances, "it was like waiting for a bus. We waited . . . until they came along . . . and then we photographed them."

Then, in late August 1981, Cooper received a phone call from Frances in which she asked if he would come down again to Ramsgate to visit her.

Hoping she might at last be prepared to turn over to him the fifteen-thousand-word essay she had once written on the fairies, Cooper dutifully turned up, driving all the way down from Yorkshire, arriving late on a Sunday evening in September 1981.

The next day Frances asked him to drive her to nearby Canterbury, where she went into the cathedral, leaving Cooper in a café across the street.

When she rejoined him, Cooper says she seated herself opposite him, "hands on chin, a thin, amused mouth, and brown eyes behind round specs regarding me intently."

Launching into the subject of his interest, Cooper began talking about other fairy accounts—trees and streams and types of fairy life—when Frances interrupted him. "What d'you think of that first photograph?"

Cooper's mind flicked to the world-famous snap of Frances surrounded by sprites as she looked at the camera.

Frances's eyes met his with amusement: "From where I was, I could see the hatpins holding up the figures. I've always marveled that anybody ever took it seriously."

Cooper says he gulped his coffee as his pulse accelerated. The truth at last!

"That first photograph always haunted me," said Frances. "I swore to Elsie I wouldn't tell anybody. But last month Glenn [Elsie's son] confronted Elsie with the Shepperton picture [from the 1916 gift book], and Elsie admitted she'd copied cutout figures from it. Glenn persuaded Elsie to confess, then rang up my daughter Kit and told her."

"What about the other four photos?" Cooper asked, steadying himself. "Are they fakes?"

"Three of them," said Frances. "The last one's genuine. Elsie didn't have anything ready, so we had to take one of them building up in the bushes."

"So that's the first photo ever of real fairies?"

"Yes."

When Cooper was told that *The Unexplained* would cease publishing early in 1983 he decided to write up the "truth" as he had learned it from Frances at Canterbury Cathedral. The magazine's editor, Peter Brooksmith, agreed and also commissioned an article from Fred Gettings on how he had come across the Shepperton illustration in the *Princess Mary Gift Book* of 1916.

Both articles appeared in December 1982, entitled "Cottingley. At Last the Truth."

Curiously, no one remarked on the fact that fairies, which are reputed to take on shapes familiar to their viewers, would naturally emulate the Shepperton illustration so familiar to the girls.

Frances and Elsie, says Cooper, stonily severed contact with him. Frances curtly called him a traitor over the phone and hung up.

It was she, following *The Unexplained* articles, who then decided to be the first to make a public confession. She telephoned the *Times,* and the interviewer produced a story with the well-known first photograph, headlined "Photographs Confounded Conan Doyle. Cottingley Fairies a Fake, Woman Says." The story described how stiff paper cutouts and hairpins had been used.

Frances nevertheless continued to maintain that the last photograph was of real fairies, taken by herself.

Elsie at first refused to comment on the article but later received a reporter and cameraman at her Nottingham home. There she was snapped in the act of cutting out a fairy figure from cardboard.

A few days after the *Times's* disclosures, says Cooper, a reporter from the *Manchester Daily Express* put an end to the whole affair: "Fairies?" he quoted Elsie as saying with a laugh, "No. I don't believe in fairies. Never have and never will."

A smiling photograph of the eighty-one-year-old Elsie accompanied the article under the headline: "The Biggest Fairy Story of Them All."

Yet after Frances died in July of 1986 at the age of eighty, her daughter claimed her mother had maintained until the end "that fairies were real; she never changed her mind."

Cooper, whose faith was only partly shaken, went on to write a book on the Cottingley saga, explaining that Elsie's later dismissal of fairies "was, I guess, the device of a tired and ailing old lady not wanting to be bothered by reporters anymore."

What was in play, of course, was the same old routine practiced over the centuries by an orthodoxy determined to wear down the resistance of heretics. Anyone who dares to challenge established beliefs knows the game is stacked and that he or she must either recant or follow in the footsteps of such noble martyrs as Hypatia, Giordano Bruno, Joan of Arc, or the millions of souls tortured and immolated in this century by one side or the other in their hot and cold wars.

And there the story might really have ended had it not been for Geoffrey Hodson, who was to devote a lifetime to validating not just the Cottingley fairies, but the whole world of nature spirits as seen by those who can describe its tenuous realms with the aid of spiritual insight, a tale that leads out of darkness toward the light.

4

Seeing Is Believing

The original publicity surrounding the investigation of the fairy photographs led to increased interest in Hodson's clairvoyant powers. In January of 1923 a group of wealthy theosophists in London formed a scientific group to "correlate modern scientific views with Theosophy." They invited Hodson to collaborate with his remarkable clairvoyant abilities.

The Theosophical Society, brainchild of that fabulous but controversial Russian psychic, Helena Petrovna Blavatsky, had been founded in New York in 1875 with the help of American journalist-author Colonel Henry Steel Olcott, who was fascinated by the occult. Blavatsky, born in the north Caucasus in 1831 to a Russian army colonel and a princess descended from early Russian rulers, claimed to have lived from childhood in two worlds. One was physical, the other spiritual, and the latter was peopled by visible and invisible companions. She tells how one of these manifested to her in the flesh when she was sixteen as she strolled in London's Hyde Park. Appearing in the guise of an Indian rajput known as Prince Koot Hoomi, he told her she would one day come for training to his ashram in the Himalayas, a prophecy that seemed improbable at the time.

Married by her parents at seventeen to a Russian general three times her age, Blavatsky, to avoid the nuptial bed, escaped in disguise to travel the world, sustaining herself for years by performing feats of apparent magic. In India and Tibet she claimed to have acquired, as promised by Koot Hoomi, a considerable knowledge of arcana under the instruction of a series of adepts and to have been initiated into the mysteries.

In Paris in 1873 she was told by her "masters" to go to New York to found the Theosophical Society for the purpose "of collecting and diffusing knowledge of the laws which govern the universe." Early members of the society included Thomas Edison, inventor of the electric light bulb, and General Abner Doubleday, supposed originator of the game of baseball.

The term *theosophy* or *divine wisdom* referred in those days to a strain of mystical speculation associated with the kabbalah and the writings of occultists such as Paracelsus and Robert Fludd. On the premise that no religion was higher than truth, the society's intention was to "reconcile all religions, sects, and nations under a common system of ethics based on eternal verities." Colonel Olcott spoke of "freeing the public mind of theological superstition and a tame subservience to the arrogance of Science." His further object was to forge a multinational, multiethnic, multidenominational body of men and women firmly united in "brotherly love" engaged in altruistic study, work, and goodwill, bent on accomplishing what other societies, such as the Freemasons, only promised: fraternity of membership without distinction of race, creed, or social position. Blavatsky, aware that the social conditions of poverty, misery, and disease afflicting large masses in Western countries rendered impossible the improvement of either their bodies or their spirits, wanted the society to be a living protest against the gross materialism of the day, against careless indifference, material luxury, selfish indulgence, and general lack of kindness, justice, love, or caritas.

In New York Blavatsky produced her first major theosophical text, her monumental *Isis Unveiled*, subtitled *A Master-key to the Mysteries of Ancient and Modern Science and Theology*. Olcott maintained that the book, which postulates humans as spiritual beings and chronicles the human race through eons of karma, was inspired astrally or telepathically by highly evolved masters; he describes Blavatsky's pen as flying over the paper until she would stop, "look out into space with the vacant eye of a clairvoyant seer, shorten her vision as though to look at something held invisible in the air before her, and begin copying on her paper what she saw."

The first edition sold out in ten days and was called by Manly P. Hall—in his own right an encyclopedic writer on the arcane—"the most vital literary contribution to the modern world." *Isis* was followed shortly by *The Secret Doctrine,* two volumes totaling sixteen hundred pages, the first entitled *Cosmogenesis,* the second on *Anthropogenesis.*

Theosophy claimed to teach the essential truths found in all religions so that it might appeal equally to Christians, Buddhists, Hindus, Parsis, Hebrews, and Muslims, who, in fact, thronged to the society while retaining their own religion.

Bright lights in the society were Annie Besant and Charles W. Leadbeater. Besant, then in her forties, known as "Annie militant," was a rebel, free thinker, radical activist, Fabian Socialist, crusader for women's rights, and a brilliant orator. Asked by William T. Steed, editor of the *Pall Mall Gazette,* to review *The Secret Doctrine*—of which Steed could make no sense—Besant devoured its sixteen hundred pages and became a theosophist overnight, "dazzled, blinded by the light in which disjointed facts were seen as part of a mighty whole, and all my puzzles, riddles, problems seemed to disappear. In a flash of illumination I knew that the weary search was over and the very truth was found."

Besant met Blavatsky in London in 1887, became her acolyte almost immediately, and after her death in 1891 succeeded her as head of the Theosophical Society. Passionately involved with the political liberation of India, Besant spent many years in the subcontinent, eventually becoming elected president of the Indian National Congress.

Charles W. Leadbeater, best known as the enfant terrible of theosophy, whose major contribution to the society was a dozen lucid books on the subject, liked to travel the world decked out in the purple robes of a bishop of the Liberal Catholic Church, sporting crosier and jeweled cross.

In England the Theosophical Society began to publish a wealth of detailed information on conditions this side and the other of death, on the nature of etheric, astral, and mental bodies, on the laws of human growth and of karma, on the purpose of existence, and on the swiftest way to reach the goal of human evolution, the source of all this arcana being clairvoyance in its various forms.

Thus far, three basic kinds of clairvoyance had been described by Leadbeater. Simple clairvoyance enabled its possessor to see whatever "astral or etheric" entities happen to be around him or her but not distant places or scenes belonging to any other time than the present. Clairvoyance in space he described as the capacity to see scenes or events removed from the seer in space, too distant for ordinary observation or concealed by intermediate objects. Clairvoyance in time allows its possessor to see objects or events removed in time; that is to say, it is the power to look into the past or the future, all of which is said to be recorded in fine cosmic material known as Akasha, Sanskrit for "ether." The records are described as being of planetary, solar, galactic, and cosmic events from the beginning of time, down to such details as Caesar's thoughts and imaginations when directing his legions. On the astral plane, says Leadbeater, the recorded pictures are occasionally endowed with motion. On the higher mental plane they appear as an endless succession of moving cinematography pictures.

Amazing as such feats of clairvoyance may be, there is no denying their existence, though the explanation of them may seem as tenuous as of the weak force of nuclear physicists. Theosophical literature describes many levels of clairvoyance, the most elementary being "etheric sight," a faculty said to operate through an etheric counterpart to the physical eyes by means of an "etheric retina" situated, as described by Hodson, just behind the physical one: it enables its user to see the aura surrounding the human body.

Occultists describe the etheric body as resembling the physical body in form, interpenetrating it and extending slightly beyond it, consisting of a substance finer than matter in the gaseous state. A ghostly bluish pink, somewhat darker than peach blossom, it appears to be luminous and fluidic. In lieu of organs it is streaked by currents of diverse colors, predominantly orange and yellow. Densified, it reflects light, becoming visible, as in psychic photographs, even tangible. Everything living is considered as having an etheric body whose function is to give "life" to the physical body, which, left to itself, would crumble into dust—as at death.

More subtle than etheric sight is astral sight. Astral matter being finer than etheric matter, the astral body interpenetrates both the etheric and the physical, filling in between. To the occultist, the astral body appears as an egg-shaped cloud in perpetual inner movement surrounding the physical body, disappearing gradually as it nears the ground. Its function is to make sensation possible, embracing desire and emotion, serving as a bridge between our etheric body and our spiritual "self"—between mind and matter—taking on all the colors of the rainbow according to the passion by which it is animated. The astral body serves to endow the etheric body with consciousness, without which it would remain in a state of sleep. In short: life belongs to the ether body, consciousness to the astral body, memory to the actual ego. What for the physical body is death, for the etheric body is sleep and for the astral is oblivion. Astral sight, more subtle than etheric sight, requires no specialized organs; one sees objects equally well behind and beneath one, without needing to orient the head.

Leadbeater points out that simple clairvoyance can go from sudden flashes of insight to full possession of etheric and astral vision. The most striking change produced by etheric sight is the appearance of inanimate objects, most of which become transparent. A brick wall seems to have a consistency no greater than a light mist, enabling the viewer to see what is going on in an adjoining room, describe accurately the contents of a locked box, read a sealed letter, or, with a little practice, find a given message in a closed book.

With etheric vision solid ground becomes to a certain extent transparent, enabling the viewer to see to a considerable depth, much as if through fairly clear water. One can watch a creature burrowing or distinguish a vein of coal or metal, providing it is not too deep. Animate objects are equally altered by etheric sight: humans and animals become in the main transparent, so that one can watch the action of the various internal organs and, to some extent, diagnose their diseases.

To draw a distinction between etheric and astral sight, books about clairvoyants had to coin new words: etheric vision is described as "throughth," meaning the ability to see through opaque objects, whereas astral vision is described as "withinth," meaning a sort of four-dimensional sense of seeing an object from all sides at once and from inside as well. Comparing etheric to astral viewing, Leadbeater points out that a cube of wood with writing on all sides viewed with etheric vision would be transparent like a cube of glass, and one could read the writing on the front, whereas the writing on the back would appear reversed, the sides being illegible unless the cube were turned. Viewed astrally all the sides would be visible at once, right way up, as if the cube were flattened. "Yet you would see every particle of the inside, not through the others. You would be looking at it from another direction, at right angles to all the directions that we know."

Astral sight, to theosophists' eyes, is thus comparable to viewing in the fourth dimension. Astral observers would have no difficulty reading any page of a closed book, because they would not be looking through all the pages, as they would etherically, but would be looking straight down on one page as if it were unique. The same feat, says Leadbeater, would present difficulty to one using etheric sight because each page would have to be looked at through all the others. It is etheric sight, says Leadbeater, that enables observers to perceive, more or less clearly, the denser etheric bodies of the lower orders of nature spirits, which are still too rarefied to reflect any of the rays within the spectrum of ordinary light; among these he includes most of the fairies, gnomes, and brownies. The vaster kingdom of nature spirits appertains to the more refined astral plane, and astral vision opens a whole new world to the observer. "Anyone possessing astral vision in its fullness," says Leadbeater, "will be able to see by its means practically anything in this world that he wishes to see. The most secret places are open to his gaze and intervening obstacles have no existence for him if he changes his point of view."

Hodson, armed with both etheric and astral vision in a highly developed state, was considered of inestimable value to the London group of theosophists. To take full advantage of his gifts, the group divided into several sections, each concerned with a specific branch of scientific thought: psychology, healing, anthropology, geology, psychic investigation, diagnosis of disease. To assist in these investigations the Hodsons sold their house in Preston and moved to London.

One of the first experiments Hodson was asked to perform was along the lines previously explored by Besant and Leadbeater for *Occult Chemistry*, a subject about which Hodson had as yet little knowledge. Several gases in as pure a state as possible were prepared in numbered glass tubes, and Hodson was asked to investigate each one clairvoyantly, the first being oxygen.

Like Leadbeater, Hodson described the atoms he viewed with his siddhi powers as whirling, shooting centers of energy. Like Leadbeater, he managed to make them stand still for detailed examination. As Hodson focused his consciousness within the oxygen atom, he said he experienced a sensation similar to that of gazing outward into the solar system from a planet. He was greatly struck with the similarity of the construction and the relativity of magnitude, finding that the change of consciousness resulting from the very high magnification produced the illusion that when the atom was thus examined from a point within it, it seemed as immeasurably large as the solar system.

Hodson described the oxygen atom as an ovoid shape surrounded by a spiral flow of force. Within the ovoid he said he could see that one-fifth of the space was occupied by what he described as a pillar around which a double spiral was formed by the rapid revolution of small globules, one-sixtieth the diameter of the surrounding ovoid. Within the central pillar Hodson described "a golden, sun-like focus through which an incalculable supply of energy wells up and out from within the atom, as if it were pouring forth from a higher plane to a lower."

Hodson's power of magnification was astounding considering that the size of an atom of oxygen in relation to a person is comparable to that of a person to a galaxy. Handed a tube of chlorine without being told its contents, Hodson described greenish atoms of a bent dumbbell shape, with radiating ends, oscillating together in pairs as if linked, their movements reminding him of dancers, a description that tallied with the one given in *Occult Chemistry*. Hodson further described twelve funnels at each end of the chlorine bar, the sides of the funnels being "areas of flow of force." Twelve was the number of funnels noted in *Occult Chemistry*.

And Hodson's range of vision was equally impressive. Asked to investigate two white powders that, though their chemical composition was quite different, appeared to be identical when viewed with ordinary sight, Hodson had no difficulty clairvoyantly differentiating the two powders as sodium sulfate and magnesium sulfate.

Additional examples of his capacities included detecting the passage of an electrical current through a wire without physical knowledge of whether the switch was on or off. He could also observe different emanations from the north and south poles of magnets as well as detect such radiations in the dark.

A practical use for Hodson's clairvoyant vision was demonstrated in the field of bacteriology. In a series of experiments starting in November of 1927, cultures were made from intestinal bacteria derived from a number of persons, bacteria capable of causing such diseases as Morgan's, Proteus's, Gaertner's, and dysentery. All the cultures were diluted by homeopathic process to the thirtieth potency, at which level it was almost impossible to detect the presence of anything but the distilled water in the dilution. Placed in glass tubes and numbered, the dilutions were submitted to Hodson for clairvoyant investigation. In each case, though the nature of the dilution was unknown to anyone present during the investigation (so that thought transference or mind reading could be eliminated), Hodson was able to note a connection between the vial and the person from whom the contents had been drawn, accurately describing sex, age, and other particulars of the patient. Unlike the famous American psychic, Edgar Cayce, who could only prescribe while in a trance, Hodson, wide awake, could correctly enumerate the qualities of the homeopathic remedies submitted and discern their ascertained powers "with a swiftness that was amazing."

Another remarkable talent was his capacity for accurately locating the relative position of the planets of the solar system on any particular day. This feat provided a rational explanation of how such ancient peoples as the Maya were able to construct extraordinarily accurate calendars, covering thousands of years, giving the correct location of the known planets at any given time without the benefit of sophisticated astronomical instruments.

December 7, 1928, at 11:30 A.M., Hodson was asked to explore the solar system with his clairvoyant powers and to observe the angular positions of the planets and their relative distances from the sun. Unknown to Hodson, a plan of the solar system had been drawn up in the form of a clock face, with the position of the sun taken as one o'clock and that of the earth as six o'clock. The heliocentric positions of the planets were then distributed among the hours as recorded in·the nautical almanac for the date of the meeting. Hodson accurately placed Uranus at 8:30, Neptune at 3:00, Mercury at 1:00, Mars at 6:00, and Jupiter at 7:00. Thereafter he repeated the observation on a number of other occasions, always·accurately able to clairvoyantly observe the angular positions of the planets and their relative distances from the sun.

Psychometry, the art of divining facts concerning an object, its source, and its background merely through contact with or proximity to the object itself, is described by Leadbeater as deriving from astral sight, though dependent on etheric radiations. The psychometrist develops a rapport with a place and an event occurring there, or having occurred there, by means of a material object that, as occultists explain it, is still etherically connected to the spot from which it was taken. As Leadbeater explains the phenomena, every material object throws off radiations in all directions, and these radiations are continually being recorded on a higher, finer plane, the Akashic.

Hodson carefully described his method of psychometrizing an object from some area remote in time and space, simply by holding it for scrutiny close to his brow chakra, or "third eye." "If I am examining a fossil, at first I see small pictures of its environment before my eyes, then a change may occur, and the vision ceases to be a picture and becomes my environment so that I seem to be present, reliving the events. . . . There is a sense of immediacy; one is there in the scene, and I have even felt the temperature in my physical body." But one cannot take action, says Hodson: "If I am asked whether the creature I see has a tail, and he happens to be sitting down, there is nothing I can do about it, except wait till he gets up and allows me to see; I cannot exercise any additional occult powers to see through the body and observe the tail."

One of the most effective ways of validating psychometric data obtained clairvoyantly is by means of archaeological digs. This was the case with Hodson's psychic exploration of the great buried metropolis of Teotihuacán outside Mexico City, which flourished two millennia earlier around the great structures known as the Sun and the Moon Pyramids.

In 1956, when nothing of the ancient city was visible above ground, Hodson stood atop the Sun Pyramid and described ceremonies dating from between 500 B.C.E. and 500 C.E., performed there by priests robed in brilliantly colored feathers for a thriving city that thereafter showed signs of decline. Hodson pictured the great metropolis as divided into quarters, with the lower classes in poor houses and the higher classes in more lavish ones nearer the temples. The buildings he saw as flat-topped, constructed of adobe and stone, though many were not roofed over. He further described long, straight roads that crossed at right angles.

Not until the mid-1960s was it possible for Rene Millon, professor of anthropology at the University of Rochester, to obtain sufficient funds from the National Science Foundation in Washington, D.C., to prepare an aerial photogrammetric map of the entire buried area of Teotihuacán and to establish the exact dimensions of the ancient city, verifying Hodson's description as remarkably exact. Millon found a city that at the height of its development around 500 C.E. covered some twenty square kilometers, an immense and well-planned city laid out on a grandiose scale, teeming with people, one of the largest preindustrial cities in the world, vaster than the imperial Rome of the Caesars. Millon's map of Teotihuacán showed a city at the peak of its power split into four squares with parallel crisscrossing streets. Thereafter, as reconstructed archaeologically, signs of degeneration appeared, with indications of a great holocaust around 750 C.E. that reduced the once-great city to a ghost town. By the time Cortés arrived at the beginning of the sixteenth century, the entire area had been covered over with dirt.

In December of 1957 in New Zealand, Hodson was invited by Dr. D. D. Lyness, a Member of Parliament with a degree in chemistry, to cooperate in a further series of clairvoyant investigations of the atom. The results were published in a pamphlet by Dr. Lyness entitled *Some Recent Clairvoyant Research in New Zealand*. Therein Hodson described his method of examining graphite at various levels of magnification. "My preliminary sight of the specimen is as black powder, telling me that I am still at the dense physical level. Then the will to magnify is applied. The first result is the vanishing of the black powder and its replacement by a field in depth of immeasurably minute pinpoints of light in very rapid motion in all directions." For Hodson the whole of space was filled with these minutest moving points of light. "Sometimes there are tiny explosions in the their midst, giving a flash of light. I can see this background with eyes open or closed."[1]

In the hope of extending the scope of *Occult Chemistry*, Dr. Lyness conducted a further series of experiments with Hodson in Australia during 1958 and 1959 aimed at identifying a single electron, a particle far smaller than the "atoms" described by the earlier theosophists. Were a carbon atom to be blown up to the size of the great city of Teotihuacán, its electrons would relatively be the size of a pea! With little hope of observing electrons unless from an abundant source, Lyness provided Hodson with a cathode ray tube in which a stream of electrons could be projected between the poles of a strong horseshoe magnet, which could deflect the stream. As the position of the magnet was varied, Hodson could correctly describe the direction of the deflection.

Part of the beam, as Hodson described it—more in the language of a tank officer than of a particle physicist—appeared to be made of rushing particles, with a sort of spiral moving like an eel around it, thickening and thinning with a series of wave-crests "as if you had a wire wound round another wire, and this second wire . . . consists of rapidly moving particles. But they don't go along with the wire, the big wire. They go on going round and round and round, as if the wire, the main one, went through it."

Commenting on Hodson's analysis, Professor Smith remarked that he could hear Hodson grasping for words, uttering unfinished sentences, then breaking off to replace them in more suitable terms.

Individual electrons spotted by Hodson appeared as elongated particles, definitely spinning like the smallest constituents of matter discovered by Leadbeater and Besant, their "ultimate physical atoms," only

---

1. Hodson's description tallies with the remarkable work of French biologist Gaston Naessens, developer of an effective cure for cancers of many sorts; his avant-garde microscope enables him to observe living blood plasma with greater resolution than is possible with an electron microscope, revealing thousands of tiny specks of light, to which he has given the name "somatides"; these he believes to be the prime manifestation of biological life.

very much smaller. Hodson described one as having a spiral movement. "I can't give you any relative sizes—it has a double spiral movement in it. . . . Somewhat like the sweet chestnut with its cover round it.That is to say, it hasn't got a smooth surface, it's radiating itself; it is radiating rays and lines of force all round itself and these spike out for a distance of about one, two, three—about a sixth or eighth of the diameter, sideways diameter, of the object. . . . But don't think of anything like a chestnut covering.They are very much closer than that."

Perhaps the most significant part of Hodson's vision of spiraling electrons was his description of how the electrons ought to move in a cathode ray tube as originally predicted by the Austrian physicist Erwin Schrödinger, inventor of wave mechanics. This was something—as noted Dr. Lyness—that Hodson was not likely to have known.And the power of Hodson's magnification, far greater than that of any microscope then devised, may be gauged by the fact that the electron's radius was finally measured in 1990 as less than .000000000000000001 inches!

Lyness's reaction to these experiments was to state that the results indicated that Hodson was actually observing electrons as they obeyed the laws of deflection in a magnetized field, leaving no doubt that he was actually seeing what he described so vividly and dramatically:"His sincerity and integrity shine through his words."

The most powerful method for analyzing objects at a distance developed by both Hodson and Leadbeater involved the ajnic chakra, or "third eye." Leadbeater found a way to make out of astral matter a definite connecting line to some remote object; it would act as a telegraph wire to convey vibrations by means of which "all that is going on at the other end can be seen." He claimed that by human will it is possible to polarize a number of parallel lines of astral atoms reaching from the operator to the scene that he wishes to observe.All the atoms thus affected are then held for a time with their axes rigidly parallel so they form a kind of temporary tube along which the clairvoyant may look.

The view of a distant scene observed by means of this "astral current," says Leadbeater, "is not unlike that seen through a telescope. Human figures usually appear very small, like those on a distant stage, but despite their diminutive size they are as clear as if close by."

Leadbeater adds that by this means it is sometimes possible to hear what is being said. His complaint was that astral sight, when cramped by being directed along what is practically a tube, is limited very much as physical sight would be under similar circumstances. However, it still shows auras, says Leadbeater, even at that distance, "and therefore all the emotions and most of the thoughts of those under observation."

This form of distant viewing does not require the viewer to leave his physical body: there is no projection of his astral vehicle or of any part of himself toward that at which he is looking. He simply manufactures for himself a temporary astral telescope.

Hodson's results were achieved by focusing the "sight" of his brow chakra in a manner analogous to shifting the focus of his dense physical eye. This he accomplished by the yogi practice of vivifying the chakra with kundalini, the specialized energy residing in the base chakra, described by occultists as one of the forces emanating from both the sun and the center of the earth and lying dormant in humans in the etheric matter near the base of the spine. To clairvoyant vision, kundalini appears like liquid fire as it rushes through the human body, spiraling like the coils of a serpent to vivify the chakra, bringing astral experiences into physical consciousness. The pituitary body when fully working is said to afford a perfect link between astral and physical consciousness. The process, said Hodson, conveys to the consciousness of the investigator a sensation interpreted as "sight," a feeling that the third eye "sees" patterns of light just as does the retina of the dense physical eye. The substance to be investigated is then brought about four to six inches away from the spot between the eyebrows and thus within the open end of the chakra. "This accurate location is essential to me."

Hodson described projecting from the center of his third eye a tube like Leadbeater's to magnify etheric objects almost indefinitely. "Kundalini is deliberately forced into the frontal brain in general, and into the pituitary body in particular. Thereafter it is driven by will down the funnel of the ajna chakram until this part of the mechanism is considered to be sufficiently 'electrified.'"

This tube, which Hodson called the "ajnic microscope," he described as being denser than the rest of the chakra, gray in color, and movable by willpower within the mouth of the chakra. It seemed to Hodson to consist of what Leadbeater called E4, the densest etheric subplane. Hodson would place the tip of his ajnic microscope inside the substance to be examined and then determine the required magnification. But, unlike an ordinary microscope, Hodson's etheric tube had to be projected and held in contact with the object under observation, and this by willpower, which required a considerable effort of concentration. Not only that, but the degree of magnification was not conveniently fixed by a wheel or knob. This obliged the investigator to learn to mentally control the focus and to recognize at what level of magnification he was operating.

Hodson commented on the tremendous effort involved in this work with the ajnic microscope, so tiring he felt that mistakes were bound to occur after a while. He described his whole body as trembling with the power of kundalini, saying the maximum effort called for was truly heroic.

For ordinary psychometry and magnifying clairvoyance, Hodson said he used only the ajna chakra, not the ajnic microscope. "When using the ajna chakram the physical eyes are closed, and the physical disappears from view under inspection by astral or mental sight."

This was the faculty used by Hodson for his long excursion into the world of nature spirits. "If I want to see the form of the fairy or gnome, I must use the ajna faculty at the etheric or astral level. But to determine what it is doing demands full use of astro-mental faculties of the ajna chakram. However. . . I used to see fairies inadvertently, and found that I was unconsciously slipping into the use of the ajna. . . . The same kind of thing happened when I looked at fairies and gnomes in earlier years. Occasionally they would stand still for me, but usually they were darting about, not noticing me; yet I could get a still picture of one for examination, if I so chose."

5

Deep into Fairyland

Between his involvement with the Cottingley fairies in 1921 and his move to London in 1923, Hodson spent much of his spare time studying nature spirits wherever he could find them in the English countryside. Given his remarkable track record in using clairvoyant powers to analyze atoms, diagnose patients, psychometrize archaeological objects, and explore the solar system, his detailed descriptions of the world of nature spirits take on new light, incredible as may be the picture he lays out.

Already in September of 1921, a few miles from his house in Preston, in a glade of beautiful old trees, "touched with autumn tints, a stream flowing gently, and the whole bathed in autumn sunshine," Hodson described coming upon a field densely populated with fairies, brownies, elves, and "a grass creature between elf and brownie, but smaller, less evolved."

By this time Hodson was following the classical custom of dividing the world of nature spirits into four main categories according to the predominant element of their makeup—whether earth, water, air, or fire; but he was quick to point out that there were innumerable different species, often overlapping.

None of these nature spirits, said Hodson, had fixed solid bodies, since their essence was of the astral plane, but they were able to "materialize" vehicles out of heavier etheric matter, using for models the thought-forms concocted by local peasants and children, occasionally imitating other forms they may have seen and admired. To see these spirits required at least etheric sight and preferably astral and higher.

To Hodson, with his well-developed etheric and astral vision, the fairies he found in the field near Preston, similar in many ways to the ones he had seen with the girls at Cottingley, were among his favorites because they expressed "light-heartedness, gaiety, and joie de vivre." With keen pleasure he watched as they flitted from place to place. They appeared as delicate female forms dressed in a white, clinging, sheeny material of fine texture, "bearing something which they give to the grass or the flowers at each stop, putting out a hand to touch where they come to rest, as if applying some substance."

In the garden at Preston in October 1921, Hodson spotted a specifically beautiful fairy clothed in iridescent shimmering light. "She is decidedly fair in coloring," he noted, "full of laughter and happiness, very open and fearless in expression, surrounded by an aura of golden radiance in which the outline of her wings can be traced. There is also a hint of mockery in her attitude and expression, as of one who is enjoying a joke against the poor mortals who are studying her."

Suddenly, said Hodson, her manner changed and she became serious, giving him a better notion of her function by stretching out her arms to perform an act of concentration that had the effect, as Hodson witnessed it, of reducing the size of her aura and of turning it inward on herself. Having maintained this condition for about fifteen seconds, "she releases the whole of the concentration of energy, which pours forth in all directions in streams of golden force, and appears to affect every single stem and flower within its reach."

At the center of a clump of chrysanthemums, the fairy appeared to Hodson to reinforce the vibration already there, probably, he thought, as a result of previous similar activities on her part. "Another effect of this operation has been to cause the astral double of the whole clump to shine with an added radiance, an effect which is noticeable right down to the roots."

Other earth spirits, less appealing but still of interest, appeared to swarm over a nearby field; they were principally brownies, gnomes, elves, and mannikins. In his notes Hodson described brownies as varying in height from four inches to a foot, usually in the guise of little old men, short, squat, and round, invariably dressed in medieval style: brown coat with bright buttons, facings of green, knee breeches, rough stockings, heavy boots or long, pointed shoes, and heads covered by pointed deerskin caps like old-fashioned nightcaps.

These brownies gave Hodson the impression of rustic tillers of the soil, red-complexioned, with gray beards and gray brows, eyes small and beady. A group wearing aprons like blacksmiths pretended to use spades and picks to delve into the earth with great earnestness, but Hodson could not tell from their expression of mock seriousness whether they regarded these endeavors as work or play.

A few months later, in the lake district on the western shore of Thirlmere, in a thick wood of oak, hazel, and beech, Hodson found a large colony of brownies, varying little in appearance, swarming over the steep side of one of the crags. In among the roots and rocks he could distinguish a number of tiny houses, just beneath the surface of the soil, quite perfect in shape, mostly wood and thatch, with windows and doors. As the brownies went in by the door, Hodson watched them put off their brownie form to descend into the earth in a relatively formless state.

With etheric sight Hodson tried to enter one of these picturesque houses, but once he was past the door the illusion of a house disappeared, leaving only darkness streaked here and there by fine lines of "magnetism."

The houses did not seem to belong to any individual or group. Any member of the colony could use them to pass in and out through the door in a make-believe pantomime of domestic life, though Hodson could see no female brownies, only males, all exceedingly self-centered, seemingly lacking in communication with one another.

Back in Preston, Hodson became aware of the presence in the house of a nature spirit of the brownie family, five or six inches tall, dark brown, eyes round and black. He first observed it in the kitchen on a shelf over the stove and later in the hall and the living room; it was noticeable by the occasional flashes of etheric light that accompanied its rapid movements. Hodson says the brownie acted as if it had adopted the family and that, unlike others of its species, it was bright, youthful, and clean shaven.

The gnome would enter the house from the garden and run about without any clothes, occasionally turning its body dark green. Approaching Hodson, it appeared to enjoy standing in his aura as if receiving an "etheric showerbath." When it finally climbed onto

Hodson's knee he says he felt a tremor, a distinct coldness, and a very slight weight. Hodson described his diminutive visitor's fragile ethereal makeup as "possessing less consistency than a puff of wind." Yet his form was perfectly outlined, details sharply defined.

That same autumn of 1921 in the fields near Preston, Hodson spotted some gnomes, a species also generally found on or just beneath the surface of the earth among the roots of trees and plants. In contrast to the brownies, Hodson sized up these creatures as over two feet high. They were thin and lanky, either black or peat brown, rough complexioned with small, black eyes, cadaverous in appearance, lantern jawed, and their legs were bent stiff at the joints, giving the impression of extreme old age. Possibly, he thought, they were leftovers from Atlantis, not a pleasant type of elemental.

Hodson described several other kinds of gnomes, some only a few inches high, all earth creatures, capable of moving unimpeded through rock, some moving across the earth with their feet below ground, none able to rise much above their own height into the air.

When Hodson tried to contact these gnomes in their subterranean world, they appeared to dissolve and somehow lose their individuality, melting as they sank below the ground into a common essence. This indicated the tribe was animated almost entirely by a group consciousness or herd instinct. Forming themselves into globules of this essence, they moved about the earth quite freely, yet upon rising above the ground they instantaneously manifested as fully shaped gnomes. Hodson, unable to attribute this metamorphosis to any intelligent effort, assumed it to be more or less automatic.

Still in the lake district, while Hodson was observing other nature spirits, his attention was drawn to a large rock, beneath which he says lived a more imposing gnome, gray bearded, with a coat reaching just below his waist, carrying a light, not unlike a candle, that shone with a yellow gleam. Hodson watched the gnome descend into the earth, two or three feet below the stone, where it moved about without obstruction, its whole manner and appearance changing as soon as it was below the surface.

Deep within another nearby rock, large and solid, Hodson sensed what he called the "evolving consciousness" of another type of gnome, much larger but less developed, some ten to fifteen feet high. Apart from eyes and mouth, it manifested only as a formless blotch of color, its body barely suggested. To Hodson's etheric sight the creature appeared encased in transparent rock, through which it was only vaguely aware of its surroundings. The only power of volition it appeared to possess was to slowly change the focus and direction of its dim and limited consciousness. Yet its presence, says Hodson, gave individuality to the rock, noticeable as a magnetic vibration on the physical plane.

Nearer home, Hodson spotted what he described as a tree gnome, about two feet, six inches high, which assumed the gnome shape as it prepared to leave the tree for a short excursion into the field. With cadaverous features, long and sharp, cheekbones high and prominent, and eyes elongated into almond shape, the gnome moved swiftly—at not less than twenty miles an hour, according to Hodson. It picked its way óver the grass, taking long strides, lifting its legs high in the air. But the distance it could travel appeared to be limited by the "magnetic contact" it retained with the tree, as if it were using the etheric body of the tree to form its own body. To Hodson the trunk of the tree without the gnome looked like an empty cylinder. As the gnome reentered through a "doorway" on the south side it discarded its gnome form, becoming homogenous with the tree.

Contacting the gnome's consciousness astrally, Hodson found that it had lived a very long time, the passage of which made little or no impression on it, either mentally or physically, for it appeared to live very largely in the present, with no room for anything but joy in its mind, permanent and stable, not needing the companionship of its kind.

In another field near Preston Hodson came across a different set of "dancing" gnomes at a lower stage of development than the tree gnomes. They were much smaller, only four to six inches high, and quaint in their antique movements. Unlike the tree gnomes, they were not solitary but lived and played in groups, their antics and games varied and grotesque.

Gaily colored little fellows, their beady dark eyes gleaming as if they were experiencing inward ecstasy, they held hands and swung from side to side, an oscillating movement "seemingly purposeless on the physical plane," according to Hodson, but which appeared to produce for them a highly pleasurable astral sensation.

Hodson could see that it had the effect of disturbing and exciting their astral body—a cloud of unorganized matter roughly twice the size of the physical. Radiations from the center of this astral body (approximately at the solar plexus) swept through their whole astral body in waves and ripples, causing its colors to become more intense, allowing the gnome to enjoy to the fullness the effects produced.

With yet another type of earth spirit, the elf, Hodson says his experience was limited; elves did not seem to be common in his area. The ones he had encountered racing about the ground under the old beeches in the woods at Cottingley in August of 1921 had been only a few inches high, hands and feet out of all proportion to their bodies, legs thin, ears large and pointed, differing from other nature spirits chiefly in that they did not appear to be clothed in any reproduction of human attire. To Hodson their bodily constitution consisted of one solid mass of gelatinous substance, entirely without interior organization, surrounded by a small green aura. Small oval wings of a glistening semitransparent substance, not used for flight, nevertheless trembled and quivered at every movement.

In a glade a few miles from Preston Hodson did find such elflike creatures, diminutive, only an inch or so high. Very numerous, they made a curious chattering sound as they moved through the grass wholly absorbed in exploring the fairy pathways in what to them was a jungle. Their auras caused the etheric double of the grass to vibrate more quickly as they passed. As Hodson watched these grass elfin fly short distances in a clumsy way, with feet pointed down and forward, more like a swing than a flight, a succession of tiny globules of light steadily issued from their heads, which Hodson perceived as thought-forms, all exactly the same, connected by a thread of light, as if the elves were talking to themselves.

Mannikin is the name given by Hodson to all the fairy people he encountered of male appearance whom he could not classify as either gnome, brownie, or elf but who exhibited some of the characteristics of each, together with certain specific features of their own. He found mannikins in connection with trees, hedges, bracken, grass, heather, and wildflowers, perhaps the most common fairy type in England with many varieties in different parts. Bracken and grass mannikins he found nearly always dressed in green with little green caps, pointed ears, and chubby faces like three-year-old children.

Red mannikins, four to six inches high, sporting bright crimson tights, could enlarge themselves almost to human size, but only with great effort and only for a relatively short time. In a colony of thousands they were trotting about a field, tiny and shy, merry and playful, dancing to form geometric figures that Hodson believed gave expression to some force flowing through them to produce an added sense of happiness and life.

Mannikins concerned with trees he usually found "living" in the trunk and branches, just inside the bark, through which they could pass for work in connection with the growth and coloring of the branches and leaves. Occasionally one would flash out from a tree, hover in midair, "perhaps to absorb vital essence from the air," then return to give it to the tree. Numbers of little mannikins could be seen working on the outside of the leaves and branches of a large beech, occasionally flying to the ground as if fetching some substance to take back to the tree and weave into the texture of the smaller branches and leaves. These mannikins would then fly to an adjacent tree of the same genus, there to repeat the operation. Others puttered about on the surface of the ground, amid the undergrowth and fallen leaves.

When Hodson tried to communicate with individual mannikins, he found their intelligence to be very primitive, below that of the animal, imitating humanity but without understanding the meaning or purpose of their mimicry. He observed them go through the motions of speech and even appear to shout loudly but was unable to catch any sound from their wide-open mouths.

Unlike with the more stable gnomes or fairies proper, Hodson found that if too intense a scrutiny was directed toward the mannikin it would lose its equilibrium, become confused and helpless, and finally disappear, either to a safe distance or into a higher, astral, dimension.

Hodson says he twice came across mannikins who were by no means pleasant, with prominent features, large noses, slanting eyes narrowed to slits, and unpleasant, malicious, leering expressions.

Infinitely more attractive to Hodson were spirits of the water, known as undines or nymphs, invariably naked and female, with delicately molded bodies.

In the ocean shallows he found sea nymphs more keenly alive than spirits of the land, in shape just like a human female of radiant beauty, but not winged like land fairies. These he found living in colonies both under the sea and on the surface, riding the waves and sometimes sinking into the depths with cries of joy. He could hear them call to one another in loud voices, "crying in exaltation as the life forces of which they are composed arouse in them an almost unimagined joy."

Constantly changing into brilliant and relatively formless flashes of light, then back again to human form, these sea nymphs, says Hodson, had no permanent etheric body but were able to assume a temporary one for contact with the physical plane. Their center of consciousness appeared to be a brightly burning flame in the head as they joyfully bathed in the powerful magnetism of the sea, absorbing some of the magnetic force and, after a moment's assimilation, discharging it. Their existence appeared to Hodson to be vivid in the extreme, far beyond anything possible to anyone living in a dense physical form as they continued to absorb and discharge force, their astral body swelling to twice its normal size, enormously quickened by the experience.

Hodson caught one sea fairy momentarily motionless, eyes blazing, arms outstretched in a shimmering aureole of white light, fully charged with force that radiated six feet in every direction, rejoicing in the sensation of vitality. The force, when discharged, carried with it for Hodson the impressed vibration of the sea spirit. As the sensation waned, the process was repeated.

Other fairy forms, in human shape, were described as scurrying over the surface of the water, among them small sea fairies, riding the waves, rejoicing in the electric vitality borne in with the incoming tide. More active and "virile" than land fairies, they "manifested a quality of fierceness in their exhalation and joy, as if taking on the power of the sea."

Larger varieties, much farther out from land, appeared as green etheric monsters, fishlike, yet unlike any fish known to Hodson, with head and body, but no resemblance to the human shape, transparent as glass, shining with a weird green light of their own. They seemed to rise up from the depths, slow and heavy of movement, gazing vacantly as if with an obtuse and limited intelligence.

Far down in the depths Hodson could see huge filamentoid, vegetablelike, etheric forms with little or no external consciousness drifting about with the currents. Even farther out to sea he spotted a group of great sea devas, heads crowned, huge, solemn, majestic rulers of the seas, faintly reminiscent of the classical Greek rendition of the sea god Neptune.

Watching the incoming tide on the west coast of England in April of 1922, Hodson could see up the coast and out to sea. The air was densely populated with countless sea spirits at various levels of evolutionary progress, from smaller human-shaped beings, rejoicing among the breakers, through the orders of large sea spirits resembling both fish and birds but usually with human heads.

It seemed to Hodson that as the electric vitality of the incoming tide increased, hosts of sea spirits would clothe themselves in etheric matter in order to participate more vividly in the marvelously refreshing and vitalizing magnetism created and released as the tide came higher and higher.

He described them as rushing toward the breaker line to enter the tidal magnetism as it discharged upward and forward during the whole period of flow, increasing to a peak at high-water mark. As they entered the magnetic field, sea spirits became visible in human shape, giving off brilliant flashes of white light. Slowly they absorbed the magnetism, experiencing a sensation of extreme delight up to a stage when even their ethereal organism could contain no more. A moment's pause as they assumed an expression of the most radiant joy and vivid vitality, surrounded by an aureole of light, then, at saturation point, the whole force dissipated in something like an electric discharge. Slowly the creature faded out of etheric vision in a state of dreamy inaction, retiring once more to the astral plane.

When the ocean reverted to the comparative quiet of low water, the beings, said Hodson, retired to the astral plane to "dwell upon the stimulating joys through which they have passed, and await the turn of the tide to once more repeat the vivid experience."

Hodson came across inland water spirits, definitely female and always nude, near rivers, streams, and falls. At Whitendale in April of 1922 Hodson sat in a heather-covered bower beside a waterfall that flowed between two huge stones to fall five or six feet to moss-covered rocks. There he set about studying water fairies. The tallest was about eight inches high, but all could increase their size to about two feet, some with rosy-colored auras, some pale green. Hodson saw them as diminutive human females, entirely nude, their long hair streaming behind them; a garland of small flowers around their foreheads, beautiful but utterly remote from human life. Because they were more subtle and quick in their movements and changed their form with bewildering rapidity, it was hard for Hodson to attract their attention or influence them in any way as they played in and out of the fall.

Flashing through the fall from different directions, they called out in wild tones, rising almost to a shriek, sounding to human ears—only faintly—like a shepherd's call across an Alpine valley, a sound Hodson believed he could represent by the series of vowels E-O-U-A-I, ending with a plaintive and appealing cadence: Wagner's Rhine maidens to a T.

With delight Hodson watched as the undines traveled up the fall against the stream or remained motionless within it, generally playing and flashing through it, passing in and out of the great rocks without experiencing any obstruction. When a cloud passed from the face of the sun and the fall was again bathed in brilliant light, the creatures appeared to experience an added joy, increasing their activity and their singing.

Hodson found less evolved undines, a foot high, their slim bodies supple and graceful, constantly assuming poses of great beauty as they floated in the midst of the fall or hovered just on the edge of the spray, rising like bubbles in water, body upright, limbs straight, drawing vitality from the sun and the falls until charged to bursting point, making a strong effort to compress and contain the vital energy until it became too much for them. At the summit he could see them flash free into the air, releasing the concentrated accumulated energy with a brilliant display of color and light, radiating joy and delight in all directions, "thrilling at the moment of discharge with delirious pleasure, as the energy impinges visibly on the surrounding rocks, bracken, and trees, which means growth for them and for the scenery in which they live." Hodson found the undine's expression at that moment of discharge to be especially beautiful, particularly in the eyes, flashing with dazzling radiance, expressing rapturous joy and a sense of abnormal vitality and power: "At the magical moment of release she experiences an ecstasy and exaltation beyond anything possible to mere mortals dwelling in the prison of the flesh."

The condition, says Hodson, is immediately followed by one of dreamy pleasure in which the consciousness is largely withdrawn from the physical plane and centered in the astral plane of emotion. The form becomes vague and indistinct until, having assimilated the whole experience, the undine reappears and repeats the process.

Their life, says Hodson, appears to consist of a continued repetition of what he called the three fundamental processes of Nature: absorption, assimilation, and discharge. Wilhelm Reich, in his *The Function of the Orgasm*, describes what he calls "the pulse of life" as "mechanical tension—bio-electric charge—bio-electric discharge—mechanical relaxation," concluding that "the orgiastic function, together with the known effect of the sun on a living organism . . . shows the living organism to be part of non-living nature."

And the similarity between the undine's experience and the human orgasm leads to the assumption that by having puritanically stunted our sexuality we may have short-circuited what could otherwise be a naturally rhythmic joie de vivre.

In the Lake District in June of 1922, by a waterfall in a bower surrounded by bracken and rocks, Hodson found another veritable fairyland, this time of more classical water nymphs. The main spirit of the falls appeared in the form of a female, again quite nude, full-sized and of singular beauty, differing from the undines previously observed in that she was much larger and had a more highly developed intelligence. Pink wings rose from her shoulder blades, small in proportion to the body, inadequate for flight, which could not have been their purpose. When first seen, this nymph, or "spirit of the falls," sprang out of the solid rock, to hang poised in the air before disappearing.

Hodson described her as like a marble statue come to life, pale rose-pink, hair fair and shining, features beautifully modeled, eyes large and luminous. To Hodson their expression had something of the wild, though the glance was not unkindly. He describes a rainbowlike aure-ole surrounding her as a halo surrounds the moon, almost spherical, consisting of evenly arranged concentric bands of soft yet glorious hues, the colors too numerous and in far too rapid movement for Hodson to detail. Her aura seemed to contain all the colors of the spec-trum in their palest shades, rose, green, and blue predominant, the bands outlined with golden fire.

Above the spirit's head Hodson noted a powerful upward flow of the force that interpenetrated her aura in a fan-shaped radiation, com-ing apparently from a brilliant golden point in the middle of her head, slightly below the level of the eyes, vibrant with her life. To Hodson the creature seemed to ensoul the rocks, trees, ferns, and mosses as well as the actual waterfall itself—a description from which one might deduce that the creature was in fact dispensing Reich's "orgone" or life force to her immediate surroundings.

Though it may be hard to believe that Hodson could encounter na-ture spirits even more energetic than these nymphs and undines, he had still to describe the sylphs. Creatures of the air rather than of earth, water, or fire, sylphs are connected to wind, cloud, and storm, their bodies entirely astral, human in form but somewhat below human height, quite asexual, their faces strangely beautiful, strong, vital, and controlled in spite of their apparent reckless abandon as they desport themselves, traveling at great speed across the sky, ten to fifteen miles in a flash, reveling in the force of the wind. Of these spirits of the air Hodson found many varieties, differing in power, intelligence, habits, and appearance, some floating near the surface of the earth, others hardly approaching it, disliking the human realm.

Hodson noted that sylphs frequently lost all semblance of human form, seeming to become whirling masses of force and vital energy, suddenly manifesting graceful winglike formations, long streaming curves, a suggestion of waving arms, of hair flying in the wind. Two blazing eyes would appear in a face of unearthly beauty "combining exaltation, intoxication, ecstasy, and fierce virility of power."

In the course of 1922 Hodson observed many different species of sylphs, varying in size, power, and evolutionary position, noting a certain fierceness in their joy as they shrieked to one another, their cries sounding like the wild whistling of the wind, much like Walkyries.

Sitting on the edge of a wood of very old larch and pine near Ewehurst in late 1922, Hodson could view a wide panorama stretching to the south downs. In a strong southwesterly he spotted sylphs at play, their gambols consisting of long, swift, straight rides down the wind for miles; or they would twist, turn, and dart suddenly upward, then fall in breathless dives that ceased abruptly just above the treetops, then equally swiftly ascend thousands of feet into the air. Hodson watched one sylph descend slowly to a few feet above the ground. It was a being of transcendent beauty, about eight feet tall, nude, asexual, but of the masculine type, perfectly modeled, beautifully proportioned, surrounded by a radiating aura three times its size, poised just above the top of wavering grasses. The sylph's natural body was found at the astral level, iridescent, changing, pulsating with astral forces, but not limited to a fixed or definite shape, capable of materializing on the etheric level into a beautiful male or female form to work among plants, animals, or even human beings.

Contact with the consciousness of this sylph suggested to Hodson a state of concentrated energy similar to that found within the atom: incalculable energy, awe inspiring it its potency, yet harmless because confined to prescribed channels of flow. The sylph's center of life appeared to be a chakra in the solar plexus area, marvelously radiant, from which the colors of the aura flowed outward in waves. Other lines of force streamed away from its body, dividing at the shoulders in winglike formations that extended above the head.

Raising its hands, the sylph seemed to Hodson to appeal to him to leave the limitations of the flesh and rise with it to higher levels of space and consciousness. The experience convinced Hodson that even the most exquisite moments of joy and exaltation possible to humans must be far below the intense dazzling vividness of existence normal to the sylph. Sadly, Hodson commented on life in the flesh as being dull and limited within its heavy, unresponsive human form.

Of the fourth category of nature spirits, salamanders, or spirits of fire, Hodson was less poetic, describing them as varying considerably in height, appearing to be built of flame, the form constantly changing, yet suggestive of human shape, eyes alight with fiery power, ears sharply pointed, "hair" streaming back like tongues of flame as they dived steeply into the flame of physical fire, flying through their element.

Their triangular face, when not veiled by flickering orange-red auric flames, seemed to Hodson distinctly human in appearance but quite inhuman in expression, with upward-slanting eyes lit by "an unholy delight in the destructive power of their element." Latent in the focal points of heat wherever it may manifest, fire spirits are grouped according to color—red, orange, yellow, or violet—all seen as subject to Agni, Lord of Fire, the active fiery intelligence considered the basis of fire in the solar system.

It remained for Rudolf Steiner, an early theosophist, later progenitor of the Anthroposophical Society, to bring to life the fire spirits and their extraordinary role of destruction and recreation. Fire in his philosophy is the fundament of all things, spiritual and physical, created and controlled by the highest in the hierarchy of creative spirits in the universe.

6

Worldwide Fairyland

Whereas Hodson, self-effacing author of a dozen books, depicts fairyland with the finesse of a hard-point etcher, Leadbeater, talented occultist, popular lecturer, thirty-third-degree Mason, former Anglican priest, and self-declared bishop of the Liberal Catholic Church, paints a broad colorful canvas with bold and convincing strokes. In contrast to Hodson's parochial consorting with domestic British spirits, Leadbeater displays the cosmopolitan panache of a world traveler.

Having observed all sorts of exotic specimens around the globe, Leadbeater speaks of an immense number of subdivisions of nature spirits varying in intelligence and disposition just like human beings, their diverse races inhabiting different countries, the members of one race tending to keep together. Some he describes as being common in one country, rare in another, while others are to be found almost any-where. All have their own colors to mark the difference between tribe and species, just as birds have different plumage, and, as with birds, the most brilliantly colored are found in tropical countries.

And whereas humanity occupies but a small part of the surface of the globe, "entities at a corresponding level on other lines of evolution" not only crowd the earth, says Leadbeater, "but populate the enormous plains of the sea and the fields of the air."

With gusto he contrasts the vivacious, rollicking orange-and-purple or scarlet-and-gold mannikins that dance among the vineyards of Sicily with the gray-and-green creatures who move more sedately among the oaks and furze-covered heaths in Brittany or the golden brown "good people" who haunt the hillsides of Scotland.

Noting that the emerald green variety is most common in England, he recounts having seen them in the woods of France and Belgium, though a bare hundred miles away in Holland hardly a one was to be seen. Yet the same mannikin could be found in Massachusetts and on the banks of the Niagara River. On the vast plains of the Dakotas, Leadbeater says he spotted black-and-white mannikins not seen elsewhere, whereas California could boast of a unique white-and-gold species.

Remarking on the diversity of nature spirits in the Australian provinces of New South Wales, Victoria, and tropical Northern Queensland, Leadbeater found the most frequent type encountered was a distinctive creature of "a wonderful luminous sky-blue color."

In Java he found the most common to be two distinct types, both monochromatic, "one indigo blue with faint metallic gleamings, the other a study in all known shades of yellow—quaint, but wonderfully effective and attractive." Another local variety was gaudily ringed, like a soccer jersey, with alternate bars of green and yellow. In the Malay Peninsula he found creatures with similar outfits, only striped red and yellow, and on the other side of the Straits of Sumatra, green-and-white ones.

On the great island of Sumatra, Leadbeater found a pale heliotrope tribe that he had seen only in the hills of Ceylon. And down in New Zealand he found the specialty to be a deep blue, shot with silver, whereas in the South Sea Islands he ran into a silvery white variety "which coruscates with all the colors of the rainbow, like a figure of mother-of-pearl."

Traveling in India, Leadbeater found all sorts of mannikins, from the delicate rose-and-pale-green type or the pale-blue-and-primrose variety of the hill country to the rich medley of "gorgeously gleaming colors, almost barbaric in their intensity and profusion," characteristic of the plains. The subcontinent also harbored the black-and-gold type more often associated with the African desert as well as a species resembling "a statuette made out of a gleaming crimson metal, such as was the orichalcum of the Atlanteans."

In the immediate neighborhood of volcanic disturbances, such as on the slopes of Vesuvius and Etna or in the interior of Java or on the Sandwich Islands or even in Yellowstone Park in North America or on the North Island of New Zealand, Leadbeater consistently found a curious variety of mannikin that looked as if it had been cast out of bronze and then burnished. This type he considered a survival of a primitive variety, representing an intermediate stage between the gnome and the fairy.

Altitude above sea level appeared to affect the distribution of nature spirits; those belonging to the mountains scarcely ever intermingled with those of the plains. In Ireland Leadbeater noticed a definite line of demarcation between different types. The lower slopes, like the surrounding plains, "were alive with an intensely active and mischievous little red-and-black race which swarms all over the south and west of Ireland, being especially attracted to the magnetic centers established nearly two thousand years ago by the magic-working priests of the old Milesian race to ensure and perpetuate their domination over the people by keeping them under the influence of the great illusion." By tradition, Milesians, led by two Spaniards, were the last invaders of Ireland and are regarded as the ancestors of the present inhabitants.

Half an hour farther up the slopes, not one of the red-and-black mannikins was to be seen. Instead the hillside was "populous with the gentler blue-and-brown type which long ago owed special allegiance to the Tuatha-de-Danaan." The latter, in Irish tradition, invaded Ireland before the Milesians and were reputed to have used great supernatural forces by means of which they defeated their predecessors, the Firbolgs. Defeated by the Milesians, the Tuatha-de-Danaan are said to have retired into the sidhe, or fairy mounds, becoming confused in Irish folklore with the fairies.

On the actual summit, says Leadbeater, no nature spirit of either type ever trespasses on the space "sacred to the great green angels who have watched there for more than two thousand years, guarding one of the centers of living force that link the past to the future of that mystic land of Erin."

Nature spirits, according to occult lore, have no phenomena corresponding to what humans mean by birth and death. A fairy, says Leadbeater, appears in this world full-sized, as does an insect. It then lives its life, short or long, without any appearance of fatigue or need for rest, without any perceptible change of age as the years go by.

As for the length of life of nature spirits, it is said to vary greatly, some having very short, others much longer lives than humans. All, like humans, are subject to reincarnation, though their condition makes the working of it slightly different.

During their tenure on earth, nature spirits have the advantage that in etheric life there is no need for food. The body of a fairy is described as absorbing the nourishment it needs without effort, straight from the surrounding ether. This nourishment, according to Leadbeater, is not actually absorbed, but rather a change of particles is constantly taking place with particles that have been drained of their vitality being cast out to make way for others full of it. And though nature spirits do not eat, they are said to obtain from the fragrance of flowers a pleasure analogous to that which people derive from the taste of food. To the nature spirits, says Leadbeater, aroma is more than a mere question of smell or taste; they bathe in it until it interpenetrates their bodies, reaching every particle simultaneously.

A nature spirit's body is described as having no more internal structure than a wreath of mist, so they cannot be cut or injured. As neither heat nor cold has any painful effect on them, they are seen to play as happily among the falling flakes of snow as under "the level lances of the rain," dancing with equal pleasure in the moonlight or glorying in the glow of sunlight, as content to float idly in the calm of a summer afternoon as to revel in the rushing wind. Fire spirits are distinct for liking nothing better than to bathe in fire, rushing from all sides to any conflagration, to fly upward with the flame over and over with wild delight.

Among nature spirits there appears to be no sex, no disease, no struggle for existence, exempting them from the most fertile causes of human suffering. Bodily pain is said to come to a nature spirit only from an unpleasant or inharmonious emanation or vibration, but the elemental's power of rapid locomotion enables it easily to avoid such hazards. Both Leadbeater and Hodson think we would see many more nature spirits if it weren't for their rooted objection to the proximity of human beings, an objection shared by all but the lowest types of nature spirits. Most, say the two theosophists, dislike and avoid humankind, whose members appear to them to be ravaging demons, despoiling and destroying wherever they go, wantonly killing—often with awful torture—all the beautiful creatures that nature spirits love to live with.

Man cuts down trees, tramples the grass, plucks flowers and casts them aside to die, and replaces the lovely wild life of nature with hideous brick and mortar and the fragrance of flowers with the "mephitic vapors of his chemicals and the all-polluting smoke of his factories."

Not only do we thus bring devastation to all the nature spirits hold most dear, but, Leadbeater warns, most of our habits and emanations are distasteful to them, giving them the same feeling of disgust that we would have if a bucket of filth were emptied over us. "For them to be near the average man is to live in a perpetual hurricane—a hurricane that has blown over a cesspool. Can one wonder that they should dislike, distrust, and avoid us. Can you be surprised that fairies shrink from us as from a poisonous reptile?"

In his discourse on nature spirits, Leadbeater highlights the role of evolution in their development, with a continual "upward movement" from lower to higher states. The gnome deeply buried underground he sees tending toward the surface before making the leap to fairydom, then, at a third stage, joining the enormous host of water spirits, eventually graduating through the air and fire spirits into the realm of angels.

Fairies of the land, according to Leadbeater, are recruited not only from the ranks of gnomes but also from the less evolved strata of the animal kingdom. This line of development just touches the vegetable kingdom in the shape of minute fungoid growth, then passes onward through bacteria and animalculae of various kinds, through the insects and reptiles, up to the birds, and only after many incarnations joins the fairies.

Another type of tiny fairy described by Leadbeater has a different origin: one of the commonest forms is like a tiny hummingbird, often seen buzzing around flowers very much like a hummingbird or bee. These charming creatures are beings, says Leadbeater, of another evolutionary line, destined never to become human. The life that animates them he describes as having come up through grasses and cereals such as wheat and oats, and later through bees. "Its next stage is to be en-souled as a beautiful fairy with an etheric body to live on the surface of the earth. Later still they will become sylphs and salamanders with only astral bodies, on their way to higher levels."

Although, says Leadbeater, there is a good deal of overlapping be-tween kingdoms as spirits evolve, the progression is rational. "A life which ensouled one of our great forest trees could never descend to animate a swarm of mosquitoes, nor even a family of rats or mice. On the other hand such a step could be appropriate for that part of the 'life-wave' which had left the vegetable kingdom at the level of the daisy or the dandelion."

With nature spirits, death, say occultists, is not as it is with humans. Instead, there comes a time when a spirit's energy seems exhausted, and it becomes tired of life. When that happens its etheric body grows more diaphanous until it is left as an astral entity to live for a while in that world among the spirits who represent its next stage of develop-ment. From that astral life, it fades back into its group soul before being provided with another astral and etheric body suitable for the devel-opment of another life.

Leadbeater describes another group of elementals that look after flowers. These, though beautiful, are really only thought-forms "created by a greater being in charge of the evolution of the vegetable king-dom." Not really living creatures, or only temporarily so, they have no evolving to do, no reincarnating life. When they have done their work they dissolve into the surrounding atmosphere, just as do human thought-forms.

Leadbeater explains that when one of the "great ones" has a new idea connected with the kingdom of plants or flowers under his charge, he creates a thought-form to carry out the idea. This usually takes the form of an etheric model of the flower or of a little creature that hangs around the plant or the flower all through the time that the buds are forming and gradually builds them into the shape and color to match the thought-form. But as soon as the plant has fully grown or the flower opened, the creature's work is over and it dissolves.

According to Hodson, the prime function of the nature spirits in the realm of plants is to furnish a vital connecting link between "the

stimulating energy of the sun and the raw material of the form-to-be."
The growth of a plant seed, regarded as the customary and inevitable
result of its being placed in a warm and moist soil, would never take
place, says Hodson, if the fairy builders were absent. "Nature's crafts-
men must be present to weave and convert the constituents of soil into
the structure of the plant."

The normal working body of a fairy or sprite engaged in assisting
growth process, according to Hodson, is not of the human nor of any
other definite form. "They have no clear-cut shape and their working
bodies can be described only as clouds of color, rather hazy, somewhat
luminous, with a bright spark-like nucleus. They cannot be defined in
terms of clear-cut form any more than you could describe a tongue of
flame. It is in this kind of body that they work, inside, that is, interpenetrating, the plant structure."

Hodson further describes these cloudlike bodies as being of the nature of a magnetic field, and their work on cell growth and the circu-
lation of sap is much like "the movement of iron filings by a magnet,
the magnetic influence being supplied by the currents of their own
vital energies."

Some of the nature spirits are seen to work above ground and some
among the roots below. Others appear to specialize in color, responsible for the "painting of flowers, the needed brush being the streaming
motion of their own cloud-like bodies."

Observing some bulbs growing in a bowl, Hodson described large
numbers of small submicroscopic "etheric creatures" moving about in
and around the growing plants, visible etherically as points of light,
playing around the stems and passing in and out of the growing plant.

"They have the power to rise into the air to a height equal to that
of the plant, but I have not seen any rise further than that. They absorb
something from the atmosphere, re-enter the tissue of the plant and
discharge it. This process is going on continually: the creatures are entirely self-absorbed, sufficiently self-conscious to experience a dim
sense of well-being and to feel affection for the plant which they regard as their body. They have no consciousness apart from this. The
bulbs give the impression of great power and concentrated energy.
The color is pinkish-violet, with a more intense light in the center, and

from this center the flowing force previously described radiates vertically upwards, carrying with it at a much slower pace the moisture and other nutrients. The little nature-spirits do not confine their energies to one plant or even to one bowl—for I see them flitting about from one bowl to another."

Hodson further explained how these diminutive creatures vitalize a plant. "When the process of absorbing is taking place they become enlarged 'and appear like pale violet or lilac-colored spheres, some two inches in diameter, with radii of force flowing from a central point within the sphere. The ends of these lines extend slightly beyond the circumference. Having expanded to the largest size which they are able to reach, they return close to the plant, enter it, and begin to discharge the material, or vital force, which they have absorbed." Hodson describes a natural "etheric vital flow" from the half-grown plants as reaching fully two feet above them, and on this vital flow the tiny creatures play and dance, tossed up and down by the flowing force, in which they appear to rejoice.

Hodson also describes seeing a process of absorption by the plants, with etheric matter flowing toward them from all sides. In some cases he saw feebly waving tentacles extended from the "etheric double" of the plant; through these, etheric matter was absorbed. These tentacles are described as hollow "etheric" tubes, slightly curved and slightly wider at the mouth, pale gray in color. The longest he could see extended four to six inches from the plant and were from a quarter inch to a half inch in diameter.

Occult teaching holds that "etheric" matter vibrates at rates that are too fine to be measured or tested by physical means yet is still substantial. It is divided into the four progressively finer levels coined by Leadbeater—E1, E2, E3, and E4—all of which take form and act according to discoverable laws. The even finer "astral" material of which the more basic body of the nature spirits is formed is said to consist of a spherical, many-colored aura surrounding the delicate "etheric form."

Normally, says Hodson, the consciousness of a fairy creature functions upon the astral plane, or "form" plane, rather than the "life" plane of etheric matter. The astral body of the creature is self-luminous, every atom of it a glowing particle of light, with streams of force radiating to build up wings of radiating energy. When a more objective self-expression is entered upon, the creature clothes itself more or less instinctively in the matter of the ether. This culminates in the temporary creation of an etheric body, "ensouled, inter-penetrated, and surrounded by its astral creator."

The denser "etheric vehicle" is taken on, according to occult tradition, for at least two reasons: an etheric body worn by a nature spirit gains for it an added sense of individuality or entity. Otherwise it feels unselfconsciously diffused throughout a group. Also, by closer contact with the physical world, the etheric vehicle provides an increased vitality and vividness of life, and this gives pleasure. The etheric body of a plant, say occultists, is created—before the physical body—out of energy organized according to a thought-form or prototype, which holds and molds the grosser material. The etheric vehicle also lasts longer, well after the plant's physical body begins to disintegrate.

To build these etheric bodies, nature spirits are required to emerge from the more tenuous astral level into the denser etheric level, where they become easily visible to clairvoyants. In the etheric they are said to dance, play, and see one another and, to some extent, human beings, whom they imitate and on occasion become attached to if the human is sufficiently sensitive to respond to their presence and even communicate with them.

Most illuminating is Hodson's remark that to etheric sight, although some of the nature spirits are less than a quarter of an inch in size, "they may be sub-microscopic from the point of view of solid measurement."

This relativity of size adds an eerie aspect to the clairvoyant's venture into fairyland. When Sir Arthur Conan Doyle completed his study of the evidence adduced by Gardner, Hodson, and others as to the nature of the spirit world, he felt himself to be "on the edge of a new continent, separated not by oceans but by subtle and surmountable psychic conditions."

This new multidimensional world, beyond the limiting confines of our three dimensions, was to be further explored and charted by Leadbeater, Besant, and other psychics as they blazed a trail for physicists deeper into the sinews of the atom.

7

Occult Chemistry

The thrust of my thesis is simple: if Hodson's clairvoyant faculties could enable him to "see" inside an electron, and if Annie Besant and Charles Leadbeater could accurately describe the inner makeup of the known chemical elements, then their descriptions of nature spirits would have to be taken seriously. But first I had to be sure there really was an acceptable correspondence between the theosophists' description of material atoms and the "reality" of orthodox physicists.

To find out I went in search of the first qualified theoretical physicist to reevaluate the theosophists' pioneering work in *Occult Chemistry*, . Dr. Stephen M. Phillips, a professor of particle physics. Phillips's book *Extrasensory Perception of Quarks*, published in 1980, while dealing with the most advanced nuclear theories, including the nature of quarks, postulated particles even smaller than quarks as yet undiscovered by science. Analyzing twenty-two diagrams of the hundred or so chemical atoms described in *Occult Chemistry* by his two co-nationals at the turn of the century, Phillips found it hard to avoid the conclusion that "Besant and Leadbeater did truly observe quarks using ESP some 70 years before physicists proposed their existence." What is more, their diagrams indicated "ultimate physical particles" even smaller than quarks.

By the time I discovered Phillips on the southern coast of England in the seaside resort of Bournemouth, he had checked another eighty-four of the theosophists' atoms: all were seen by him to be 100 percent consonant with the most recent findings of particle physicists. Every one of the 3,546 subquarks counted by Leadbeater in the element of gold could be correctly accounted for by Phillips. Were Phillips's conclusions to be substantiated by his peers, it would adduce evidence that the theosophists with their yogi powers had effectively opened a window from the world of matter into the world of spirit.

Prompt and committed approval of Phillips's conclusions had already come from the noted biochemist and Fellow of the Royal Society, E. Lester Smith, discoverer of vitamin B_{12}. At home in both the mathematical language of physics and the arcane language of theosophy, Smith spelled out his support in a small volume, *Occult Chemistry Re-evaluated*. And Professor Brian Josephson of Cambridge University, a Nobel Prize winner in physics, was sufficiently impressed by Phillips's radical thesis to invite him to lecture on the subject at the famous Cavendish Laboratory in 1985.

Yet few in the ranks of orthodoxy had the courage to risk their positions by supporting anything so wild as the notion that psychics could see better into the basic constituents of matter than could physicists armed with billion-dollar supercolliders.

Already at the end of the last century when the theosophists first directed their clairvoyant vision upon the atoms of the chemical elements, they had found themselves up against contemporary physicists who still thought of atoms as the "solid, massy, impenetrable, movable particles" about which Newton had conjectured two centuries earlier and which the Greek philosopher Democritus had envisaged as tiny, hard, indivisible balls that no one but God could dissect.

The most that the renowned French chemist Antoine Lavoisier could realize—before losing his head to the guillotine in 1794—was that the same element could exist in three states: solid, liquid, and *"vapeur."*

Newton's view was only slightly improved upon in 1808, three years after Nelson defeated Napoleon at Trafalgar, when the Englishman John Dalton declared the atom to be the basic unit of all chemical elements—such as hydrogen, oxygen, nitrogen—and that each element had its own particular weight. In Dalton's day, some forty elements were known, though no one had a clue as to the size or makeup of an atom.

By 1831, as Louis-Phillippe ascended the French throne in the guise of a citizen king, physicist Michael Faraday in England produced an electric current by rotating a copper disk between the poles of a magnet. To define a unit of this nonstatic electricity, the Irish physicist George Johnstone Stoney coined the name *electron*—not that either Faraday or Stoney had any idea what an electron might look like or what size it might be, let alone what electricity might be.

Only in 1898, three years after the theosophists had begun their psychic investigation of the atom, did Professor Joseph John Thomson, experimenting in his laboratory at Cambridge University, suddenly conclude that the luminous rays emitted by his cathode ray tube did not consist of charged molecules of gas but of fundamental particles that must be part of all matter. Nailing this first truly elementary particle, separable from Democritus's uncuttable atom, Thomson called it after Stoney's "electron," thereby inaugurating the science of particle physics.

Meanwhile, Leadbeater and Besant, approaching matter from their own point of view, using their siddhi powers to peer into the heart of chemical atoms, had entered a mysterious world still pluperfectly invisible to orthodox physicists. Their method had been described in the second century B.C.E. by the Indian sage Pantanjali in his *Yoga Sutras*, where he explained how to "obtain knowledge of the small, the hidden or the distant by directing the light of a superphysical faculty." Ever since, Eastern yogis have been using this siddhi form of perception described as "magnifying clairvoyance." The trick consists not in actually magnifying a small object but, conversely, in "making oneself [or rather one's viewpoint] infinitesimally small at will."

Phillips, analyzing the theosophists' claims, concluded they could vary the size of the images at will and that there appeared to be no limit to the level of magnification attainable, although a practical limit was set by the ability of the viewer and by the strain felt when viewing magnified objects. Unlike other forms of extrasensory perception, this particular state, though taxing, says Phillips, could be induced or terminated at will.

Among the first elements investigated by the two psychics was hydrogen, considered the lightest and simplest. As Leadbeater reduced his viewpoint to a subatomic level, he was able to describe to Annie

Besant—squatting on the floor, ready with sketch pad—an ovoid body within which appeared a pattern of two interlaced triangles whose corners held smaller spherical objects, six in all. Each of these spheres contained three points of light, which appeared as three-dimensional particles. The whole structure was seen to rotate on its axis with great rapidity, at the same time vibrating as its internal bodies performed similar gyrations.

This observation, made in 1895, says Phillips, was remarkable enough because the property of spin in atomic particles was as yet unknown to science. To slow down the spinning and quivering of their "chemical atom"—as the theosophists believed it to be—Leadbeater claimed a special form of willpower that enabled him to hold the object still enough for closer examination. Both Leadbeater and Besant subscribed to the theosophical view that in the physical plane of our normal reality, matter exists in seven distinct states: solid, liquid, and gaseous, plus four finer "etheric" states, the latter visible only to clairvoyants. They therefore believed that what they were studying as they progressively disintegrated chemical atoms were their various "etheric" levels, 1, 2, 3, and 4, until they reached a particle that, if further attacked, disappeared from their field of vision. This precious particle they called an "ultimate physical atom," or UPA. As the atoms of all the elements they investigated—from hydrogen to uranium—consisted uniformly of UPAs in different numbers and arrangements, they surmised, quite naturally, that these must be the smallest, fundamentally indivisible, constituent of matter and concluded that their disappearance must be from the etheric into the finer astral.

Eighteen such UPA particles appeared in their hydrogen "chemical atom" and 290 in their atom of oxygen. Held steady by Leadbeater, these minute UPAs were found to be uniformly composed of ten distinct, convoluted, closed spiral curves or "whorls," three of which appeared brighter and thicker than the other seven, the latter changing color incessantly as the whole heart-shaped UPA pulsated and spun on its central axis.

Counting and recounting the coiled strands of ten whorls, Leadbeater consistently came up with 1,680 turns of each heliacal whorl, making a total of 16,800 in each UPA, a number to which

Leadbeater attached great significance—correctly, as matters turned out later, much later.

Both Leadbeater and Besant noted two varieties of UPA, one a mirror image of the other, labeled by them male and female or "positive" and "negative." The two UPAs differed solely in the direction taken by the ten whorls spiraling around, down, and up again through the core in ever tighter spirals, the male ones moving in a clockwise direction, the female counterclockwise.

Force in the male atom seemed to well up as if from another dimension—"from the astral plane," as the psychics put it. A corresponding force seemed to disappear from the female atom back into the astral.[1]

Another surprising feature—as illustrated in *Occult Chemistry*—appeared to be common to all the UPAs disintegrated by the psychics from all the known chemical atoms: all appeared to be enclosed in a "wall" or a "hole" in space. Pulled out of this surrounding "hole" by the psychics' occult power, the UPAs invariably flew apart "as if released from great pressure," the contents being "extensively rearranged into astral matter." This feature was not rationally comprehensible to orthodox science until the 1980s with the further development of supercolliders and the discovery that space, rather than being a void, appears to be a plenum.

To pursue their analysis of chemical elements, the theosophists found they did not need to have the targeted element in a free state. By an act of willpower they could sever the bonds of chemical compounds to release their constituent atoms. Common salt (NaCl) thus provided ready specimens of both sodium (Na) and chlorine (Cl). For harder-to-come-by specimens, the two theosophists relied on their close friend, Sir William Crookes, England's most eminent chemist, who provided them samples in a pure state.

In 1907, during a summer holiday in Germany, their Hindu associate, Charles Janarajadasa, with an M.A. from Cambridge University,

1. In the language of modern physics, these ins and outs of energy would be labeled "sources and sinks of magnetic flux." But such language had not yet been invented by physicists.

managed to locate for them in the Dresden Museum a source of rare minerals. But when Leadbeater found it distracting to try to make a detailed clairvoyant examination of each specimen on the spot in the bustling museum, he discovered another system. He found that at night he could visit the museum "in one of his subtler bodies" yet still manage to dictate his observations to Jinarajadasa as the latter, still in the physical, took notes and made sketches.

A race was thus triggered between theosophists and orthodox physicists to discover the true nature of matter, the former by delicately employing their yogic vision, the latter more crudely by bombarding atoms with parts of atoms.

In 1909 physicist Ernest Rutherford, a big, gruff New Zealander with a walrus mustache, set the pace in his laboratory in Manchester when he found that the element radon naturally and spontaneously emitted particles to which he gave the name "alpha" (later discovered to be the nucleus of a helium atom bereft of its electron mantle). By placing a source of alpha particles in a lead case with a narrow hole, Rutherford was able to aim emitted particles at a piece of very thin gold foil, which deflected the path of the particles onto a surrounding wall of zinc sulfide. The zinc sulfide then gave off a flash of light each time it was struck by an alpha particle.

From this procedure Rutherford was able to deduce that the only thing that could be knocking the alpha particle off course would have to be a more massive particle, positively charged, and that this particle must be the nucleus in each gold atom, occupying a very small volume in the center of the relatively large atom, actually less than 1 percent. For this discovery—that Democritus's solid atom had a hard, separable nucleus—Rutherford received the 1909 Nobel Prize for physics, along with the title of baron from a grateful King Edward VII.

Yet Rutherford's nucleus was just what the theosophists had been viewing for some time with their siddhi powers and describing in great detail in various publications, although, as later developed, theirs were actually pairs of nuclei, duplicated by the disturbing act of clairvoyant observation. In 1908, well before Rutherford proposed his nuclear model of the atom, and twenty-four years before another physicist, James Chadwick, actually discovered the neutron—a discovery that led scientists to conclude that atomic nuclei must consist of neutrons and protons—the two theosophists had accurately depicted the number of protons and neutrons in the nuclei of both arsenic and aluminum. Yet neither they nor their contemporary scientists yet knew that atomic nuclei differed from one another only by the number of protons and neutrons they contained.

During this same period, fifty-six more elements were studied and described by the theosophists, including five as yet unknown to science—promethium, astatine, fancium, protoactium, and technitium—plus six isotopes, though it was not then known that an element could have atoms of more than one weight: its isotopes. Isotopes consist of nuclei with the same number of protons but a different number of neutrons, and an element can have as many as ten or more isotopes. Neon (mass number 20) and a variant meta-neon (mass number 22) were correctly described in The Theosophist in 1908, some six years before Frederick Soddy, another British physicist, introduced the concept of isotopes to science, for which he, too, received a Nobel Prize.

The theosophists, whose estimates of the atomic weight of elements, specified to two decimals, showed remarkable agreement with accepted scientific values, were simply describing what they could see with the use of their siddhi powers. As later physicists admitted, there was no scientific reason for them or anyone else to suspect a second variety of neon and certainly no purpose in the theosophists fabricating one. What Leadbeater and Besant were trying to accomplish was merely to bring what they were seeing inside their "atoms" into line with the table of elements formulated in mid–nineteenth century by the Russian chemist Dmitri Ivanovich Mendeleev. The table predicted that if elements were appropriately tabulated by atomic weight, they would fall into groups of families having similar chemical properties. The theosophists simply came across the isotopes as they noted that elements in the same group in the table, with the same properties, all had the same complex geometric shapes, which they painstakingly depicted in their diagrams.

With few exceptions, all the inner structures of their "chemical atoms" appeared in seven basic shapes: spikes, dumbbells, tetrahedra, cubes, octahedra, bars, and star groups. All the inert gases appeared to be star shaped. The five Platonic solids—the only completely regular solid geometric figures in nature—were all to be found in the theosophists' archetypal atoms and molecules. None of this, however, could be corroborated by contemporary physicists, still waiting for the development of X rays, the electron microscope, and supercolliders.

The result of the theosophists' work was published by Annie Besant in 1908 in a series of papers in *The Theosophist,* followed by the first edition of *Occult Chemistry.* A further twenty elements were studied by Besant and Leadbeater at the headquarters of the Theosophical Society in Adyar, Madras, and a second edition was published in 1919. It was edited by Janarajadasa, who amusingly describes a party of theosophists moving off into the woods with rugs and cushions every afternoon when the weather was fine so that Leadbeater and Besant could make their siddhi investigations while the others sat around listening or reading. By 1933, the year before Leadbeater died, all the then known elements—from hydrogen to uranium—and several unknown isotopes had been studied and depicted, along with an assortment of compounds. Besant's drawings are still in Adyar, mounted in a special book, as are Leadbeater's drawings, all with the relevant correspondence. From this material Janarajadasa put together the 1951 edition of *Occult Chemistry.*

Yet the book was totally disregarded by the scientific community. And because it claimed to show particles far smaller than protons, a concept at that time hopelessly at odds with orthodox science, the book could safely be disregarded as fantasy. Also, as Professor Smith points out, few physicists had even heard of *Occult Chemistry.* Books by theosophists were read mostly by theosophists, few of whom had the training in orthodox physics required to support their beleaguered colleagues.

When Janarajadasa was asked what he could do to remedy the situation, he answered, "Nothing. Wait until science catches up."[2]

---

2. In a letter to Professor F. N. Aston, inventor of the mass spectrograph, an instrument for detecting isotopes, Janarajadasa had pointed out that Besant and Leadbeater had discovered the neon-22 isotope four years before neon was found scientifically to have an isotope and that the helium-3 isotope announced by Aston in 1942 had been described in *The Theosophist* as early as 1908. Aston sent back a cursory reply: "Dr. Aston thanks Mr. Janarajadasa for sending his communication of January 8 and begs to return same without comment as he is not interested in Theosophy."

Orthodox physicists, unable without siddhi vision to see inside atoms, could pursue Rutherford's method only by bombarding atomic nuclei with atomic particles in a determined effort to break up a nucleus and find what it contained. Their best projectiles were electrons and protons, the former easily obtained by heating up a wire to incandescence, the latter by removing an electron from an atom of commercially available hydrogen. Either particle could then be sufficiently speeded up with an accelerator to shatter a targeted nucleus.

Man-made accelerators are designed to propel particles around a circuit to increase their energy and mass. In principle, all one needs is a standard car battery with terminals connected to copper plates a short distance apart in a vacuum. An electron from the negative terminal will invariably jump the gap toward the positive terminal, gathering energy as it jumps. If the positive terminal is made of wire screen, most of the electrons slip through to create a beam of electrons. Repeat the process along a several-mile circuit, add a million-volt battery (plus magnets to keep the electron beam from wandering off its steeplechase track), and you can accelerate electrons to an energy of several million volts. These can then create an impact strong enough to smash the nucleus of the atom into which they collide.

Physicists analyze the debris, not directly, as did the theosophists, but by means of a black box in which the scatterings are parsed by sophisticated electronic equipment. More and more expensive colliders were built in the 1950s and '60s, including Stanford's Linear Accelerator Center, known as SLAC, and Europe's Center for Nuclear Research, known as CERN, and Fermilab outside Chicago, named after the Italian-born physicist Enrico Fermi, developer of that super-incubus, the atom bomb. From these multimillion dollar colliders issued man-made particles by the thousands, mostly infinitesimal ephemeral particles that disappeared in microseconds—as little as a billionth of a trillionth—though a couple of hundred heavier particles remained substantial long enough to be called hadrons (from Greek for heavy) and were given Greek-letter names such as sigma and lambda. Many of these, being synthetic varieties of protons and neutrons, were not much use in determining the basic substance of matter: whereas a natural proton can last virtually forever, atom-smashed hadrons vanish under scrutiny. And in any case, none matched the theosophists' UPAs, of which they counted nine in a proton.

The first indication of a possible reconciliation between what the theosophists described and what the physicists might concede only came in the mid-1960s when a particle smaller than a proton was mathematically postulated by theoretical physicists. In 1964 Murray Gell-Mann at the California Institute of Technology and George Zweig at CERN independently proposed the existence of what they referred to as "mathematical structures": three smaller constituents of a proton Although such postulated particles—quirkily called quarks by Gell-Mann—were mathematically "logical constructs" based on the patterns of hadrons or organized protons and neutrons that appeared in the black boxes, they showed too many unlikely features to be taken seriously by the rest of the scientific community.

Believing in quarks, said eminent professor of physics Harold Fritsch, required the acceptance of too many peculiarities, not the least of which were their unconventional charges: the new mathematical theory required quarks to have not integral but an unheard-of fractional charge of $2/3$ or $-1/3$. So far all particles had been measured in whole-number multiples of the charge of an electron.

In view of this attitude, what was later to become accepted by science as one of the great theoretical breakthroughs of the century had to be ushered in as a joke during an amateur cabaret show in Aspen, Colorado. As reported by Barry Taubes in the publication *Discover,* Murray Gell-Mann jumped up from the audience on cue and babbled wildly what seemed like nonsense about how he had just figured out the whole theory of the universe, of quarks, of gravity, and of everything else. "As he raved with increasing frenzy, two men in white coats came on stage to drag him away, leaving the audience in laughter."

Even the manner in which the new particles were named was enough to incite ridicule. The word *quark* in German describes a special kind of soft cheese and is synonymous with *nonsense*. Gell-Mann claimed it was the number three that led him to introduce the word, inspired by a passage from James Joyce's *Finnegans Wake:*

Three quarks for Muster Mark! Sure he hasn't got much of a bark
And sure any he has it's all beside the mark.

Reaction to the quark model in the theoretical physics community
was also far from benign. "Getting the CERN [European Center] report published in the form that I wanted," wrote Gell-Mann (later to
receive the Nobel Prize for physics), "was so difficult I finally gave up
trying. When the physics department of a leading university was considering an appointment for me, their senior theorist, one of the most
respected spokesmen for all of theoretical physics, blocked the appointment at a faculty meeting by passionately arguing that it was the
work of a 'charlatan.'" To which Gell-Mann added, modestly, "The
idea that hadrons [protons and neutrons], citizens of a nuclear democ-
racy, were made of elementary particles with fractional quantum numbers did seem a bit rich. The idea, however, is apparently correct."

And correct it was. At SLAC, where protons were routinely being
bombarded by electrons at very high energy, an alert technician noted
within a proton three rapidly moving pointlike constituents. Could
these be quarks?

When the experiment was repeated at Fermilab and at CERN using
muons as projectiles (muons are identical with electrons, only two
hundred times heavier and ten times as energetic), the conclusion was
inevitable: a proton consists of three quarks.

What the theosophists sixty years earlier had seen so clearly with their
siddhi vision could be revealed only now to physicists. The magnitude of
the effort this required can be judged by the fact that to study one
atom the physicists needed one electron-volt of energy, but to reveal a
quark—whose radius they estimate at .000000000000000000001 of
a centimeter, or a million times smaller—required ten billion electron-
volts. As for the theosophists' UPA, or "subquark," it was still clearly many
dimensions smaller.

By the end of the 1970s the physicists' model had developed into six
different kinds of quarks, five of which had been identified and given
the Alice-in-Wonderland "flavors" of up, down, charm, strange, and
bottom. The last, and heaviest, remained elusive until mid-1994 when

physicists at Fermilab discovered "top" quark, leading Dr. P. K. Iyengar, eminent scientist and former chairman of the Indian Atomic Energy Commission, to finally give the theosophists a modicum of credit when he remarked, "The top quark discovered recently substantiates that occult chemistry is a phenomenon which exists and should be accepted as such."

Further, to differentiate the newly discovered quarks, physicists assigned them three different colors—red, blue, and green—though they were quick to point out that the choice had nothing to do with our ordinary perception of color. It was just a conventional way of labeling differing mathematical qualities encountered by theorists.

So quarks were a fact, validating—better late than never—the theosophists' diagrams of three such particles to a proton.

As the proton was seen to be made of two ups and one down quark, the neutron of one up and two downs, this gave the proton a positive charge of 1.0, leaving the neutron neutral with a charge of 0.0. With three quarks to a proton, add an electron and you have an atom of hydrogen. It—as all the other elements—turns out to be made of nothing but quarks and electrons. The whole universe must therefore be put together basically with but two quarks—one up and one down—plus the electron.

And quarks? Of what are they made?

The problem propelled Phillips into some abstruse mathematical calculations, which inexorably led to the conclusion that quarks must consist of subquarks, also three in number—just as the theosophists had presaged with their UPAs. For these postulant-particles Phillips coined the name *omegons*.

This omegon theory was reassuringly backed by Dr. Lester Smith as being "straight orthodox science founded upon recent theory of quantum chromodynamics which could be and was offered for publication in a scientific journal." Duly accepted, it appeared under the typically abstruse title of "Composite Quarks and Hadron-Lepton Unification."

It was at this point in his mathematical quest that Phillips came across the theosophists' book in California, with its "hydrogen atom" clearly depicted with six quarks, each of which showed three ultimate physical atoms for a total of eighteen—described by them as the basic building blocks of nature. But why eighteen instead of the nine omegons that appeared in Phillips's mathematical model? Why the doubling effect in an otherwise remarkable match?

For many long hours Phillips puzzled over the discrepancy until he realized that what the theosophists might have been viewing was a diproton, normally an unstable and short-lived amalgam of two hydrogen nuclei. But to account for how the theosophists could have come upon such an anomaly required more searching. Finally Phillips came up with a solution based on the modern theory of quantum physics—unknown to the theosophists at the turn of the century—of a dynamic interplay between observer and observed. The actual act of capturing atoms for observation and slowing down their "wild gyrations" must have profoundly disturbed them. This interplay, Phillips reasoned, must have released the tightly bound quarks and omegons from the nuclei of two atoms and merged them into a single chaotic cloud, analogous to extremely hot plasma, which then condensed into the double nucleus observed. In support of the hypothesis, Dr. Smith noted that normally this could be done only at exceedingly high temperatures such as those postulated to have been prevalent 10^{-6} seconds after the so-called Big Bang. But "cold plasma," he pointed out, can also exist: in it the strong forces between omegons come back into play, causing them to recombine and condense into a new stable grouping: the theosophists' double-imaged atoms.

Rewardingly, once this doubling-up effect was taken into account, every other element described and illustrated by the theosophists in *Occult Chemistry*, including compounds and crystals, fell into its proper place in the periodic table with the requisite number of constituent particles. With their siddhi powers, the theosophists had accurately described every known element years before the physicists and in a few cases even before these elements were scientifically discovered.

Not only were the theosophists vindicated, so was Phillips. With deserved satisfaction, and no fear of rebuttal, he could categorically state, "The new patterns derived by application of the rules of theoretical physics tally perfectly with the diagrams which illustrate *Occult Chemistry.*"

In opening a window for the physicist into the world of matter, Leadbeater and Besant left open an even wider door into the realm of the spirit—there, like it or not, to ponder on its gnomes and elves, its sylphs and undines.

8

Orthodox Cosmos

Adeptly clairvoyant, clairaudient, and clairsentient, Leadbeater and Besant claimed to have learned from Indian and Tibetan masters to break through to continuous "astral consciousness, with the body awake or asleep," and thus be able to investigate "the constitution of superphysical matter in the structure of man and the universe, as well as the nature of occult chemistry."

To these two investigators the basic constituent of matter, an ultimate physical atom, or UPA, smaller than a proton, smaller by far than a quark, appeared as "a little miniature sun," dual in nature, positive, but with a negative mirror image. Ovoid in shape, each consists of ten closed stringlike spirals made up of progressively smaller "spirillae." Its ever-diminishing spirillae consist of millions of dots of energy whirling in and out from what the investigators called a fourth-dimensional astral plane, entering the male UPA and exiting the female. "Bright lines" or "streams of light" that linked the UPAs were called by the theosophists "lines of force."

Leadbeater specialized in the geometric arrangement of these UPAs, identifying and counting their number in each element examined, while Annie Besant studied the configuration of the "lines of force" linking and holding together the groups of these particles. Force, said Leadbeater, "pours into the heart-shaped depression at the top of the UPA and issues from that point, and is changed in character by its passage as it rushes through every spiral and every spirilla, changing shades of color that flash out from the rapidly revolving and vibrating UPA." These color changes appeared to Leadbeater to depend on different activities of the ten whorls, each of 1,680 spirillae, as one or another was thrown into more energetic action. To ascertain the number 1,680, Leadbeater says he meticulously counted the turns in each whorl in 135 different UPAs selected from numerous substances. Each whorl of the first spirilla he found to be a helix made of seven smaller circular whorls of second-order spirillae, and so on, through seven orders, each finer than the preceding one.

By willfully "pressing back and walling off the matter of space," Leadbeater identified the seventh- and last-order spirillae as consisting of seven "bubbles" spaced evenly along the circumference of a circle, bubbles he referred to as existing in the invisible plenum of space and to which he gave the name "koilon," from the Greek word meaning "hollow." Leadbeater calculated that each major whorl consisted of about 56 million bubbles, which gave a total of some 14 billion bubbles for each UPA. The theosophists therefore concluded that all matter in the ultimate analysis must consist of bubbles or holes in space, "like pearls upon an invisible string." It was a description that two generations later would tie them to the most advanced and challenging concepts of modern physics: the superstring theory and the Higgs field theory, on the cutting edge of physics, both clearly presaged by Leadbeater and Besant a century earlier.

The Higgs field theory is a sort of revenant. Way back in the middle of the nineteenth century, in the time of James Clerk Maxwell, physicists felt the need for a medium that would pervade all space and through which light and other electromagnetic waves could travel. To satisfy these requirements, they postulated ether: an all-pervading, infinitely elastic, massless medium, poetically the personification of the clear upper air breathed by the Olympians.

What happened to this elixir or quintessential underlying principle? Einstein, with his special theory of relativity, sent it to join phlogiston in the dustbin. Yet, like the memory of an amputated limb, the need for ether spookily persisted. What now replaces it for the theoretical physicist is a controversial "field" named after a young physicist from the University of Edinburgh, Peter Higgs, the full dimensions of which are yet to be known. Some physicists believe it to consist of fundamental particles such as the electron; others believe it to be composed of quarklike objects. A third group believes the Higgs particle to be a bound state of "top" and "antitop" quark.

But why, asks Leon Lederman—eminent particle physicist, author of *The God Particle*—hasn't Higgs been universally embraced? Tartly he replies, "Because Veltman, one of the Higgs architects, calls it a rug under which we sweep our ignorance. Glashow [professor of particle physics at Harvard], a toilet in which we flush away the inconsistencies of our present theories."

Yet physics will not work without the equivalent of a Higgs field.

The notion is simple enough: all space contains a field, the Higgs field, which permeates the vacuum and is the same everywhere. The word *vacuum,* says Dr. Smith, may make the reader's mind boggle. Normally used to indicate a space from which air or any other gas has been removed, vacuum is used by physicists in the same nonliteral sense as they use *color* or *flavor* to describe mathematical properties that cannot be expressed in ordinary language, such as properties of quarks and omegons.

Search for a Higgs field "in the vacuum of space" developed after all efforts had failed to find a clue to the origin of mass, mass being described by physicists as "a body's resistance to acceleration," quaintly measured in "slugs."[1]

Lederman hints that the function of the Higgs particle is to give mass to massless particles, mass no longer being considered an intrinsic property of particles but a property acquired by the interaction of particles with their environment. Pervading all space, says Lederman, the Higgs field is "cluttering up the void, tugging on matter, making it heavy." Waxing both sinister and fey, he describes the problem: "We believe a wraithlike presence throughout the universe is keeping us from understanding the true nature of matter. . . . The invisible barrier that keeps us from knowing the truth is called the Higgs field. Its icy tentacles reach into every corner of the universe. . . . It works in black magic through a particle, the Higgs boson, or God particle."

---

1. A slug is a unit of mass equal to the mass accelerated at the rate of one foot per second when acted upon by a force of one pound weight.

To find their sneaky entity, Lederman and his fellow physicists have come up with no better system than to rev up their colliders to attack atoms with ever more powerful artillery, hoping thus to produce more particles—sleptons, squarks, gluinos, photinos, zinos, and winos—whose mass, spin, charge, and family relations they can then catalogue along with the particle's lifetime and the product of its decay.

All of this has cost taxpayers billions of dollars, half a billion alone for an accelerator at Fermilab. Fermilab's collider-detector facility, known as CDF, lavishly housed in an industrial hangar painted blue and orange, was designed to accommodate a five-thousand-ton detector instrument. It took two hundred physicists and as many engineers more than eight years to assemble what Leon Lederman, one of its distinguished directors, describes as a ten-million-pound Swiss watch, the electric bill for which runs to more than ten million dollars a year.

By the 1990s the CDF was employing 360 scientists as well as students from a dozen universities and national and international labs and was equipped with 100,000 sensors, including scintillation counters, organizers, and filters. A special computer was designed to sort through the atomic debris, programmed to decide which of the hundreds of thousands of collisions each second are "interesting" or important enough to analyze and record on magnetic tape. In one millionth of a second the computer must discard, record, or pass data into a buffer memory to make way for the next item. Data encoded in digital form and organized for recording on magnetic tape at the rate of 100,000 collisions per second in 1990–91 were expected to increase to a million collisions per second some time later in the 1990s.

Already the system stores close to a billion bits of information for each event: in a full run the information stored on magnetic tape is equivalent, as reported by its director, to five thousand sets of the *Encyclopedia Britannica*. It then takes a battalion of highly skilled and motivated professionals armed with powerful workstations and analysis codes two or three years, says Lederman, to do justice to the data collected in a single run.

The primary task of these Higgs field players is, of course, to locate the ball they're supposed to be playing with. To accomplish this apprentice sorcerer's mirage they envisaged an even more powerful collider, one with an even longer circuit, larger source of energy, and bigger punch to produce an even smaller particle: a superconducting supercollider circling fifty-four miles through the wasteland of Wasahachie, Texas, its generator to produce not billions but trillions of electron volts—at a cost to the public of several billion dollars.[2]

With this leviathan Lederman hoped to nail his God particle to the establishment barn door by the year 2005. But the theosophists appear to have found it already in what Leadbeater calls his "koilon, the true aether of space," the medium in which the bubbles of his UPAs are but holes. In orthodox physics the latest breakthrough, developed at the end of the 1970s, was formulated to demonstrate that quarks and antiquarks, the antimatter counterparts of quarks—if regarded as pointlike magnetic charges—were held together by "strings" or tightly knit bundles of magnetic "flux," lines of force analogous to the magnetic field around a magnet embedded in the Higgs field permeating all space. This Higgs medium was seen as squeezing together the magnetic lines of force into tubes of magnetic flux.

But this model didn't quite work; so back to the drawing board. By 1984 a "superstring" theory had been formulated to eliminate the abnormalities: its basic premise replaced points as the smallest existing particles with tiny strings. All fundamental particles (including quarks) were regarded as different quantum states of strings, strings with no ends known as "closed" superstrings, all interacting with one another by joining together to form more closed superstrings, in a maze of Chinese boxes.

For some time, says Phillips, this second model was thought to be physically unrealistic. But in 1985 a new kind of closed superstring was discovered, the "heterotic superstring." Occupying nine mathematical dimensions of space, it not only became the most studied model by physicists but, as Phillips demonstrates, has remarkable similarities with Leadbeater's ultimate physical atom.

Omegons, of course, are nothing but the UPAs so carefully depicted by the theosophists back in 1895 as emitting and receiving "bright lines" or "streams of light." Annie Besant, responsible for reporting how

2. The project was quashed by Congress in early 1994.

groups of UPAs were bound together, depicted hundreds of stringlike configurations or "lines of force" linking UPAs. Such diagrams, as Phillips points out, are essentially identical to pictures of subatomic particles appearing in physics research journals today.

Having established in his book that UPAs are the as yet undetected constituents of "up" and "down" quarks in the protons and neutrons of atomic nuclei, Phillips realized in 1984 that there are similarities between features of the UPA and a superstring that suggest strongly that the former are simply subquark states of the latter.

In the summer of 1984 two physicists, John Schwarz and Michael Green, respectively at the California Institute of Technology and London's Queen Mary College, made what Phillips calls "an exciting discovery." By treating fundamental subatomic particles as extended objects that look like pieces of string rather than as single points in space, they eliminated a long-standing problem afflicting quantum field theory. This, however, required that space-time have ten dimensions instead of Einstein's four. The theory that emerged from this breakthrough, as described by Phillips, pictures the basic particles of matter as a kind of vibration taking place along closed curves in a ten-dimension space-time continuum. All known particles, such as electrons, neutrinos, quarks, and photons are conceived as vibrational and rotational modes of these stringlike curves or superstrings.

According to this new theory, the physical properties of particles depend upon the nature of the curled-up or "compactified" six-dimensional space that exists at every point of ordinary three-dimensional space. One of the simplest models of such a six-dimensional space is a "six-dimensional torus" or doughnut in which at every point of three-dimensional Euclidean space there are six mutually perpendicular one-dimensional circles around which the superstring winds as it moves through space.

In what amounts to a major breakthrough, Phillips points out that

1. just as each of the ten whorls of a UPA is a closed curve, so the favored model of a superstring is that of a closed string or curve;

2. each of the 1,680 coils in a UPA whorl is a helix wound around a torus, and each of the latter's seven turns is another helix wound

seven times around a smaller torus, and so forth. There are six orders of progressively smaller helices, each one winding seven times
around a circle at right angles to the circular turns of adjacent
orders. This matches one of the models of the hidden "compactified," six-dimensional space of superstrings considered by physicists, namely the six-dimensional torus. Each order of helix is
simply the winding of a string about the six differently sized, circular dimensions of a six-dimensional torus.

To counter possible objections from string theorists, Phillips shows
that a superstring is not *one* string (as theorists currently assume) but is
a bundle of *ten* separate, nontouching strings identical to so-called
bosonic strings, which some physicists believe are more fundamental
than superstrings and for which quantum mechanics predicts all of
twenty-six dimensions. According to Phillips, the UPA is the subquark
state of a superstring, each of its ten whorls being a closed twenty-six-
dimensional bosonic string, the lowest six tornoidally compactified dimensions of which manifested to Leadbeater as the six higher orders of
helices, making up each of the 1,680 turns of a whorl.

All of which leads Phillips to a cogent conclusion. "The excuses for
disbelieving the claims of psychics," asserts Phillips, "are irrelevant in
the context of their highly evidential descriptions of subatomic particles published in 1908, two years before Rutherford's experiments
confirmed the nuclear model of the atom, five years before Bohr presented his theory of the hydrogen atom, 24 years before Chadwick discovered the neutron and Heisenberg proposed that it is a constituent
of the atomic nuclei, 56 years before Gell-Mann and Zweig theorised
about quarks. Their observations are still being confirmed by discover-
ies of science many years later."

Once more the theosophists, using descriptions of matter more
comprehensible than the abstruse mathematical symbols of the academics, let alone their Alice-in-Wonderland verbiage, appear to have
stolen a march on the physicists.

9

Inside the Electron

At this point there appeared on the scene another psychic with an even more particulate blueprint for the Higgs theory and its superstring bedfellow. In 1991 Phillips was contacted by a Canadian psychotherapist in Toronto, Ron Cowen, who had recognized in Phillips's book pictures similar to the mental images he experienced during the Buddhist meditations he had been practicing for twenty years. Ron Cowen claimed that his siddhi or micro-psi ability manifested in 1985 during meditation while studying the Theravadan Abhidhamma, an ancient Buddhist text. Could this psychic, Phillips wondered, adduce insights into the nature and mechanics of quarks?

Some years earlier, atom smashers at SLAC had identified the particle that carries the force required to keep quarks glued together as they whirl around in their proton prison: aptly the SLACkers christened it a gluon. Gluons are members of the family of energy particles—such as photons and pions—collectively known as bosons after the Indian physicist S. N. Bose, to distinguish them from more material particles—such as protons, quarks, and omegons—collectively called fermions in honor of Enrico Fermi. The zero-mass gluon was seen to be absorbed and emitted in continuous streams by quarks, creating a binding force, progressively stronger with distance, that keeps the quarks permanently trapped within protons and neutrons.

In Phillips's model his omegons, or subquarks—three to a quark—are equally confined by the same absorption and emission, only of "hypergluons," particles analogous to gluons. As physicists picture protons to be triplets of quarks held together by Y-shaped strings of gluons, Phillips pictures quarks as triplets of omegons held together by Y-shaped hypergluons. Only how to substantiate his theory?

Intrigued by the prospect of further validating the nature of the Leadbeater and Besant UPA, or subquark, Phillips traveled to Toronto to the Dharma Center, a Buddhist meditational retreat, where he tape-recorded Ron Cowen in several many-houred sessions as the psychic used his remarkable talent to delve even deeper into the microscopic world of superstrings and gluons.

In a detailed paper—of which the following account is but a précis—Phillips describes how Ron, given a capsule of hydrogen, but without being told what it contained, used his ESP to penetrate the glass and capture an object that gave him the impression of consisting of two overlapping triangles with spheres at their corners—clearly, says Phillips, two hydrogen nuclei, precisely as described by the theosophists.

Already Ron was validating the theosophists' observations by noting the diatomic gas molecule he had chosen to collapse into a brief "chaos" before reforming it into a facsimile of the "atom" described by Leadbeater and Besant. What they had observed—it was now clear to Phillips—were not the actual atoms but restabilized forms created from pairs of atomic nuclei destabilized by being viewed psychokinetically.

Pulling apart the triangles of what were evidently quarks in the hydrogen nucleus, Ron increased his magnifying power to scrutinize one of the corner spheres, which contained what looked to him like three walnuts joined together into a fan-shaped cloverleaf by three looping threads or strings: precisely the triplet of UPAs that the theosophists called a "hydrogen triplet"—today's quark.

Ron said two of the walnuts were facing him, whereas the third faced away. He got a snapshot of one walnut having flipped its axis, sensing that the others had also done so simultaneously. All three walnuts now took turns at being odd-man-out, the rhythm of flipping being regular with both walnuts and threads attached to them. This synchronized random flipping of three UPAs in a hydrogen triplet, or quark, says Phillips, is remarkable confirmation of the superposition principle of quantum mechanics. All known particles in the universe are divisible into two groups: particles of spin $1/2$, which make up matter—protons, quarks, electrons—and particles of spin 0, 1, and 2, which provide the forces—gluons, photons, pions. The indefinite spin state of each spin–1/2 subquark pointing in opposite directions at different instants in time but coordinated in such a way as to create a quark-bound state with overall spin of 1/2, indicates, says Phillips, that Ron was observing the quantum nature of spin.

Taking a closer look at one walnut, Ron saw that two threads came out of it, one of which appeared fainter than the other. The clearer one looked like a tangled, twisted piece of string, which could be pulled out into a straight line with little effort and which, on being relaxed, resumed its tangled state.

Thinking he would see a spiral within one of these strings, Ron magnified it. Instead he saw a stream of bubbles flowing back and forth so quickly he could not observe the moment they reversed direction. As the bubbles came out of the walnut in single file to move along what looked like a tube, some form of energy appeared to expand them to their maximum over a distance of up to ten bubble diameters. Then the current reversed.

That Ron should be able to see and describe such a bubble was amazing enough, the diameter of the walnut-subquark being somewhere in the neighborhood of .0000000000000000000000000000000001 cm.

Fastening his attention onto a single bubble, Ron saw that as it moved through the tube the tube rotated one instant in one direction, next in the opposite, clockwise as the bubbles moved away, counterclockwise as they moved toward him, though again he could not distinguish the actual instant of transition. Estimating the distance between successive bubbles as about six times the width of a bubble, Ron noted that as each bubble passed, the tube seemed to collapse very slightly, its edges no sharper than the boundary between two liquids.

Managing to move along with a bubble—obviously not moving his physical body but his viewpoint—Ron saw that it was shaped like a fat doughnut, with an indented sort of cap that led the bubble's motion and trailed a tail. Wanting to see what was happening close up to one of the walnuts, Ron approached a thread that appeared to link two walnuts. Inside the thread, close to the walnut's outer surface, he found himself moving in a graceful spiral. Down he went, like Alice in

Wonderland, through the coils of the UPA, about three times counter-clockwise, then along another spiral in a clockwise sense, feeling himself being swept along, losing count of the turns. Deciding to follow the rotation of the thread as seen from outside rather than by moving along it, Ron went back up to the top of the UPA and got out of its vortex. This enabled him to establish an essential feature of the threads: they were one single thread.

Following a few clockwise turns, as seen from above, the path went down a narrow vortex, made a very tight turn, came up around itself in a 180-degree turn, went back up, winding about itself for perhaps another half turn, then made a violent corkscrew motion and passed out through the wall of the walnut-UPA as what appeared to be a meandering second thread. This established that the two separate threads observed outside the UPA were actually part of one continuous thread. At no time was a break seen in the path. So where did the bubbles come from and where did they go? Moving back close to a thread, Ron noticed that as a bubble in the thread entered the walnut it got suddenly larger and became a puff of mist. This occurred at the surface and caused a slight shock wave to dissipate inside the walnut while the bubble disappeared before reaching the graceful gentle curve inside its host. On the other side of the walnut, relatively smaller bubbles streamed gently out through the other end of the thread, appearing as if from nothing.

On closer inspection, the bubbles seemed to Ron to be created in the corkscrew spiral near the exit because there was no sign of bubbles at the start of this spiral. As the bubbles flowed back into the walnut, instead of forming a puff like those entering from the other thread, they simply shrank down to nothing.

Whenever bubbles reversed direction, the tail would fade away, to reappear on the opposite side. On the bubble's bow, small concentric circles like shock waves formed along the surface, like a cap. Bubbles seemed to consist of nothing but a boundary surface, with no structural features inside. Bubbles in what to Ron was thread number two started out as mere squiggles of energy, pointed at both ends. Then the squiggle got fatter, turning into the stable tadpole shape.

To Phillips this bubble was clearly a gluon, zero mass, all energy, another form of the particle envisaged by physicists as binding quarks into a nucleus. The threads emanating from a walnut were clearly tubes of magnetic flux, that is, vortices in the ambient superconducting Higgs vacuum along which were being channeled lines of magnetic flux emitted by the magnetic monopole UPAs or subquarks.

Phillips found it significant that the bubbles were seen to be spinning because both gluons and their hypothetical counterparts (hypercolor gluons) are posited by physicists as having an intrinsic spin angular momentum of 1. Their streaming back and forth along a thread—or flux tube—Phillips explained as resulting from their virtually continual emission and absorption by the UPAs at each end of the flux tube.

So it appeared that the theosophists' dots of light in lines of force were, as seen by Ron, actually spinning doughnut-shaped particles (spin–1 gluons) that did not enter the UPA but were created and destroyed at the boundary by the walnut-shaped surface enclosing it. This indicates, says Phillips, that particles of energy such as gluons are single strings, whereas spin–1/2 particles of matter such as subquarks and electrons are bundles of ten strings—a difference, says Phillips, that has yet to be discovered by physicists.

Time will tell. Meanwhile Phillips wondered if Ron could shed light on a particle more fundamental than the UPA of the theosophists, the electron. Phillips says the reason Leadbeater and Besant didn't notice and describe electrons is that while they were preoccupied with observing the double nuclei of their enormously bigger "atoms," the infinitesimally smaller electron would have been flying past in the enormous void of the atom, since the electron's size, relative to the nucleus, is that of a BB lost in a six-acre field. Whereas the physicists' chemical atoms are measured in ten-billionths of a centimeter, weighing a millionth of a billion-millionth of a gram, the atom's nucleus, 100,000 times smaller and five trillion times denser than uranium, occupies no more than a trillionth of what is 99.9 percent empty space. There, the electrons, 1,800 times lighter still than the lightest nucleus, are posited as scurrying around at 99.99995 percent of the speed of light.

Of all known elementary particles with a finite mass, the electron is the smallest and the lightest, its one millionth of one trillionth of a meter width being the closest thing to a point particle, a sizeless geometric point still having mass. Absolutely stable, electrons are not known to transform or transmute themselves, under any circumstances, into other bits of mass. The lightest of particles among nonzero mass particles, it could also be the oldest, estimated by physicists to be older than the universe. Its only nemesis is the positron. If they meet they both vanish, exploding into two massless photons and a massless neutrino.

In relation to the constituents of an atomic nucleus—protons, neutrons, quarks, and potential subquarks—the electron requires for its examination a magnifying power far greater than was developed by Besant and Leadbeater to view their ultimate physical atoms, considered to be the size of subquarks in the nucleus of a chemical atom.

Ron focused on the material in his shirtsleeve and searched for electrons. As recorded on the tapes, he zoomed down into a cloud of them and saw that they seemed to be moving in circular orbits. Capturing one, he noted its pretzel shape: a bundle of threads with a hole or vortex at the top, much like the UPAs he had analyzed, only much smaller, each encased within an egg-shaped, transparent, glass-like shell.

Entering a shell, he saw what looked like a string of beads. Something made him shudder, and he explained it was a kundalini-type energy coming up from the base of his spine. He saw that what looked like beads were in fact the folds of spirals. Capturing a bundle of these threads, he saw a hole or vortex at the top. Following the spiral of a thread, he saw that it made between two and three revolutions, the third not being quite full. But he could not see how the outer spirals returned at the bottom into the central inner spirals.

Examining the threads, he got the impression that there were two—perhaps three—thicker whorls and some finer ones. Their undulations impeded closer observation. The threads were separated by a "trough" filled with haze, which continued all the way up the electron, getting narrower before disappearing back down into the center vortex. There the troughs twisted in a way he could not readily clarify.

The width of the largest spiral in the sheath of threads was about one-tenth of the spiral diameter, perhaps a little less, with a small gap between each turn, but there were too many turns to easily count. Examining one of the thinner threads, or minor whorls, Ron saw an even finer spiral inside what looked like a tube and remarked that there was a "wind" inside the spiral that swept him down it. He could not see this wind, only feel it, confined as he was to the central one-third of the spiral.

As Ron zoomed further in, he saw an even smaller spiral, more tightly wound, its turns almost side by side. The wind blew down these smaller spirals as well. Counting from the first type of spiral, Ron moved through six or seven orders, his voice becoming fainter as he counted.

At last he saw bubbles, just as Leadbeater had reported in the UPAs, almost spherical in shape. All had the same spin: clockwise seen from above. The top of each bubble appeared quite dense and dark, with a small dimple. The lower portion was transparent. As Ron floated down through the dimple deep into the bubble he sensed "a kind of quality of intelligence ... a kind of consciousness" and suspected he had drifted into another kind of space, very large and otherwise featureless.

In the body of the bubble Ron noticed a circular vortex-type activity, but unlike a whirlpool the motion did not seem to end at a point. Then he found himself in an opaque or foggy space where he could see nothing. Dropping through it, he came to the trumpet end of the bubble, but when he wanted to go back up to the edge, he could not do so. He seemed to be forced along a closed path that took him back to where he had been before. Going around in circles, he felt his motion was programmed or guided, for he could not control it or stop it. Unable to leave the closed circuit, Ron decided the only way out of his predicament was to stop his meditation.

Reviewing his experience, Ron saw that one way he could distinguish electrons from UPAs, despite the similarity of the structure of their whorls, was that the electron had no strings emanating from it and appeared less energetically active than the UPA. Yet both the electron and the UPA shared the property that their whorls consisted of higher orders of spirillae arranged as coils within coils. The essential difference lay in the winding of the electron's strings, which decreased progressively, as did the size of the pitch and thickness of the helices.

That the electron should display higher-order spirillae that wind themselves in helices just as they do in the UPA was to be expected, says Phillips, because both particles are different states of a superstring: the UPA with its ten whorls is a bundle of ten closed, twenty-six-dimensional strings; electrons are superstrings without flux tubes emanating from them; gluons are single bosonic strings.

Ron Cowen's observations indicate, says Phillips, that space has more than the six higher dimensions predicted by superstring theory, dimensions consistent with recent attempts by some string mathematical theorists to build superstrings out of more fundamental twenty-six-dimensional bosonic strings, sixteen dimensions of which are compactified.

Ultimately, as visualized by Ron, both UPA and electron consist of bubbles that are actually tori, the same "bubbles" described eighty years earlier by Leadbeater as "holes in koilon, the true aether of space." The discrepancy between the spherical bubbles observed by Leadbeater and the doughnuts seen by Ron is explained by Phillips: "Ron's doughnut was spinning very rapidly and its torus shape was noticeable only when he slowed down its rotation. Leadbeater did not notice its spinning and so had no reason to stop its motion; all he saw was the blurred imaged of a sphere created by a fat torus with a small hole as it rotated and tumbled in all directions." But the difference in topology between a sphere and a torus, says Phillips, is crucial. Ron's torus (seen as a bubble by Leadbeater) is actually a two-dimensional cross-section of a string that extends into fourteen more dimensions of space, and this would be consistent with the sixteen-dimensional torus, one of the model spaces that have been considered by string theorists.

This space is generated by sixteen mutually perpendicular one-dimensional circles and has the topological property that a journey along any one dimension leads back to the starting point—precisely the property of the cyclic motion in which Ron found himself trapped.

When Ron found himself lost in what he sensed was a different kind of space, in a bubble deep in the heart of an electron, "a space with a kind of intelligence . . . a kind of consciousness," he tentatively speculated that this consciousness "had left a doorway into . . . a larger intelligence, a universal intelligence."

To occultists, of course, nothing exists but consciousness, be it in innumerable subtleties of degree. As for the force that holds both the UPA and the atom together, to Phillips it is bosons exchanged between subquarks from the same quark, and gluons exchanged between subquarks belonging to different quarks. What Ron confirmed was that Leadbeater's "lines of force" were actually spinning, tubular surfaces (vortices in the superconducting Higgs field) through which flowed spinning particles (spin-1 gluons) that did not enter the UPA but were created and destroyed at the boundary of the walnut-shaped surface enclosing it.

To Leadbeater: "The force does not enter the UPA from outside. It wells up within—which means it enters from higher dimensions." As he explains the phenomenon, dimensions of space are merely limitations of consciousness, and a sufficiently developed consciousness is entirely free from such limitations, with the power of expression in any number of dimensions. "Each descent into denser matter shuts off perception of one of these dimensions. By the astral level it is limited to four dimensions; further descent into the physical world limits it to three."

Reverse the process, remove the limitations, and the universe becomes endowed with greater depth, richness, beauty, and harmony: in all its beauty, grandeur, divinity, it is already there, always. It is we who change as we increase or remove our limitations.

Fortunately, the limits appear to be arbitrary. If you consider the size of a superstring: .0000000000000000000000000000000001 centimeters, as estimated by physicists, and the outer limits of the observable universe to be under 100000000000000000000000000000 centimeters, the theosophists' and Ron Cowen's feats place humans midway between one and the other extreme, with the amazing faculty, developed through siddhi powers, of being able to shift consciousness toward either extreme, annihilating space.

As for time, it appears to be just as illusory: a photon emitted by a remote galaxy billions of years ago knows already as it approaches earth whether to behave as a wave or a particle when detected by a human observer. And in quantum mechanics, if an electron interacts with another electron, a relation is maintained between their quantum states irrespective of however far apart they may wander in the universe. This means—and it is something Einstein didn't like—that if you observe an electron and discover the direction of its spin, the direction of the spin of the other electron, by some sort of magic, will be simultaneously decided, in the opposite direction, no matter where it may be.

Eastern Cosmology

The wisdom of the East, as codified in the Vedas and the Upanishads—resurrected by theosophists at the turn of the century and made available in translation to the West—is based on a fundamental mystery, considered "incomprehensible to intellect and unconveyable by words," qualified as the "Absolute" or "Ultimate Reality." As the same mystery appears to haunt both the world of physics and of mathematics, nothing may be lost by following the occult tradition as it depicts a universe miraculously springing from this Absolute, like Egypt's cosmos from Atum's autoerotic hand or Pantagruel from Gargantua's ear. Especially is this true since this background serves to make more comprehensible the truly amazing spiritual world of Rudolf Steiner. Not an easy subject to condense without the risk of making it denser, this effort is primarily indebted to the works of Dr. I. K. Taimni, professor of Eastern philosophy in Madras, India.

Ultimate Reality, in this Eastern tradition, is seen as pure unmanifest consciousness, simultaneously, like the Higgs vacuum, a void and a plenum, the source of everything, yet beyond the range of even the highest adept. Poetically described as "in perfect balance, always perfectly integrated (in no way differentiated), serenely harmonized," it is seen as a synthesis of all possible opposites, the source of everything manifest or unmanifest, eternally the same, though remarkably cyclical in its manifestation, appearing and disappearing in vast alternating cycles of creation and dissolution. It is a world like that the medieval mystic Meister Eckhart spun out of stardust by a predicateless Godhead behind God, unknowable not only to humans but to itself, essence and potential of all things.

The concept of an Absolute that is simultaneously boundless infinite space and an ideal dimensionless point is made more manageable by a mathematical analogy: if a sphere is repeatedly contracted it must ultimately be reduced to a point, a dimensionless ideal entity without magnitude either of length, breadth, or thickness. To the rational mind such an ideal point is self-evidently the limit in the direction of the infinitesimally small, whereas boundless space constitutes the limit in the direction of the infinitely large. Ultimate Reality, say the Hindu sages, exists in both point and space but in neither exclusively, its "consciousness" alternately expanding and contracting between one and the other, sweeping through all the intermediate states to emerge as a wave of expansion and contraction into a negative world. The ultimate space must therefore be the opposing eternal vestures of Ultimate Reality, for, as both scientist and occultist agree, nothing exists without its balancing negative state, including negative space, negative time, and negative matter.

An ideal point is basic to the Hindu concept of cycles of manifestation, for it is required as a device through which to fluctuate and through which each newly manifested universe can be projected, a sort of door between the void of the Absolute and all the states of both the unmanifest and the manifest. The extraordinary properties of a point are best grasped by venturing into the subtler world of more dimensions than the standard three of the physical world. To the occultist an ideal point serves for the meeting of any number of different planes, and as any number of points can coexist within one another, a point can contain within itself an infinite number of other points, hence unlimited planes and dimensions.

To use another mathematical analogy: if zero represents the boundless, infinite, empty space known to Hindu sages as Mahakasha, then one represents the eternal dimensionless point, or Mahabindu—*Akasha* being space, *Bindu* a point, and *Maha* the great. And with this concept comes an explanation for the basic source of energy, ranging all the way from that of the far-flung galaxies to the heart of every atom.

The eternal point, Mahabindu, or one, by drawing apart from its static center—in some miraculous but patently energetic way—two poles, produces the number two, foci of the primary differentiation of Ultimate Reality into what the Hindus describe as consciousness and power, symbolized by the god Shiva and the goddess Shakti. Shiva stands as the static principle—potential, changeless, stable—and Shakti as the dynamic, kinetic source of movement and change. Yet the duality remains inseparable: as logically explained by Hindu sages, there can be no power without will, no activity without potential energy, no change without a changeless substratum, no action without a will to change. As will is concerned with the end, so power is concerned with the means of attaining that end. Will without power to provide the means is helpless. Power without will to provide the end, and continued concentration of that end, is purposeless.

From these two Hindu divinities all the polarities in the manifest universe are seen to be derived: positive-negative, father-mother, space-time, energy-matter, attraction-repulsion, electron-proton. By their mutual action and reaction, and by their balancing of opposites, the fabric of the universe is woven. But in this occult cinemascope it is only when something called "mental space," or Akasha, comes into existence that a manifested system—one of universes, galaxies, and solar systems—can be created. As mind is seen to be no more than "a disturbance in consciousness," what is needed to manifest a universe is another dual polarity, one of self and not-self. To achieve this further schism, consciousness is described as producing, out of itself, two streams, one the basis of subjective phenomena, the other the basis of objective phenomena, the former related to the perceiver, the latter to the perceived, there being no phenomena without a seer to witness what is seen. Shiva provides the viewer, Shakti the raw material for what is viewed. And so develops the next polarity of mind-matter. Summed up by occultists: "Matter floats and functions in a sea of Mind; Mind functions in a sea of Consciousness; Consciousness functions in the void or plenum of the Ultimate Reality."

And so we come to the world as we know it, or think we know it. When integrated consciousness reacts through any viewing vehicle produced by Shiva-Shakti with any matter produced by Shiva-Shakti, the result of the interaction, say the Hindus, is mind, the basis of all experience. With consciousness as the highest aspect of reality, and matter the lowest, mind comes in between. And the link between mind and matter lies in the nature of the perception by consciousness of a world outside itself.

For consciousness to unfold its potentialities as it descends from the unmanifest into manifestation, its descent must be preceded by the formation by Shiva-Shakti of a manifested system in different grades of mind and matter. This, in theosophical terms, becomes the realm of the supreme creator, the Cosmic Logos, a realm achieved through what is described as cosmic ideation. Such ideation, or the projection from a state of consciousness of something outside itself, is compared to an artist creating a picture in his mind. So long as the picture is only in the mind, it remains potential; once the picture is actually drawn, it goes from the realm of the mind to that of an object.

In this theology, for the cosmos to come into being, the "Father-Mother" principle, symbolized as the number two, produces the "Son," symbolized as three. In Meister Eckhart's vision, from the predicateless Godhead proceed the three persons of the Trinity, conceived as stadia of an external self-revealing process. And the eternal generation of the Son for Eckhart is equivalent to the eternal creation of the world. In Blavatsky's *The Secret Doctrine* the Son of the Hidden Father is known as the Cosmic Logos. With a dual personality, partly unmanifest and partly manifest, this Cosmic Logos becomes the creator of the whole universe of manifestation, with its galaxies and solar systems, in all possible grades of subtlety, created through the medium of cosmic ideation.

Pure consciousness when it ideates and projects this manifested universe in all its different grades and infinite variety of forms is described as being present in every part of every form of the manifested universe as its basic substance, the basis of differently evolving forms. By analogy: in a world of multiform golden objects, the forms may change, but the gold remains the same. Manifest and unmanifest remain integral aspects of the Ultimate Reality.

As *logos* means "word," it is "sound" that constitutes the formative agency. Manifestation, essentially an interplay of Shiva and Shakti, of consciousness and power, is produced, with sound as the instrument of the static positive principle of Shiva's consciousness and light as that of the dynamic, negative principle of Shakti's power. Shakti's function is to provide the structural raw material of the universe in the form of "light," or what scientists call radiation, with an average frequency for visible light calculated at some five hundred trillion oscillations per second! To the occultist, these are merely wavelengths in the medium of the mind, with mind in turn an outgrowth of consciousness.

Shiva's function as consciousness is to give material form to Shakti's light by bottling it up in atoms and molecules so as to control and coordinate the building and maintenance of form; this is seen as being accomplished by Shiva through the agency of "sound"—not the sound we hear on earth, but a cosmic form of vibration that produces a field of influence undetectable with physical apparati. This sound, or *Nada* in Sanskrit, is described as vibration in the medium of Akasha, or space. It is not mere empty space but "mental" space containing within itself an infinite amount of potential energy, which can find expression in any and all the kinds of vibrations needed in a manifest system. This infinite potential for producing vibrations of different frequencies in any intensity or amount is attributed to the fact that hidden within Akasha is ubiquitous consciousness, and consciousness, which is "self-determined, integrated, and free," can produce of itself an infinite amount of energy through the medium of mind, a notion intolerable to physicists, who maintain that energy can neither be destroyed nor created.

A peculiar fact pointed out by physicists is that when matter is produced from the materialization of energy, equal amounts of matter and antimatter are formed simultaneously. Conversely, when matter meets antimatter both are extinguished in an explosion that produces light. And the extent of the energy released can be gauged by the fact that the interaction of one proton with one antiproton produces a staggering 1.8 billion electron-volts of energy.

All the forces such as gravitation, magnetism, and so forth, are also seen by occultists as derived from sound, and though predominantly static they also have a dynamic character that gives rise to waves. And since waves cannot exist without a medium of some kind, they must, say occultists, exist in the mind. According to this doctrine, motion exists in only three kinds: rhythmic, nonrhythmic, and no-motion or stability. From the interplay of these, all forms are derived, just as all possible colors are derived from the three primary colors: red, yellow, and blue.

To the Vedic Hindu, the atom is nothing but imprisoned light that is released as free light and other forms of energy on breaking up the atom in atomic fission. When the light of Shakti becomes bound by Shiva with the noose of sound, the basis of all the atoms of the elements is born in Akasha in the sinews of quarks (or subquarks) and electrons. As explained by Steiner, the physical atom bears the same relationship to the force of electricity that a lump of ice bears to the water from which it has been frozen. The atom of physics, says Steiner, is nothing but frozen electricity. And what is electricity? "It is exactly as human thought, only viewed from inside and from outside"—as with astral vision. Even more stunning is Steiner's notion that each atom in the universe contains in miniature the plans for the next world in the next round that is to succeed the present. "The Logos," says Steiner, "is continually slipping into the atom and thus the atom becomes the image of the future plan."

Down the ladder of creation from Cosmic Logos comes the Manifest Logos and with it—in contradistinction to cosmic ideation—logoic ideation, from which a manifested system begins to unfold in terms of time and space. Space, it is explained, is more basic than time because one has to have mental space in which to have mental images that change and so produce time. Both space and time must depend on the mind and its mental images. When the mind is without images there is neither space nor time, only basic Reality, of which consciousness, mind, and matter are but three projected aspects.

In Hindu philosophy the Manifest Logos, though a single personality, appears in three separate aspects: as Brahma the creator, Vishnu the preserver, and Mahesha the regenerator. In the production of the different realms of manifestation this threefold Manifest Logos is said to use three distinct forms of energy: fohat, prana, and kundalini—all derivatives of Shakti and therefore all mysteriously linked.

When Brahma, the Third Logos, or third aspect of the Manifest Logos, makes his appearance, his first activity, related to the form side of Nature, is described as the creation of the five lower planes of existence—atmic, buddhic, mental, astral, and physical. As the basis for these "material" aspects, Brahma uses what the Tibetans call fohat and what Helena Blavatsky called cosmic electricity, an energy she relates to magnetism and gravity, qualified as the occult potency of sound, imbued with thought. It is this soniferous, creative, propellant force that is defined as the Logos or word. All changes of a material nature, even in the human body, are considered to be dependent upon and be brought about by this cosmic electricity or fohat and its related forces.

The Second Logos, Vishnu the Preserver, concerned with the "life" aspect and the evolution of vehicles, is described as using prana, a vital force derived from the sun, part superphysical, part physical, responsible for and underlying all life processes—much like Steiner's world-ether. On the physical plane, prana builds up all minerals and is the controlling agent in the chemico-physiological changes in protoplasm that lead to differentiation and the building of the various tissues of the bodies of plants, animals, and humans; it makes of the physical body a living organism in contradistinction to an insentient aggregate of matter and force. Without prana the body would be nothing more than a collection of independent cells. The blending of astral prana with physical prana creates nerve matter, which gives the power to feel pleasure and pain. Pranic centers are the glandular and nerve centers in the physical body and the chakras in the etheric and astral bodies. Flowing pranas act as the link between body and soul. Controlling prana by thought, yogis succeed in controlling their bodies.

As the material instrument of the Second Logos, or Vishnu, prana is posited as enabling the raw material of kundalini, created by the Third Logos, Brahma, to be worked up into "living" vehicles with the inherent capacity for growth and for acting as instruments of mind in various degrees of development. As Brahma, the Creator, evolves more and more complex atoms and molecules for the different planes, Vishnu, the Preserver, takes these atoms and molecules and organizes them into living bodies, which can serve as vehicles for mind and consciousness.

Meanwhile the First Logos, Mahesha, concerned with the unfoldment of consciousness, uses kundalini, which, as explained by Hodson, serves not only as the active principle in all procreative procedures but also for the awakening of the faculties of abstract thought, intuition, will, and their expression in the brain, including clairvoyance and clairaudience. The seven layers of kundalini, says Hodson, correspond to the seven planes and states of consciousness, the arousal of each layer bringing about entry and awareness in the corresponding plane and state.

To Gopi Krishna, Indian sage and author of several books on consciousness and kundalini, the kundalini mechanism "is the real cause of all so-called spiritual and psychic phenomena, the biological basis of evolution and development of personality, the secret origin of all esoteric and occult doctrines, the master key to the unsolved mystery of creation, the inexhaustible source of philosophy, art, and science, and the fountainhead of all religious faiths, past, present and future."

So it is that the First, Second, and Third Logoi, working together on the different planes—for indeed they are conceived to be one divinity—produce differing densities of matter, differing subtleties of mind, and the differing measures of time and space. All of this to constitute the realm of the Manifest Cosmic Logos, who, with sound as the instrument of will, controls, regulates, and directs all the forces and energies of the system, including those of myriads of dependent solar logoi throughout the wide, wide cosmos. Yet each solar logos is considered an independent spiritual ruler over its own solar system, each a relative microcosm reflecting and expressing the consciousness of the paramount Cosmic Logos. According to occultism, our sun is the physical abode and instrument of such a solar logos described as a divine being whose consciousness pervades our solar system at all levels.

In this great tapestry of occult science, as cosmic and then logoic consciousness descend lower and lower into the realm of manifestation in the form of progressively lower states of mind, sound descends in different forms of energy in order to produce the world of forms, bringing about interaction among them, with perception of form remaining a mental phenomenon based on consciousness.

The necessary power for this descent—derived from the original self-initiated drawing apart of Shakti from Shiva—is transformed and stepped down to lower levels, just as electric energy at high voltage is stepped down by transformers, through the intervention of different kinds of spiritual, mental, and material mechanics. Below the solar logos come the successive hierarchies of spiritual beings who embody spiritual principles and powers in different degrees and combinations.

As consciousness differentiates into states of mind of different degrees of subtlety, and power into specific powers, what the Hindus call devis, devatas, and devas come into being. They represent, by analogy, the different colors of the spectrum derived from white light or the Ultimate Reality. Though separate and distinct, they are seen not as being independent of one another, but rather as manifesting in many levels of mind and matter of different densities.

Our solar system in turn is peopled by billions of evolving individual souls, known to theosophy as monads. And as it is a tenet of the occult doctrine that consciousness at any level must manifest through an "ideal" point, and as an ideal point can contain an infinite number of other points, the consciousness of monad, solar logos, and Cosmic Logos, though operating on different levels, separately and without interference, are seen as all centered in the Great Point, Mahabindu, existing eternally in the Absolute. The notion is comparable to the innumerable conversations carried over a fiber-optic cable with equal clarity and lack of interference, all accessible to the cosmic switchboard.

Through the Great Point an infinite number of universes, solar logoi, and monads are envisaged as continuing to appear eternally, starting with basic electrons and protons, evolving through various stages in eons of time to become countless solar logoi in the cosmos, countless centers of consciousness, all reflections of the Ultimate Reality. This same Ultimate Reality, differentiated along two separate lines, is credited with producing, on the one hand, an infinite number of spiritual monads and, on the other, an infinite variety of material planes for ensheathing and evolving these monads, the main purpose for the evolution of forms being to provide more efficient vehicles for evolving mind and unfolding consciousness.

Individualization is posited as taking place by separation of an individual unit from a "group soul," for without a ray of separate consciousness there can be no separate monad. To separate such a unit of consciousness, say occultists, there must exist around it a sheath of matter, however subtle, even but one atom thick. This leads to the formation of the causal body; and so a human soul is born. The monad, or human entity, then descends to lower planes to unfold its divine potentialities before working its way back—somewhat dazedly, perhaps—up the ladder of existence.

According to the teachings of the occult doctrine the unfoldment of the monads is one, if not the, reason why the manifested universe comes into existence, each individual monad being considered a differentiated aspect of the one reality, "fragments of the Divine Life, children of the Most High." Hence they are called "sons," to show they have the same status and nature as the Son or Cosmic Logos and that there must exist "an intimate and exquisite" personal relationship between the Divine Parents and each individual soul.

Considered to be eternal, each monad is granted the potential of becoming a logos as the result of its unfoldment. This makes of the monads microcosmic representations of a solar system with the same nature, powers, and potentialities as the macrocosm or the Cosmic Logos. The ultimate destiny of the monad is therefore to become a solar logos.

All the facts revealed in this occult doctrine point to the eternal continuance of the monadic individuality with its uniqueness, the whole of reality in its infinite depths or levels being hidden in its completeness and full splendor within each individual soul, each monad receiving impressions from the divine mind according to the development of its corresponding vehicle.

Basic to the occult doctrine is the subtle and essential concept that monads must develop in freedom so that they learn to cooperate with the divine will not from outer compulsion but from inner choice, born of experience and enlightenment. As Richard Leviton puts it in his brilliant analysis of the Steinerian philosophy, *The Imagination of Pentecost:* "Spiritual beings must love; only humans can choose to."

To which Steiner adds his heartening dictum: "The more human love there is on earth the more food there is for the gods in heaven; the less love the more the gods go hungry."

Elementary Beings

Many years before the formulation of anthroposophy, and well before Leadbeater or Hodson appeared on the scene, Helena Petrovna Blavatsky, founder of the Theosophical Society, laid down the secret doctrine about "elementals." Though invisible to human beings, they were, she said, the true cause of all that takes place behind the veil of terrestrial phenomena.

To endow matter, about which nothing is really known, said Madame Blavatsky, with an inherent quality called force, or energy, the nature of which is still less known, "is to create a far more serious difficulty than that which lies in the acceptance of the intervention of 'nature spirits' in every natural phenomenon."

To Blavatsky, nature spirits, which she defined as cosmic agents, each confined to its own element of earth, water, air, or fire, "exist in the etheric and can handle and direct etheric matter for the production of physical effects as readily as humans can compress air for the same purpose with a pneumatic apparatus. They condense etheric matter so as to make themselves tangible bodies, which they can cause to assume such likeness as they choose, taking as their models the portraits they find stamped in the memory of the persons present."

This belief in nature spirits, revived by theosophists, flourished in every civilization of every age. The mythologies of Persians, Mongolians, Chinese, Japanese, Indians, and Egyptians as well as many tribal peoples abound with accounts of spirits, benevolent and malevolent.

The Greeks had nymphs, dryads, and sprites of fountain and forest. The ancient Celtic druids had tree spirits, inhabiting sacred groves of ash, oak, and other trees. The Irish have their leprechauns; Teutonic tribes were convinced of the reality of the Nibelungen gnomes and dwarves.

Christendom, in an effort to eliminate the pagan world, turned the Great God Pan into a devil, his world of nature spirits into goblinesque fiends. For fifteen hundred years the true essence of the spirits of nature was relegated to the care of witches, gypsies, or the secret laboratories of the alchemist.

The first to retrieve such spirits from enforced obscurity was the Swiss alchemist Philippus Aureolus Theophrastus Bombastus von Hohenheim, better known as Paracelsus. Born in the canton of Schwyz in 1490, a contemporary of Martin Luther, Paracelsus was perhaps an even greater reformer than his Saxon peer in that he tackled medicine and physics as well as religion. Like Luther, he also broke the tradition of his day by choosing to write a treatise on nature spirits, not in the academic Latin of his compeers, but in his own vernacular German. It was to become the prime source of innumerable works by later authors.

Following the concepts of classical cultures, Paracelsus divided the world of nature spirits into the standard four elements of earth, water, air, and fire, calling them elementals because each was considered to be composed of a single one of these classic elements. Grouping his elementals into races and division, he assigned each to performing innumerable useful tasks within its natural realm. "They represent," explained the Swiss physician, "certain forces fulfilling a role in nature, and are not created without purpose."

Not limiting himself to the study of what had been written in the past, Paracelsus went deeply into nature to study the subject firsthand. Unlike his peers, trapped in the narrow limits of contemporary scholasticism, Paracelsus sought solutions to the mysteries of nature by personally pursuing his data wherever he could find it, from gypsies, witches, faith healers, herbalists, or anyone who claimed knowledge of the healing arts. He liked to visit hermits living in huts or caves: he believed the old tales of isolated religions would have meaning for those who had the wit to examine them. "Whosoever would understand the book of nature," said Paracelsus, "must walk its pages with his feet."

Boldly determined to clear the way for a modern understanding of the mechanics of nature, Paracelsus scandalized his fellow doctors and academicians at the University of Basel by burning the books of Avicenna and Galen before a class of students, informing them instead—as would Rudolf Steiner some centuries later—that each person possesses within himself the powers and latent faculties necessary to become aware of a many-dimensioned universe.

On this basic notion, Manly P. Hall, the Western philosopher and adept, in a monograph devoted to Paracelsus's mystical and medical philosophy, commented that it "will mean the ultimate conquest of space through the realization that there is no such thing as space, but merely an infinite expanse of the unfolding areas of visible and invisible, known or unknown life, energy, and substance." To which Hall added, "There is no vacuum in the universe, and the nearest thing to a vacuum, according to Paracelsus, was the brain of one of his fellow professors at Basel University."

Four hundred years later, in Paracelsus's own Swiss canton, and almost coincident with Hodson's exploration of the fairy world in Britain, Rudolf Steiner added his own basic lectures on the role of nature spirits in the growth and development of the mineral, vegetable, animal, and human kingdoms.

Born to Austrian parents in a remote village of Croatia in 1847, Steiner was clairvoyant from childhood but had a hard time convincing his family that beyond the world of matter lay another whole world of the spirit. To master both worlds he trained himself at the Technical University of Vienna very thoroughly in physics, mathematics, biology, and chemistry, devoting his spare time to optics, botany, and anatomy. Aware that science, as taught in the academies, negating the spirit, could understand in matter only that which was dead, never the living process, he determined to debate the orthodox on their own ground by acquiring a doctorate in philosophy. His thesis was simple: a new, exact, and scientific form of clairvoyance would have to be included in the scientific approach if the half-truths of materialism were not to drag the world into a materialist and mechanistic disaster.

Exploring the world of nature spirits, Steiner opened up another dimension with fascinating details about the way in which gnomes, undines, sylphs, and fire spirits go about their part in the symphony of life. Whereas Hodson's descriptions have the vividness of an eyewitness reporter and Leadbeater's the eclectic assurance of the world traveler, Steiner's, with the benefit of his clairvoyantly developed "spiritual science," are specifically analytic, giving substance to Blavatsky's dictum that the role of nature spirits is the very essence of every natural phenomenon. In so doing, Steiner produces a canvas eerier and even more fantastic than that of any of his predecessors.

Whereas Hodson and Leadbeater describe the nature spirits as they could see them in their various lairs, Steiner goes deeper, much deeper, to explain their paramount role in human and planetary life, claiming that without these workaholic elementals the planet would be bare and sterile. Steiner's approach is simple but cogent. All that surrounds us—not only mineral, vegetable, and animal, but also we ourselves, including our bodies and our inner organs—is created and maintained by nature spirits. Without the help of friendly industrious elementals, says Steiner, we would not even be able to marshal our own thoughts. In this occult view of life on earth, elemental spirits lie hidden behind all that constitutes the physical, sense-perceptible world, making it, with their effort, truly alive. And to the degree, says Steiner, that we deny reality to these beings that whirl and weave around the mineral, plant, and animal worlds, to that degree do we lose understanding of the world, an understanding necessary to life, health, and especially to the art of healing, an art largely lost to present-day humanity.

Basic to Steiner's nature spirits are the substances and forces out of which they are composed, all derivatives of his "world-ether," of which warmth-ether is prime. Way back in the past, says Steiner, warmth-ether split into two streams: one branch ascended to form the other three ethers, light-ether, chemical-ether, and life-ether; the other branch descended to form the four elements known to Aristotle and Anaxagoras as fire, air, water, earth. Steiner's four groups of nature spirits, though classically identified with fire, air, water, and earth, are actually composed, respectively, of warmth-ether, light-ether, chemical-ether, and life-ether, whereas the elements, in line with Aristotle, are not in themselves substantial but rather forces responsible for the maintenance of the states of solidity, liquidity, gaseousness, and fieriness. Earth makes for all that is solid, from potato to ingot of gold; water all that is liquid, from mother's milk to gasoline to molten lead; air all that is gaseous, including all the chemical elements when in that stage; fire is the all-pervading element that triggers the change from one elemental state to the next. For spiritual science, fire is not, as with the physicist, a condition of movement, but something of its own, endowed with an even finer substantiality than air, so rarefied it permeates all other elements, warming or cooling by its presence or its absence. Everything that exists derives from condensed fire.

To spiritual science, elements and ethers work together in pairs: fire with warmth-ether, air with light-ether, water with chemical-ether, earth with life-ether, but from opposite polarities: elements function upward from the center of the earth, ethers down from the celestial sphere whence they originate. Fire, the subtlest of the elements, expands skyward, as in a candle or flaming oil well; fire's companion, warmth-ether, radiates down from sun and stars, stimulating growth. Air—with qualities and functions opposite to those of its etheric companion, light-ether—fills all the space between things, thus connecting them. Light-ether, on the contrary, is perceived on things, not in the spaces between. Light-ether is seen as separating things, making them distinguishable one from the other, creating distances and conditions of space. Light and space being inseparable, where there is light there must be space. Unlike light, air is chaotic, without direction. Its main characteristic is elasticity; it can be diluted almost indefinitely without loosing its cohesion. Light, the opposite of elastic, is brittle and separable and is directional as it streams from its source. Beat the air with a stick, says Steiner's follower Ernst Marti, and the air gives way to reunite behind the stick. Light is separated by a stick, and its rays do not reunite but stream off in straight lines. Air from all sides presses toward the earth, centripetally, but is not, as Steiner points out, compressible beyond a certain point; and by air, he means, of course, all that is gaseous.

The element of water, or all that is liquid, works like the other elements in opposition to its etheric partner, chemical-ether. Water is dense, continuous, always tending to the spherical, consistent throughout. Chemical-ether (or tone-ether, as Steiner sometimes calls it) is loose and divisive, discrete, erratic, separate. When rain falls into the sea, each drop is incorporated into the whole, tending to the spherical; the same applies to honey, mercury, magma. Chemical-ether tends to separate, create distances, form nodes, make buoyant rather than cohesive. Music, chemistry, and number are all products of Steiner's chemical-ether, a force that keeps units apart while maintaining a relation between the separate parts. Through the laws of number, substances become chemically related. A tree under the influence of chemical-ether separates into branches, twigs, leaves, none touching the other, making a whole of separate parts. Water, by contrast, goes from pond to lake to ocean, amalgamating, keeping its sphericity from dewdrop to Pacific Ocean.

The last element, earth, is also described by Steiner as working in opposition to its companion, life-ether. Whereas earth expresses itself in solidity, rigidity—a solid body requires its own space—life-ether creates inner mobility, is the force of "self," generating form from within. Pouring down from the cosmos, life-ether enlivens and individualizes the fixed and solid earth, developing independent organisms, creating skin or separate sheaths as an expression of individuality. And whereas the earth element produces lifeless bodies, life-ether creates living bodies. Earth and life-ether, in conjunction, are the basis for our three-dimensional world.

Together, and in various subtle mixtures, the four ethers and the four elements make up all the spirits of nature. Gnomes, says Steiner, exist just as do electricity and magnetism; they are beings in earthly solids imperceptible to our outer senses, active throughout the world, just like human beings, but with an intellect that is much smarter, slyer, and cleverer than ours. "They consist entirely of active cleverness, active intellect, active craftiness, active logic. . . . With their steel gray figures, quite small compared to humans, almost entirely head, bent forward, they bind together all the existing gravity, and form their bodies out of this fleeting, invisible force, bodies that are continually in danger of falling apart, or losing substance."

For Steiner's gnomes the entire earth globe is like a permeable hollow space in which they can go where they please; rocks and metals in no way prevent their walking or swimming about. Only the full moon makes them uncomfortable, obliging them to enclose themselves in a sort of spiritual skin, like knights in armor in the light of the full moon.

Everywhere present in the earth, says Steiner, the root spirits—mostly gnomes and brownies—derive a particular sense of well-being from rocks and ores, which are more or less transparent to them, obtaining a different experience as they wander from a vein of metal to a layer of chalk, gaining subtly different sensations as they pass through gold, mercury, tin, silica. "They enjoy their greatest sense of well-being when they are conveying what is mineral to the roots of plants, without which the plants could not thrive."

Alive in everything pertaining to the earth, Steiner's gnomes are responsible not only for dealing with rock and metal, "but for serving as messengers to their underground world, bringing news of the outer encircling cosmos, relayed by undine, sylph, and salamander down through leaf, petal, trunk and root to the underground gnomes."

Steiner describes how at a certain season of the year, plants gather secrets from the extraterrestrial universe and sink them into the ground, spirit-currents flowing from the blossom of the fruit down the plant into the roots below, streaming into the earth. "What the sun has sent to the leaves, what the air has produced in the leaves, what the distant stars have brought about in plant structure, the plant gathers and seeps down spiritually into the ground."

It is then, says Steiner, that earth spirits turn their faculties toward the roots of plants, which have brought the sunlight down through the plant into the earth, and take the secrets of the universe into themselves. "From autumn and on through winter, in their wanderings through ore and rock, the gnomes, in full consciousness, become carriers of ideas of the universe from metal to metal, from rock to rock. The gnomes are the light-filled preservers of world understanding within the earth."

Although the predominant characteristic of Steiner's gnomes is an absolutely unconquerable lust for independence, troubling themselves little about one another, giving their attention only to their own immediate surroundings, "yet everything else in the world in which they live interests them exceedingly. They are purely sense and understanding, immediately taking in and understanding what they see and hear."

Because gnomes have this immediate understanding of what they see, says Steiner, their knowledge is similar to that of humans, but they look down on human understanding as not being complete, laughing at our groping and struggling to understand. Having a direct perception of what is comprehensible in the world, they have no need for thought. They comprehend at sight, without needing to think, and therefore find it entertaining to observe a human being "asleep"—not in bed, but in his astral and ego bodies—for they see someone "who thinks in the spirit but does not know it, does not know that his thoughts are alive in the spirit world."

Strangely, in this anthroposophical view, the gnomes do not actually seem to care much for the earth itself and would like to tear themselves free of it. But the earth, says Steiner, holds over them the continuous threat of forcing them to take a particular form, a form that gnomes do not relish, especially forms of frogs or toads. Therefore, with the fundamental force of their being, they unceasingly thrust away from the earth, and it is this thrusting, says Steiner, that determines the upward direction of the plant's growth. "Once a plant has grown upwards, once it has left the domain of the gnomes and has passed out of the sphere of the moist earthly element into the sphere of moist air, the plant develops what comes to outer formation in the leaves." Here other beings are at work, beginning with undines and sylphs.

Undines, as denizens of the chemical-ether, are active in the etheric element of water, especially on the surface of drops or other liquid bodies; their consciousness lives in the flow of the fluid element. "They are the world's chemists, without whose activity no kind of transformation of substance could be possible. They carry the action of chemical-ether into the plants which would otherwise wither above ground if not approached on all sides by undines. In a tree they stream through the fluidity of its sap."

Seen clairvoyantly as they swim and sway through the element of moisture, undines recoil from everything in the nature of the fish, as if the fish form, like the frogs to the gnomes, were a threat to them.

"Even if they do assume it from time to time, they forsake it immediately in order to metamorphose."

Plants, says Steiner, cannot be understood so long as human beings insist on ignoring the existence of the elemental nature spirits whirling and weaving around them as they grow: plants would wither if it weren't for undines who approach them from all sides, showing themselves as they weave around the plants "in their dream-like existence," bringing about a mysterious combination and separation of the substances that emanate from the leaf. Truly protean, Steiner's undines change their shape at every moment. "One can only catch a particular instant of their being. They dream continuously. As they dream of stars and sunlight and warmth, undines carry the plant further along in its formation, into the domain of the sylphs, spirits which live in the airy-light element."

Steiner's sylphs, whose bodies consist of spiritual light-ether, carry the effect of light-ether into the plants: "Their task is to bring light to plants in a loving way." And because the air is everywhere imbued with light, says Steiner, sylphs press toward the light and relate to it. Through the sylph-borne light something remarkable is brought about in the plant; according to Steiner, the power of the sylphs works upon the chemical forces where they have been induced into the plant by the undines, and there occurs an interworking of sylph light, an undine chemistry. "With the help of the upstreaming substances which are worked on by the undines, the sylphs weave out of the light an ideal plant form. They actually weave what amounts to Goethe's Archetypal Plant with their light and the chemical working of the undines."

By the rules of spiritual science, sylphs unfold and develop their being within this sound of music, finding their life-space in the moving current of modulated air. "In this spiritually-sounding element of motion," says Steiner, "they are at home, and absorb what the power of light sends into this vibrating air, feeling most in their element where birds are winging through it." In spring or autumn when a flock of swallows produces vibrations as the birds fly in a body of air, causing currents with their flight, this vibrating air, says Steiner, is as audible to the sylphs as it is to the birds. "To the sylphs it is cosmic music."

Naturally, says Steiner, those who regard the plant as something purely material know nothing of its ideal spiritual form. Materialistic science describes the plant as taking root in the ground, while above ground it develops leaves, finally unfolding its blossoms, and within the blossoms its stamens, followed by the seed bud. At which point pollen from vessels, usually from another plant, is carried over to the germ, which is fertilized, and through this, a new plant is produced, The germ is regarded as the female element and what comes from the stamens is the male. "Indeed," says Steiner, "matters cannot be regarded otherwise, so long as people remain fixed in materialism; for them this process really does look like fertilization."

Spiritual science views the process in quite another light, granting to salamanders, or fire spirits, a significant role in the life of plants, without whom there would be no so-called generative propagation of plants, no blossoming. After the plant has grown up through the sphere of the sylphs, says Steiner, it comes into the sphere of the elemental fire-spirits, inhabitants of the "warm ether" element, the salamanders. When the warmth of the earth is at its height, or is otherwise suitable, the salamanders gather the warmth together and carry it into the blossoms of the plants. The pollen, seen clairvoyantly, now provides what may be called little air-ships to enable the fire spirits to carry the warmth into the seed: everywhere warmth is collected with the help of the stamens, and is carried by means of the pollen from the anthers to the seeds and the seed vessels. What is formed here in the seed bud, says Steiner, is entirely the male element, which comes from the cosmos. "It is not a case of the seed-vessel being female and the anthers of the stamen being male. In no way does fructification occur in the blossom, only the pre-forming of the male seed."

Salamanders carry warmth-ether into the plant in the same way that sylphs carry light-ether and undines carry chemical-ether; without salamanders there would be no flowering of plants: they transform lifeless warmth into living warmth. No creature could live or reproduce without salamanders. These fire spirits, he notes, take the utmost delight in following in the tracks of butterfly flight so that they may bring about the distribution of warmth, which must descend into the earth so that it may be united with the ideal plant form. "Fire spirits love to follow insects to introduce concentrated warmth-ether into the ovaries of plants; the aura of the bee is really the fire spirit which accompanies it."

The fertilizing force, says Steiner, is what the fire spirits in the blossom take from the warmth of the world; all of this while the cosmic male seed—to be united with the female element—is resting below. In anthroposophy, earth is the mother of plants, heaven the father. "It is a colossal error," says Steiner, "to believe that the mother-principle of the plant is in the seed-bud. The fact is that this is the male principle, which is drawn forth from the universe with the aid of the fire-spirits. The mother comes from the cambium, which spreads from the bark to the wood, and is carried down from above in ideal form." (In botany the cambium is a zone between the wood and the bark of exogenous plants from which new tissues are developed.) Plant fertilization, in spiritual science, takes place through the fact that the gnomes take from the fire spirits what the fire spirits have carried into the seed bud as concentrated cosmic warmth "on the little airships of the anther pollen." Fertilization takes place in the earth during winter, when the seed comes into the earth and meets with the forms that the gnomes have received from the activities of the sylphs and undines, carrying it to where these forces can meet with the fructifying seed. What now results from the combined working of gnome activity and fire spirit activity is fructification. The gnomes are the spiritual midwives of plant production.

"With the help of what comes from the fire-spirits, the gnomes down below instill life into the plant and push it upwards. They are the fosterers of life. They carry the 'life-ether' to the root—the same 'life-ether' in which they themselves live."

Thus the plants, adds Steiner, can be understood only when they are considered in connection with all that is circling, weaving, and living around them, which, he adds, is why Goethe instinctively argued with botanists who held that fructification takes place in the blossom.

Steiner's explanation of the mechanics of bird and sylph life, far-fetched to the materialist, are only so for lack of a basic emulsifying ingredient, banished from the vocabulary of academia since the time of Plato—the notion, embarrassing to science, of the effect of love in nature. Love and self-sacrifice are to spiritual science the prime requirements for life on earth. Without the self-sacrifice of nature spirits there would be, says Steiner, no so-called generative propagation of plants.

Neither the four elements nor the four ethers, says Steiner, are creators: they are merely potential for the formation of physical substance. To become substance, something more must supervene. Two of Steiner's more eminent anthroposophical colleagues, Guenther Wachsmuth and Ernst Marti, the former in his book *The Etheric Formative Forces in Cosmos, Earth and Man*, the latter in *The Four Ethers*, struggled valiantly to make comprehensible the mechanics of "etheric formative forces." Both fell short—perhaps for fear of alienating their academic colleagues with what might sound too much like a fairy story—by failing to identify these forces for what they really saw them to be: the nature spirits of the elemental world, guided by superior spirits. Ernst Hagemann, another eminent anthroposophist, is more courageous. In his *Weltenaether-Elementar-wese-Naturreiche* he gathers together every available Steiner reference to nature spirits scattered as they are throughout lectures given over many years. These "beings"—gnomes, nymphs, sylphs, and salamanders—Hagemann clearly identifies with the formative forces that operate at the physical level to mold from element and ether the myriad forms of nature from blueprints provided for them by a hierarchy of superior spirits.

When Steiner talked of etheric formative forces, he did not mean abstract physical forces or their effects; he meant elemental beings: it is they who are involved wherever etheric forces or formative forces are in play. They are the long arm of the divinity, acting like the fingers at the end of Akhenaton's sun rays, to mold what passes for reality out of stardust—the quarks, subquarks, and electrons of the physicist—continually being poured into the cosmos by the divinity's other hand. It is a dual process most felicitously depicted by the tarot card of the Star Goddess Nuit, symbol for a cosmic channel used by cosmic energy, or Shakti, to manifest on earth. In each hand Nuit holds a jar from which to pour and mingle twin vortices of that inexplicable energy derived from the Absolute through the primordial separation of will from power.

Nature spirits create plants from the blueprint of a higher dimension, and they create the etheric body of the plants out of their own etheric bodies. But they cannot create of their own responsibility. They can only implement instructions from above, from their immediate superiors in the supervening hierarchy of spiritual beings, beginning with the devas.

12

Devas

To the Eastern mind the word *deva* conjures up a host of "shining ones," astral creatures of almost infinite variety and function, creative powers all around the world. To theosophist and anthroposophist, devas represent a lower order of angels, responsible for handling the realm of elemental nature spirits.

Along with the devas that take care of fruit, vegetables, and flowers—as described by such sensitives as Findhorn's Dorothy McLean and Perelandra's Machaelle Small Wright—Hodson and Leadbeater describe others that oversee copse, wood, mountain, and valley. Some deal in very broad outlines, vast landscapes, huge elemental forces. Earth devas are described as attending leys beneath the ground, along the plate lines and other features of the earth's crust; they have been interpreted in folklore as dragons and great worms.

The higher devas, says Hodson, know the plan: "The will of the creator finds expression in them, and they are its agents and channels in manifested Nature." The plan is then disseminated by a kind of mental osmosis to all the ranks below them, each lower group having its leader, responsible to the group above.

Though astral by nature, says Hodson, devas can assume etheric bodies and usually appear to humans in human form, though often of gigantic size, differing in appearance according to the order to which they belong, the functions they perform, and the level of evolution attained.

Gardner describes deva consciousness as being much freer than human consciousness, but he says their mentality and sense of responsibility vary according to their development. They are credited with producing thought-forms, as do humans, but theirs are deemed to be not as concrete as those of humans, though possibly put to better use as they communicate with one another by flashings of splendid color; it is a language not as definite as ours but more expressive.

Steiner describes deva impulses, emotions, desires, and wishes—invisible in humans—as effects of light: radiant, flashing with a myriad hues, like rainbows changing colors. To Hodson, the deva's aura is less defined than the human aura. The colors are more fluid, more like a flame than a cloud, and whereas human auras appeared to him as brilliant but delicate clouds of glowing gas, the devas' looked more like a mass of fire. He describes a deva's natural body at the astral level as "iridescent, changing, pulsating with astral forces," not limited to a fixed or definite shape, but often losing all semblance of human form, seeming to become "whirling masses of force and vital energy in which appear graceful wing-like formations, long streaming curves, a suggestion of waving arms, of hair flying in the wind." In the deva's consciousness Hodson found nothing that could correspond with pain, disappointment, depression, fear, anger, or desire; nor was there any sign of strain. To account for this, Hodson points out—in his quaintly puritanical language—that devas do not have to resist the "promptings of the lower nature with which the human aspirant to the spiritual life is assailed."

But like the angels in John Milton's epic poem, *Paradise Lost,* who make love to one another for the pleasure of fulfillment rather than to beget children, Hodson's angels practice union and self-identification with one another not for reproduction of the species but to share their life and consciousness with other forms of life, "attaining such a large measure of self-identification with the life and consciousness of the object of their labors that Buddhic and nirvanic power is released into both the life and the form at the level at which they are working."

Leadbeater further explains that angelic and devic beings cannot affect things on earth directly because of their higher levels of consciousness, so they use the services of nature spirits to create all kinds of objects and creatures in the material world. In the development of the earliest forms—mineral, vegetable, and animal—devas made use of fairies and elementals to evolve the most beautiful and responsive examples.

When one of what Leadbeater calls "these great ones" has a new idea connected with the plants or flowers under its charge it will, he says, create a thought-form for the special purpose of carrying out that idea: this usually manifests as an etheric model of the flower itself or as a little creature that hangs around the plant or flower all through the time that the buds are forming, gradually building them into the shape and color of which the deva gave thought. "But as soon as the plant is fully grown or the flower has bloomed, the thought-up creature's work is over and its power exhausted." It simply dissolves, because, says Leadbeater, the will to do that piece of work was the only soul it had.

To see devas, says Leadbeater, all that is required is a little clairvoyance at the right moment. And when they see a human being, says Hodson, especially one who can see them and even understand them and converse with them, they almost all show a great surprise and delight. According to the prolific writer on theosophy, A. E. Powell, devas are often near at hand and willing to expound and exemplify subjects along their own line to any human being sufficiently developed to appreciate them.

The more evolved devas who have reached the level of self-consciousness are said to become guardians of special groups of humans or even of nations; they are attached to work of importance in the scheme of evolution, either on the physical or other planes, acting as messengers who carry out the will of higher angelic beings.

As beings at a higher stage of development than humans, devas are able to work on higher levels of existence. To advanced clairvoyants they appear on the three different and subtler planes to which the Hindus have given the names Kama, Rupa, and Arupa. Kamadevas have as their lowest body the astral. Rupadevas operate on the lower mental plane. Arupadevas exist in bodies of the higher mental or causal matter. But for Rupadevas and Arupadevas to manifest on the astral plane, says Powell, is at least as rare as for an astral entity to materialize on the physical plane.

Hodson describes encounters with a variety of devas, not only tree and plant devas, but mountain devas, landscape devas, and higher-ranking devas in charge of humans and their habitations. In the west of England, after a scramble of several hundred feet up a rocky glen, Hodson came out onto an open fell facing a huge crag; there he became aware "with startling suddenness" of the presence of a great nature deva, "partly within the hillside, which seemed to be in charge of that part of the landscape."

Hodson's first impression was of a huge, brilliant, crimsonlike thing, which fixed him with a pair of burning eyes, like a huge bat with a human face, its wings outstretched over the mountainside. Seeing itself observed, says Hodson, the deva flashed into what he assumed to be its proper shape, about ten to twelve feet high, "its auric flow very beautiful, swept back behind its body in wing-like sheets from the top of its head to its feet, reaching back in graceful flowing lines."

The function of this splendid creature appeared to be to oversee the evolution of the landscape, "its powerful vibrations having a quickening effect upon the animal, vegetable, mineral, and nature spirit life within its sphere of influence." Hodson's own physical body thrilled for hours afterward with the force of the contact and the rapport established on that hillside.

Another sort of deva was spotted by Hodson on the shores of Thirlmere, on the site of an old Roman colony known as "The City." Three "lower level tree devas" were moving swiftly in an out of trees, "continuously impressing their vibrations on their wards." And so great was the power with which they moved, says Hodson, it produced the psychic effect of a sound like the running of a well-tuned motor. He found these devas' eyes preternaturally bright, looking more like centers of force than organs of vision. They were apparently incapable of seeing to any distance, their consciousness seated at a higher level, their awareness obtained by an inner sense rather than by sight.

Some of these tree spirits seemed to have associated closely with an individual tree or a lesser group of trees and to remain stationary with the charge or charges included within their auras. Others moved about at the height of the topmost branches, from where they had "established a powerful keynote for the auric vibration of the whole group of trees, making their continued presence necessary for the maintenance of the quickening, energizing force they induced." This force, on the physical plane, manifested to Hodson as a powerful magnetic influence, so marked as to be noticeable without the aid of clairvoyance.

Gardner explains how devas have their center of consciousness at the astral level and dip down into the physical plane chiefly to stimulate the life of trees and larger plants. He says they may live as the ensouling life of a tree or group of trees, like the dryads of tradition, stimulating the far slower activities of the tree with the magnetism of their bodies, circulating the sap, and so forth. Or they may be engaged in raying out strong influences over certain spots termed "magnetic centers."

Leadbeater described the spirit of a great banyan tree as occasionally exteriorizing itself in the form of a gigantic human. Beneath the tree many earth nature spirits or gnomes were running about on the surface of the ground, dark in color like the skin of an elephant, from eight inches to two feet high, of very primitive intelligence, their sense of enjoyment of life predominant.

Around the outer surfaces of the tree, in the more leafy regions, Leadbeater found a number of "leaf" nature spirits, somewhat feminine in appearance, diminutive in form, a few inches to two or three feet tall. He says they were transmitting creative form-producing impulses and stimulating energies to the outermost branches and leaves. The association of these nature spirits with the tree had the effect of impressing the form of the tree upon their auras, which made it possible for the overseeing deva to observe, correct, and influence their actions.

The deva of a tree Leadbeater described as stationed in the central trunk, its head in the upper branches, its feet below the ground; though at times it would rise high above its ward. Its consciousness completely unified with that of the tree, it could subject it, from within, to stimulating and quickening power.

William Bloom, of the Findhorn Community—where the vogue of communion with devas was revived in the 1960s—says that devas have an exact sense of what the perfect plant should be and that the changes wrought by the interference of weather, of other plants, of soil conditions, of animals, and of people are all inputs to which the deva fluidly adjusts, always clearly holding the sense of the perfectly fulfilled plant.

Thus, no matter what external interference there might be, the plant it-self is still enveloped by the ideational matrix, held by the deva, into which it may grow.

Studying what he called "the female deva of another tree," Leadbeater noted that she observed the astral double of all the physical-plane objects around her. A tree appeared to her as a dark central form, its physical shape interpenetrated and surrounded by a pale, luminous, gray light, its etheric double surrounded in turn by a violet astral aura that extended about six inches beyond the physical form. To this female deva each tree was like an engine into and through which force was flowing from the astral plane, vivifying and illuminating it—keeping it alive. "She sees at the root of the tree, just below the ground level, a golden vortex of energy where the force enters from the astral plane and from which it passes throughout the whole body of the tree."

Exploring the Cotswolds in August of 1925, Hodson encountered in a valley two miles long and one mile wide a more majestic deva, which appeared to him to be there "to help forward the evolution of the whole valley, primarily the elemental and vegetable kingdoms, but also taking an interest in the human inhabitants of the valley." In the evening of the following day, climbing the hills that rise from the valley to a point where he could look down on fields, houses, and woods—a peaceful, beautiful scene—Hodson spotted the deva hover-ing over the treetops, apparently waiting to bid him welcome.

About ten feet high, its aura—which radiated to about a hundred yards on all sides—could extend right across the valley to touch every living thing within it, giving to each, as Hodson puts it, "a share of its own magnificently vital life force, its colors brilliant and constantly changing, flowing in waves and vortices outward from its central form, from deep royal blue with red and golden yellow and green sweeping through it, followed by pale rose-du-Barry with a soft eau-de-Nil sky blue."

The deva's features Hodson described as noble and beautiful, eyes dazzling bright, more like the centers of force than eyes, not used to the same extent as those of humans for the expression of thought and emotion. The seat of its consciousness appeared to be in the middle of its head, a blazing center of light. From this center the deva controlled a host of nature spirits throughout the valley. Elves and brownies, says Hodson, could feel this control as a sudden exaltation, the source of which they could not fully comprehend, though they recognized it as a constant feature of their lives.

Hodson says he savored the deva's combination of a sense of freedom from all limitations with a humanlike capacity for tenderness, deep concern for others, even love. Among its functions appeared to be that of guiding humans who had just died to a place of peace.

Thereafter, throughout his life, wherever he traveled, Hodson described encountering great devas with whom he was able to communicate. During a lecture tour in Java in 1933, on a visit to the great Buddhist shrine known as Borobudur, Hodson realized he was in the presence of the presiding deva, "distinctly masculine and Indo-Aryan, with the golden light of Buddha shining all about him, glowing through successive spheres of soft rose, soft green, and a dazzling white aura." Here, says Hodson, was the head of devic life on the island as well as in the surrounding seas, a veritable deva king, who advised Hodson "to live intensely in the fullness of the eternal now," explaining that to a consciousness beyond time and space "all exists at once in its fully developed state."

Shortly after arriving in Australia, Hodson says he experienced another of those welcoming greetings from the local devas. In Perth, on an eminence in King's Park overlooking the broad Swan River, from where he could see the whole city and, beyond it, the Darling Range and the vast expanse of Australia, he says he was greeted by a large number of great golden devas.

The relation between devas and humans, says Gardner, is mutually beneficial, for the deva also learns from people. It is therefore up to humankind to strengthen the relationship.

William Bloom says that to work cooperatively with devic life, accuracy and 100 percent clarity of perception are not required. All that is needed is the right personality attitude. And then, over time, greater certainty and greater clarity of perception will develop.

From deva to angel, the shading appears to be of the finest. Gelda van Doren in *The Real World of Fairy* describes the matter of which an angel's body is made as being very much finer than that of a fairy, so fine that to see it requires a purer form of clairvoyance. Whereas fairies can be seen, especially out of the corner of the eye, angels, says van Doren, are rarely seen with the physical eye. Her theory is that the central part of the retina is used so much for ordinary sight that it does not respond to the more delicate vibrations of light from fairies, let alone angels, whereas the rest of the retina is fresh and more suitable for such uses.

To those who can see the angelic hosts, they appear to fill all space, a vast orchestra and choir gathered in tiers, arranged in groups, each with its own characteristic colors and cosmic chants, a sort of Jacob's ladder of development, no rung missing.

As Hodson describes them: "Every atom of their auras is glowing and shining with the appropriate hues of their particular chord of existence, and the space all around them is shimmering with the iridescent radiance of their auras and the effects of their song upon the surrounding elemental essence."

To Hodson, angels serve somewhat as electrical transformers, rheostats of resistance, stepping down the voltage from on high. "They appear to receive in themselves the primordial, creative energy and, as if by resistance to its flow, reduce the voltage, slow it down." In Hodson's romantic language: "They hear the divine song, direct and re-echo it, rank upon rank, until it is brought to a voltage where it will build instead of destroy, as it might do in its naked potency."

By self-unification with this descending "word-force," says Hodson, and particularly with such streams of power as are vibrating at frequencies that are identical with those of their own nature, the angels amplify and augment its form-producing power.

Hodson describes what he calls "the music of the divine idea" descending to the world of form, or Rupa plane. There the appropriate angel receives and reechoes it until it is "heard" at the astral level, from where it influences the elemental essence. Again it is reechoed and slowed down until it reaches the etheric world, where it uses etheric matter to assume shapes and beautiful designs. Magnetic fields of force are there set up containing geometric designs. In these lines of force the nature spirits play, thereby increasing their formative tendency as they assist in building natural physical forms, atom by atom, molecule by molecule, cell by cell. These nature spirits, says Hodson, operate instinctively, largely by playing and dancing along the lines of force, which they find stimulating, electrifying, even intoxicating.

Gardner describes tiny etheric creatures working in the grass that run about aimlessly, just "going somewhere" like gnats in the sun. Yet the busy traveling of these specks of etheric being, says Gardner, has its function: that of keeping active the vital currents in the grass and thereby stimulating growth even in that low order of plant life, even though these tiny entities have only a mass consciousness of the purpose for which they exist. He describes groups of fairy workers—brownies, elves, and pixies—working at their tasks like a hive of bees or a nest of ants, without individual responsibility, though instinctively in touch with Nature's plan.

To obtain a view of this spiritual supersensible world, says Steiner, one must organize oneself up to the level of angelic beings, learn to see the world with the kind of perception possessed by the angels. "Things that appear to us in material form are but the outward sheaths of spiritual beings. The radiant glory of the angels is far more real, not less real, than things of the physical plane."

With no physical body and no physical organs such as eyes, ears, and so on, angels, says Steiner, perceive the physical world differently. They do not see as we see: what to us is perception, to angels is manifestation. We see because an external world appears before our senses; angels are aware only of what they are themselves manifesting. When entering into connection with the world around them, they develop another form of consciousness, in a way like sleep; only they are not unconscious. They merely feel a sort of loss of self. Consciously, says Steiner, angels are aware of four kingdoms: plant, animal, human, and their own world of angels, but not the mineral kingdom: where there is mineral they perceive only a hollow.

As in their lowest being angels have an etheric body, their consciousness can descend low enough to perceive plants; hence their close relationship, especially the lower devas, with the world of plants.

In the future, says Steiner, humans will develop the consciousness of angels: meanwhile angels are the spirits that help man transform his astral body to·the point when it will be under the control of "his immortal self, the real I."

What helps a person in the continuing struggle to regain the state of grace enjoyed before the Fall is, according to Peter Lamborn Wilson, the constant intercession of a personal angel, who guards, cherishes, protects, visits, and defends its ward.[1]

It is the personal angel who guards human memory, "awakening recollections of the soul's previous earthly lives, in order to establish continuity of endeavor—of the quest and aspiration of the soul from life to life—so that particular lives are not merely isolated episodes but constitute the stages of a single path towards one sole end."

But angelic support does not mean substituting the angel's will for human will. The guardian angel is programmed never to interfere with human free will. "He is the clairvoyant helping the non-clairvoyant with respect to psychic and physical temptations and dangers."

The angel is also seen as screening his protégé from the wrath of heaven, acting as an advocate for a person, defending him or her like a mother defends her child, without regard to whether he or she be good or bad. This, says Wilson, is why traditional art presents guardian angels as winged females and why the Virgin Mother bears the title *Regina angelorum*. "Think of your angel as a luminous cloud of maternal love above you, moved by the sole desire to serve you and to be useful to you."

While to Swedenborg, Blake, and Goethe the world of angels was as real as any, by the turn of the century Steiner was describing this spiritual world from his own clairvoyant point of view, its beings as real to him as humans. His object was to show how the threshold from the physical to the supersensible can be crossed in order to communicate first with the elemental beings and then with the hierarchies in their ascending ranks and functions throughout the cosmos.

1. In biblical tradition, the period before the influence of Luciferic beings is described as the Age of Paradise. To Steiner, the Fall, or expulsion from Paradise, was conditioned by the descent of human beings out of this extraterrestrial region to the earth, followed by their entanglement in the world of the senses.

Access to this world, says Steiner, is available to all in a condition of conscious sleep: "When we have drawn our astral bodies out of our physical and etheric bodies, we are no longer unconscious, but have around us, not the physical world, nor even the world of the nature spirits, but another and still more spiritual world, a new order of spiritual beings who have command over nature and all spirits."

The world he is describing, stacked above the angels, is said to consist of eight more levels of spiritual beings whose functions are not only to run the solar system but to be responsible, operating in their hierarchical ranks, for all of creation. Nor, says he, are the functions of the hierarchies alien to the future of humanity, quite the contrary. "As humanity reaches maturity and develops its inner faculties, the direction of Nature's activities will then begin to fall into man's hands."

13

The Hierarchies

The prime Western source of descriptive material about the angelic and archangelic hierarchies is attributed to a gifted young Athenian student of Plato's writings, an intimate of the apostle Paul, known to history as Dionysius the Areopagite. According to Steiner, Dionysius was in Heliopolis in Egypt at the time of the crucifixion, and later in Athens helped found an esoteric school with Paul, which was to influence Christendom for centuries. Steiner goes so far as to say that it was through Dionysius, a great initiate, that the Rosicrucian spiritual path was prepared and that from Dionysius later Western esoteric wisdom and training was derived as well as "much of the deepest thought of the leading scholars and masters of the Middle Ages."[1]

In Steiner's version, Dionysius, teaching into his nineties by word of mouth to a small group of chosen pupils, proclaimed that space was filled not only with matter but "with realm upon realm of spiritual beings far more developed than man." These beings Dionysius divided into three hierarchies, subdivided into three levels. His lowest hierarchy, which he named the Third Hierarchy, he peopled with angels, archangels, and archai; the next higher, or Second Hierarchy, with powers, mights, and dominions, known to him as exusiai, dynamis, and kyriotetes; and the highest of all, the First Hierarchy, with thrones, cherubim, and seraphim. To Steiner it was clear that Dionysius was referring to the same spiritual beings described millennia earlier by the

1. Whether Steiner—evidently on the basis of his perusal of the Akashic Record— is correct in attributing the most important text in the history of angelology, Dionysius's *The Celestial Hierarchy*, to a contemporary of the apostle Paul, or as other scholars attribute it, to a later Neoplatonist pseudo-Dionysius is immaterial. What matters is the text.

Rishi adepts of the Vedas. This ninefold celestial hierarchy, made visible in sculpture on the south portico of Chartres Cathedral in the eleventh century and poetically depicted by Dante in his *Divine Comedy*, was made rationally comprehensible by Steiner at the beginning of this century when he described the role and function of these spiritual beings as they rise in spiritual bodies ever more tenuous and ever more powerful toward their source, the Divine.

Angels and archangels—members of Dionysius's Third, or lowest, Hierarchy—are qualified as messengers to indicate they are not carrying out tasks of their own but fulfilling orders received from superior hierarchies. And whereas archangels and archai are said to be barred from erring, "being constitutionally incapable of sinking into evil out of their own resolve," angels, because of their involvement in the human scenario, have been allowed to err as part of the process enabling humanity to develop free will.

Characteristic of Steiner's beings of the Third Hierarchy is "being filled with the spirit of the superior hierarchies, being controlled by them, carrying out what is required by them." In their inner life, says Steiner, angels of the Third Hierarchy originally had no independence to do wrong, such as humans have. As tools or automata of higher authority, they felt the force of superior hierarchies welling up in their inner being and were inspired to manifest this superior will. Unlike humans, who can shut up their thoughts and feelings within themselves, members of the Third Hierarchy were unable to hide their feelings: "Any inner thought immediately manifested externally. They could not lie or be untrue to their nature: thoughts and feelings had to harmonize with the world around them."

Then, according to Steiner, an extraordinary development occurred. "There were Angels, members of the lowest hierarchy, who wished to deny their own nature. They wished to develop an inner life of their own, to obtain independence from beings of the higher hierarchies, to have experiences in their inner nature which they did not have to manifest externally." Thus, says Steiner, were engendered the Luciferic beings who wished to be filled with their own being. But in so doing they did a service to humankind: they made it possible for human beings also to develop an independent life of their own, choosing or refusing to be tempted, to love out of choice, not compulsion.

Before the advent of Luciferic influences, the human soul, says Steiner, carried out all its activities in line with the intentions of higher spiritual beings.

Were there no temptation—as is perennially explained by adepts—humans would not have the choice of eschewing evil. Hence the important role of Luciferic beings. "The gods," says Steiner, "were able to foresee that if they continued to create only as they had done, then free beings who acted out of their own initiative would never come into being. For free beings to be created, the possibility had to be given for opponents to arise against them in the cosmic all." He then points out that one should not look for the origin of evil in so-called evil beings but in so-called good beings.

In due course, according to Steiner, the Luciferic angels, having served their purpose, will reacquire their benign angelic status. Surprisingly, he postulates 14,000 or 15,000 C.E. for this event, indicating that the Akashic Record allows its viewer access to the future as well as to the past. Ahrimanic beings, whose function is to tempt humanity to gross materialism, having served their purpose in humanity's development to freedom, may also return to the hierarchical groups from which they were expelled during the course of earth's evolution.

Yet there remained non-Luciferic, non-Ahrimanic angels, and they, together with archangels and archai, continue, according to occult philosophy, to help humanity progress to higher stages of development, stages it cannot reach on its own without help.

What is done for humanity by members of this Third Hierarchy is regarded by anthroposophists primarily as work upon the human soul, comparable to the work of a human teacher. The angel, says Stewart C. Easton in his remarkable overview, *Man and the World in the Light of Anthroposophy*, can gaze upon the development of an individual soul: "In reality there is a self belonging to each of us which is not to be found with ordinary consciousness, but has a hidden existence; it is this self which the Angel tries to guard, and to reveal to us at certain moments."

The role of angels, adds Adam Bittleston, an ordained priest of the Christian Community—a religious group following Steiner's philosophy, separate from the Anthroposophical Society but widespread throughout the world—is to care for individual human beings and to lead human souls into successive civilizations. Archangels shape these civilizations so as to provide the right experiences for those who incarnate into them. Archangels, unconcerned with single human beings, says Bittleston, bring about harmonizing influences among larger groups, among peoples, races, and so forth, indwelling the development of a nation, working primarily among its artists, thinkers, and reformers. "But just as a man's pride in his own genius is a great hindrance to his Angel, national pride blocks the work of the Archangel, producing an appalling caricature of it." Instead of fostering a healthy spirit of nationalism, Luciferic angels, says Bittleston, "turned what had been a normal feeling of unity with one's fellow countrymen into the evil that is nationalism."

In a world capable of producing a Thirty Years' War, a Hundred Years' War, two World Wars, and endless Holocausts, some heavy jousting may be in order between Luciferic and archangelic contestants for the illumination of human minds. In Steiner's mind it is still touch and go as to whether humans will make it, especially if we continue to ignore angelic prompting. His direst prophecy involves a great war of "all against all."

On the positive side stands a Bittleston analogy: "The Archangel is to the Angel like a brother who can remember very much further into the past, a past of great nobility and splendor of which he often tells his younger brother." And in yet another analogy, Bittleston sees angels as akin to patiently flowing water, archangels to the swift winds of heaven, archai to fiery spirits, enkindling and purifying love, their physical bodies only perceived in flames.

Archai—a Greek word that could be rendered as "princes"—or "Spirits of Personality," as Steiner calls them, highest members of the Third Hierarchy, are those who form successive civilizations, awakening and bringing about human "ego-consciousness"; this they are said to do in such a way that individuals can develop toward a personality on earth. In Bittleston's words: "The Archai live in glowing enthusiasm for the awakening of man into free understanding and free action: feeling himself in ancient times only as part of a tribal community, passing through stages in which he has a status given to him from outside, towards the awakening of a freedom in which he chooses the purposes and tasks of his life for himself."

And just as archangels vie to have the nations entrusted to them live as part of a great choir, each contributing voices in accord with the rest, so the archai, says Steiner, want every age to play its part in the whole span of human development, from the first beginnings to the fulfillment of history. "Seeking the eternal within the temporal," adds Bittleston, "Archai prepare for the task which lies before them when this universe will have passed away. They will then rise to the rank of world creators and bring forth from the invisible, in accord with purposes of still greater powers, a new heaven and a new earth."

As Steiner shows in his *Occult Science: An Outline,* the goal of the world-creator powers with their extraordinarily complex hierarchy of spiritual beings is none other than the creation of humankind and the creation of an environment that, in an ongoing evolution, can eventually help individual human beings to become free. "Preparation for this development entailed enormous sacrificial work on the part of the hierarchical beings in the course of which they themselves attained a higher development."

To Steiner the basic "spiritual substance" of the cosmos, his "world-ether," is generated by the various states of consciousness of hierarchical beings from primordial spiritual "warmth." World-ether, as it radiates down to the earth from cosmic heights is, in its essence, a thought-forming power, a manifestation, says Steiner, of the consciousness of hierarchical beings in differing levels, there being nothing in the universe but consciousness.

In this scenario, as the hierarchies prepared for the creation of earthly beings, they first had to secrete and sacrifice from themselves, as building material derived from world-ether, the four distinct ethers (warmth, light, chemical, and life) and the four elements (fire, air, water, and earth), sending both ethers and elements "down into the earthly realm so that the etheric bodies of the multitudinous creatures of the kingdoms of nature could be created."

Fire, source of all the other elements, is attributed to the cosmic sacrifice of "thrones," or spirits of will. "The Thrones reached such an exalted state of development they were able to let the heat substance stream from their own bodies, like silk-worms spinning threads from their bodies." Without the thrones, says Steiner, there would be no physical world at all. Thrones also produced as offspring the spiritual beings that became the devas of minerals, enduring and conservative powers that because of their high descent have, as Hodson was quick to discover, a high state of consciousness. As Steiner elucidates: "Colors in flower and leaf glow forth but pass away; the red of carnelian and the green of emerald endure as long as the earth."

But because these rarefied spiritual beings cannot directly affect things on the material plane—owing to their higher level consciousness—angels, archangels, and archai, members of the Third Hierarchy, are obliged to use the services of nature spirits, who are equipped for directly handling the four ethers on earth to create all kinds of creatures and creations, and through them the material world. So, while the devas of mineral, plant, and animal were being separated from the First and Second Hierarchies, nature spirits were being exuded from the etheric substance of the Third Hierarchy. From the life-ether of archai appeared a multitude of gnomes; from the chemical-ether exuded by archangels waves of undines; from the light-ether provided by angels, flights of sylphs. Salamanders, or fire spirits, for some arcane reason, are described as deriving from the warmth-ether exuded from the devas of animals, in turn detached from the dynamis of the Second Hierarchy.[2]

But all these beings produced by the Third Hierarchy should not, says Steiner, be properly called nature spirits because they have—as yet—no spirit, only body and soul. (By *soul* he means an astral body; by *spirit* a ruling ego as yet not developed.) Rather than nature spirits, says

2. Some salamanders, says Steiner, can originate from detached parts of animal group-souls that dare to enter too far into the physical world, becoming overly attached to a human being, such as a horse to its rider, a sheep to its shepherd, any pet to its owner.

Steiner, they should be called "very useful elemental beings." And very useful they appear to have been, and to be, as the immediate helpers of their hierarchical creators. But having no ego of their own, these beings need to be controlled by intermediary, subangelic creatures of the astral plane, the devas. The function of these supervising spirits is to ensure the accurate implementation by the egoless elementals of the blueprints passed down from the superior creating hierarchies. The etheric bodies of these astral devas (or "group souls") are also fashioned, says Steiner, like the bodies of the "very useful elemental beings," directly from the world-ether.

Yet another essential step was required for the creation of the etheric bodies of all these living organisms: a very special self-sacrifice on the part of each and every "very useful elemental being." For any earthly form to materialize and then maintain itself—in accordance with the blueprint produced by its hierarchical ideator, transmitted via the requisite deva—"very useful" elementals must allow themselves individually (or rather their consciousness) to be hypnotized or "enchanted" into the material object being created.

As Steiner explains the process, whereas these elemental beings retain their astral bodies on the astral plane, only their consciousness is enchanted down into their physical creations. For the word *enchanted* Steiner often substitutes *charmed, bewitched, condemned, imprisoned,* or *chained,* meaning a sacrifice willingly undertaken by the four groups of elemental beings in order to assume and maintain earthly physical forms.

So long as the elemental remains enchanted, the physical form is required to persist. Beings remain enchanted until they have fulfilled their task in that particular organism. They then pass their work on to another elemental being. These enchantments and disenchantments can occur in regular daily rhythms. But generally, says Steiner, elemental beings, released from enchantment, try to get back down into matter.

Elemental beings are described as constantly being enchanted into air; and when air is transformed into a liquid state they are bewitched into lower forms of existence. An enchantment of spiritual beings is always connected with the condensation and formation of gases and solids. To build up the etheric bodies of all the species planned by the creator-powers—the hierarchies—a huge amount of etheric substances was evidently required, along with a very large number of elemental beings ready to sacrifice themselves, ready to be sent down to earth to be imprisoned in fire, air, water, and earth.

Thus nature spirits, or "very useful elemental beings," descendants of the Third Angelic Hierarchy, become, under the control of devas, master-builders in the kingdoms of nature, metamorphosing their entire beings into all kinds of earthly forms, enchanted into objects and creatures until the physiological process in an organism is completed and the creature or object either perishes or dissolves, liberating the elemental.

As the various nature kingdoms became physically manifest on earth, more and more elemental beings were clearly needed to build up the etheric bodies of all the species planned by the creator powers, forms that could not otherwise exist. All earthly creatures and inanimate beings are conditioned, says Steiner, by the sacrifice of elemental beings, which have to continually enchant and disenchant themselves in order to produce the countless materializations and dematerializations without which no earthly phenomena could be: no living creature could arise, maintain itself, or perish.

Furthermore, says Steiner, as endless etheric bodies have to be filled with "physical sense-perceptible substantiality," through countless rapidly successive enchantments and disenchantments, a great many more willing elemental beings are needed.

To explain the devoted sacrifice of elemental beings, continually going into or coming out of enchantment, Steiner says that they, too, like all spiritual beings, are bent on evolving so that they may return to their spiritual home and be reabsorbed by their creator hierarchies. To achieve this, they try to please the hierarchies "bringing them knowledge of the earth."

Gods, says Steiner—meaning members of the hierarchies—are as dependent on the world as the world is dependent on them.

Seen through spiritual insight, salamanders strive toward a higher development through countless enchantments and disenchantments;

not only fire spirits but also sylphs and undines appear to experience bliss by sacrificing their lives in order to be inhaled back into their originating hierarchies, in whom they can then live indefinitely. As Steiner explains it: "Undines and sylphs have a need for death. They feel they only have a life when they die. Dying is really the beginning of life for them as they stream out of earthly matter to offer themselves to higher beings as nourishment."

Steiner's vision affords him a poetic description of the final stages and self-immolation of his "very useful elemental beings." In summer, when seas such as the Baltic begin to "blossom," as sailors call it, and the heat causes fish to decay, imparting a peculiar putrefactive smell, undines are described as being truly in their element. "This is not unpleasant to the undines as the sea becomes for them a wonderful phosphorescent play of color in every shade of blue, violet, and green. The whole decomposition in the sea becomes a glimmering and gleaming of the darker colors up to green."

Undines, so described, absorb this color into themselves, becoming phosphorescent, longing to rise upward, to soar and offer themselves as earthly substance to the higher hierarchies, to angels, archangels, and so on. In this sacrifice they are said to find their bliss, living on within the higher hierarchies.

Even the song of birds ascends spiritually into the far reaches of space "to nourish the highest of the spiritual hierarchies, the Seraphim, who then pour the song back onto earth as a blessing for man."

Meanwhile, says Steiner, dying birds fill the air with astral substance that they would like to have delivered to the higher hierarchies in order to release it from the earth, but for this they need an intermediary. "So the sylphs hover in this astrality, taking up what comes from the dying bird-world, and carry it up into the heights, to be inhaled by beings of the higher hierarchies. The sylphs flash like blue lightning through the air, and into this blue lightning—which assumes green then redder tones—they absorb this astrality and dart up like lightning flashes to be inhaled by the beings of the hierarchies, and experience immortality."

It is, indeed, a carousel of life played to the music of the spheres, La Ronde on the grandest scale.

Superhierarchies

In Steiner's celestial symphony the hierarchies are developed one from the other in a descending and condensing sequence. The highest order, or First Hierarchy of seraphim, cherubim, and thrones, composed of the prime element "warmth," produce as offspring members of the Second Hierarchy, kyriotetes, dynamis, and exusiai, who then condense warmth into light and the shadow of light, which to Steiner is represented by air. Their progeny, in turn, the Third Hierarchy, thirsting for actual darkness (rather than mere shadow) develop darkness to interplay with light and thus create the magic of color, from whose reflection arises the watery element or chemical ether. With the final condensation into earth comes life.

At this point the development of the "very useful" elemental beings through the "tying-off" of parts of the hierarchical beings, plus the mediation of the devas, produces an uninterrupted process of creation spreading across the earth to populate the mineral, vegetable, and animal kingdoms.

Closely connected with this development of the planet are what Steiner calls "spirits of the cycles of time," descended, like the devas of minerals, directly from members of the highest hierarchy, the thrones, or spirits of will. Their function is to distribute work to the lower-ranking nature spirits throughout the year, bringing about change of seasons in the various regions of the earth. It is these controllers of cycles who are credited with spinning the planet on its axis and rolling it around the sun, responsible not only for generating day and night but also for regulating the seasons and the growing and fading of plants and animals, along with all other rhythmical repetitions of temporal events.

Under their control, myriads of elementals are spread around the earth so that all four groups can be active in the creation of the physical forms of weather: undines to make raindrops; fire spirits to evaporate water; gnomes for the formation of snowflakes and hailstones.

Like architects who tell the foreman, who in turn instructs the workers, spirits of the cycles of time are charged with giving orders to the devas of plants, who evidently need direction or blueprints in order to bring forth their offspring—individual plants in etheric bodies. And just as the etheric bodies of all the nature spirits form the etheric body of the earth, viewed clairvoyantly, so the astral body of the earth teems with spirits of the cycles of time: it is into this world one plunges with one's ego and one's astral body when asleep, and—if sufficiently awake in the ego—it is these spirits one meets. When developed enough, says Steiner, "we feel ourselves not only poured out into the whole world of the Spirits of the Cycles of Time, we feel ourselves one with the whole individual spirit of the planet." Its ego, as described by Steiner, is seated at the center of the planet and consists of the egos of all the plants on earth.

The actual etheric shape of the planet appears to be molded from etheric substance by the exusiai, spirits of form, as Michelangelo might mold a statue from clay. In this occult solar system each planet has its own spirit of form, operating from the sun. Singly and in conjunction, the function of these spirits is to produce the blueprints for all etheric substance in the solar system.

To the occultist, the earth, in its physical form, never at rest, always in a state of perpetual change and movement, is endowed with consciousness, its inner being regulated by the kyriotetes, spirits of wisdom, its inner mobility dependent on the spirits of motion, the dynamis. The impulse that drives it through space and governs its movement, causing it to revolve around our fixed star, the sun, is the function of the spirits of will, or thrones, lowest members of the First Hierarchy.

And just as behind the etheric body of humans operate their astral, mental, causal, and egoic bodies, so, says Steiner, behind our planet come sheaths of more rarefied spiritual beings to form its finer spiritual bodies: egoic, buddhic, and atmic—sheaths provided for earth by the more elevated spirits of motion, wisdom, and will, as well as by the sublimest cherubim and seraphim. Working all together, these spiritual hierarchies are viewed as ruling over and guiding human evolution, but they are considered of a nature so sublime and so different from all that humans are normally concerned with "that it is only possible to come to a very distant impression of them through comparison and analogy."

Beings of the Second Hierarchy—exusiai, dynamis, and kyriotetes—whose principal abode is given as the sun sphere, are qualified by Steiner as creator spirits who, over great spaces, call life into being and transform living things over long ages. The kyriotetes are organizers, the dynamis carry out their directives, the exusiai maintain what has been formed. To Steiner, the exusiai, or spirits of form, are the same as the Hebrew Elohim, plural of *Eloha,* or god, whose work is spelled out in Genesis as the "Six Days of Creation," meaning, says Steiner, "the totality of the spiritual intelligences by whose agency all worlds and all things are conceived and are objectively manifest at all levels, manifestation occurring when ideation is impressed on cosmic substance."

Not only, says Steiner, do beings of the Second Hierarchy manifest their selfhood creatively, as do beings of the Third Hierarchy, they go further: "They detach from themselves what they create, so that it persists as an independent being." Detached from beings of this Second Hierarchy are the group souls, or devas, that animate and interpenetrate the beings of the nature kingdoms of plants and animals. With animals, each species is endowed with physical, etheric, and astral bodies, but, according to Steiner, no "I." Instead of an ego, each animal has a group ego or group soul, "a real being, wiser than man," dwelling on the astral plane, from which it directs individual animals on earth through their instinct. Other clairvoyants maintain that animals and birds can develop egos, a notion that Steiner goes along with to the extent that a person's horse or dog or parrot can develop by close association with humans. Plants, lacking both astral bodies and egos, have their group soul on the next higher plane, the lower devachan. Minerals, last to condense in the course of earth's history, are described as having their group egos on the still higher devachan. Occultists see the physical body of a mineral as an empty hollow sphere surrounded by its etheric body, which works inwardly from without; its astral body is seen as raying out through the etheric into cosmic space, from where its group ego streams back in from the devachan.

In the formation of minerals on earth there is also the influence of planetary spirits, an influence divided among the various planets, a notion perfectly clear to Paracelsus. Streams of etheric life are described by Steiner as pouring down to earth from individual planets to permeate the various earthly minerals with "inner being:" Saturn permeates lead with its etheric currents, Jupiter does likewise for tin, Mars for iron, Venus for copper, Mercury for quicksilver; silver itself is influenced by the moon, as is gold by the sun. The actual forms assumed by minerals are seen as being provided by the exusiai, spirits of form, while subtly different substances in the mineral world are obtained through the workings of the group-souls of minerals, offspring of the thrones, who use rays to modify minerals in all sorts of delicate ways from without.

Another example elucidated by spiritual science is the influence exerted on the growth of plants by differing hierarchical beings operating from both the planets and the sun, as together they interweave the forms of individual plants on planet earth. Steiner describes dynamis, or spirits of motion, working down from the various planets of our planetary system through their offspring, the devas of plants, providing a spiral influence on the formation and growth of individual plants, bringing forth the leaves in spiral patterns, which mirror their own planetary movements. At the same time a different group of devas, offspring of the kyriotetes, or spirits of wisdom, work down vertically from the sun to draw up the stalk in a direct line from the center of the earth.

When these two forces—the spiral, originated by the spirits of motion in the planets, and the vertical, originated by the spirits of wisdom in the sun—are united at the right season in what Easton calls a sort of marriage performed by the spirits of the cycles of time, offspring of the First Hierarchy, the thrones, the plant on earth is complete. Thus, an ongoing symphony is orchestrated by the spirits of the cycles of time as plant and animal life become interwoven in complex and mysterious ways with the mundane work of the elemental beings, the nature spirits, offspring of the Third Hierarchy.

Bittleston is expansive, though a touch ecclesiastical, in his description of the joint roles of hierarchical beings influencing the earth from planets and sun: "We may feel something of the greatness of the sun by turning first towards the Spirits of Form, through whom all visible things strive towards their archetypes, towards the Spirits of Movement, through whom all beings meet and part, passing through need and fulfillment, and towards the Spirits of Wisdom who give all things their meaning, their place within the whole."

The actual operating space of these hierarchical spirits is explained as being not so much a single planet as a space within the whole orbit described by each planet as seen from the earth, Ptolemaically. Angels, being closest to humans, work closest to earth, up to the orbit of the moon: archangels up to the limit of Mercury's orbit, archai to that of Venus, dynamis to Mars, exusiai to the sun. Beyond the sun, the domain of the kyriotetes coincides with the orbit of Jupiter, that of Saturn with the bailiwick of the thrones.

The sublimest hierarchy of spiritual beings—thrones, cherubim, seraphim—are seen as inhabiting space beyond the zodiac, the seraphim receiving their high-level ideas directly from the Divine Trinity; cherubim elaborate these ideas, transforming them into workable plans; thrones put the plans into practice. Known to occultists as spirits of will, love, and harmony, the members of this First Hierarchy are said to be so intimate with the source of life, "having gathered wisdom over millions of years of cosmic growth," they no longer have to receive their life from outside but can create it from themselves and give it away. The inner experience of these beings of the First Hierarchy, says Steiner, lies in creation, in forming independent beings. "To create and live through other beings is the inner experience of the First Hierarchy: here we have not only self-creators, but creators of whole worlds: creation of worlds is their outer life, creation of beings their inner life."

As Steiner elucidates the process, whatever is created by spirits of the First Hierarchy continues to exist by itself, is separated from them like a skin or shell, and becomes a being of its own, continuing to exist even when severed from its creator. Their offspring, the devas of mineral, plant, and animal, split off from their creators, are sent down into the kingdom of nature, and "as these creations become detached there is not only the creation of independent beings but of whole worlds."

How such sublime beings might appear to human eyes is indicated by the prophet Ezekiel in the course of his ecstatic visions when he describes thrones as many-colored, wheel-like structures built up in such a way as to form wheels within wheels, multicolored transparent rings, one turning within the other, the inner one with eyes. In this description, angelologist Robert Sorbello sees a indication of flying saucers, as does his Dutch colleague, H. C. Moolenburgh, in his *A Handbook of Angels,* and as does Billy Graham in his book *Angels:* all three authors relate the UFO phenomena specifically to the higher hierarchies of angels.

Most pertinent, of course, is the role of these beings in the creation of humans. Steiner describes how early in the long history of the various cosmic bodies that preceded earth the hierarchies were already instrumental in developing what was to become the human being. First came the physical body, a creation of the highest hierarchy, virtually a body of fire, exuded from their own body by the thrones, or spirits of will. Gradually, over eons, this human body condensed through gaseous and liquid stages into a gelatinous creature swimming and hovering in the earth's environment until able to descend to such parts of the earth as were already more or less solidified. As man stepped onto earth and received the first traces of mineral substance in his physical body, he gradually acquired his present form but needed, in progressive order, an etheric body, an astral body, and an ego.

The "will" exuded by the thrones when united with the "life ether" radiated by kyriotetes from their own etheric bodies (made of cosmic sun force) endowed the human being with an etheric body. Next the dynamis, or spirits of motion, with no physical or etheric bodies, their lowest body being the astral, allowed their astral bodies to surge through the human etheric body "like sap in a plant." This enabled man to manifest for himself the soul qualities of sympathy and antipathy, enabling him to feel pleasure and displeasure.

The exusiai, spirits of form, allowing their forces to flow in and out of the human etheric body, individualized this life essence, giving man a more permanent form after their own, endowing humans with a spark of their own fire: their ego or I. This allowed humans to deliberately seek what causes pleasure and avoid what causes antipathy.

Next, the archai, spirits of personality, working on the human astral body, conferred on man the appearance of personality, imparting independence. Working together with members of the highest hierarchy, the seraphim or spirits of love, they then allowed humans to observe in pictures the inner soul-states of beings in the environment, engendering the emotion of love, an emotion that was to degenerate—as man gained freedom—into the confusion between spiritual and sensual love.

Archangels, or spirits of fire, working on the human etheric body, made man aware of his own existence, developing organs of sense and the first beginnings of a glandular system. Working on the ether body, they allowed the physical body to draw nutrition from animals and plants. Angels, known to Steiner as sons of light, appeared as beings that humans can picture mentally as etheric soul-forms, or bodies of light. They give memory to man's etheric body and work on his physical body so that it can become the expression of his independent astral body.

By the end of the Lemurian Age, says Steiner, ego forces permeated the human astral body. During the Atlantean period these same forces permeated the human etheric body; in post-Atlantean evolution they came to penetrate the physical body. As this occurred, the hierarchies began to withdraw, leaving humans to their own devices.

As human bodies became distributed over the whole earth, subject to earthly influences, which vary at different points of its surface, differing varieties appeared in human forms. When the present moon separated from the earth, there ensued the separation of the sexes, the purpose of sex being to continually refine the love principle to the point of spiritualization. Someday, says Steiner, when our earth has attained its goal, all earthly beings will be filled with love. "Love will be developed in its true form initially on earth: to put it crudely: love will be bred here, and the gods, through their participation in mankind, will come to know love, just as, in another sense, they bestowed it."

Every night, when we leave our physical and etheric bodies asleep, we find ourselves in the astral world where we encounter the beings who gave us our physical, etheric, and astral bodies. Between death and rebirth we learn, says Steiner, to know these spiritual beings directly in their real spiritual essence, witnessing how they "shine forth with gentle phosphorescence, how they spread streaming warmth, how they speak out of their own essence, each spiritual form apparently different, kyriotetes differing from exusiai, yet constituting the only real things in the universe. The created world is nothing but the outer garment, the outer glory, of creating hierarchies. Actual reality is only attained with knowledge of the spiritual beings at work in the various heavenly bodies. In the stars we contemplate the bodies of divine beings, and finally the Divine in general. They are the true reality. Nothing else is real, neither space, nor time, nor matter."

Dionysius the Areopagite, following the sages of the East, carefully differentiated among the various degrees of divine spiritual beings, but, as Steiner points out, "Those who grasp the unity of cosmic wisdom are well aware of the fact that they are but different names of the same being."

15

Kabbalah Unveiled

The cascade of consciousness from Absolute to material, through logos, planet, monad, down to the heart of the electron, is subtly and mathematically depicted in that most remarkable of ancient hieroglyphs, the kabbalists' ten-branched Tree of Life.

The meaning of the word *kabbalah,* etymologically related to the Hebrew *QBL,* "to receive," is supposed to indicate secret knowledge received by word of mouth, hidden knowledge considered so profound that "few could be trusted with its essence, let alone fully understand its complexity." Tradition has the kabbalah somehow hidden in the first five books of the Pentateuch.

Many years ago Madame Blavatsky pointed out in *The Secret Doctrine* that the kabbalah, with its mystical and occult formulation of the doctrines of the Jewish religion, encoded the story of this descent of consciousness using the metaphoric language of the creation myth in Genesis.

The central books of kabbalistic wisdom, the Sepher Yetzirah, or Book of Formation, along with the Zohar, or Book of Splendor, and the Sepher Bahir, Book of Brilliance—all fruit in their modern versions of intense medieval scholarship—postulate the existence beyond everyday reality of a vast, unseen, multilayered cosmic reality, with everything in the universe connected to everything else, all in constant interaction.

The Tree of Life, with its ten branches, the so-called sephirah (plural *sephiroth*), meaning "numerical emanations," turns out, in a remarkable analysis by Stephen Phillips, to be nothing less than a mathematical blueprint of the cosmos—a notion that raises mathematics from servant of the sciences to mistress thereof. In a detailed study of these aspects of the kabbalah—compiled into a large manuscript entitled *The Image of God in Matter*—Phillips qualifies the Tree of Life as "an object of awesome mathematical power and beauty, containing the mathematics of a theory recently proposed by physicists to unify the forces of nature."

The same Tree of Life is described by theosophist Ann Williams-Heller, in her *Kabbalah: Your Path to Freedom*, as representing not a religion but a revealed truth at the core of all world religions and universal thought.

In the ancient hieroglyph the sephiroth are depicted as spheres oddly arranged in three columns to symbolize the "ten divine qualities or objective modes of the manifesting Cosmic Logos." Horizontally the spheres are separated into four layers, representing four "worlds" or four stages of the logoic involution into matter—through spirit, mind, heart, and body—each related to fire, air, water, and earth, each achieved through a different level of consciousness and differently manifested qualities.

As all life is conceived as coming from above and being sustained from above, the Tree is depicted as inverted, its branches unfolding downward as its roots reach upward into the unknown, "the never-changing yet ever-becoming absolute undifferentiated consciousness, cause of all causes."

The first of these four worlds, that of "origination," is represented by only one sephirah, topmost of the ten, or Kether, known as the Crown, symbol of the manifesting Cosmic Logos, the one-in-all, representing ultimate unity. In this rarefied atmosphere the Logos conceives and ideates plans for creation. In the second world, of "creation," the next two sephiroth, Chokmah (Wisdom) and Binah (Understanding), are awakened into the archetypal forces proceeding from the male-female polarity of Shiva and Shakti, will and power. In the third world, of "formation," the sephiroth of Mercy, Justice, Beauty, Victory, and Glory come together with Foundation to create vibrant life through sexuality. The Angels of Foundation, or Yesod, says William G. Gray in his *The Ladder of Lights,* are directly concerned with principles of fertility and fecundating behind the life forms on this planet. They are active agents of germination and gestation not only for plant and animal life but also, on deeper inner levels, for mental and spiritual births. "As Formators, they are responsible for shaping up energies intended to be expressed in terms of what we call 'life,' guiding them through the proper channels of birth. We might almost describe them as pre-birth nursery attendants who form the child in a womb or a plant coming through a seed."

All together, the nine sephiroth produce the fourth world of "manifestation," again—as above so below—represented by a single sephirah, Malkuth (or Kingdom): this is the phenomenal world of the four elements and of minerals, plants, animals, and humans. Here, where the fine matter of spirit becomes the dense spirit of matter, the all-pervading spirit of the first world is reflected in the crystallized spirit of the fourth. The primal cause has reached its final effect in life, nature, humanity.

As the Tree of Life can represent both macrocosm and microcosm, the ten sephiroth are also divided, from a microscopic point of view, into seven planes to coincide with the human chakras. In this case the tree grows upward out of the earth, which makes of it not only a map of the descent of cosmic spirit into matter but a sort of Jacob's Ladder for the individual monad to ascend, through meditation, back to reunion with the Godhead in Kether.

Together the sephiroth are connected by twenty-two paths, said by kabbalists to represent the psychological states or experiences encountered as the Logos descends into matter, or the monad ascends to higher worlds.

As can be done with most complex symbolism, the same glyph of ten sephiroth can be used to represent Dionysius's nine celestial hierarchies (plus a tenth for humankind), with seraphim or lords of love in Kether (the Crown), cherubim, the lords of harmony, in Chokmah (Wisdom), and thrones, or spirits of will in Binah (Intelligence). The rest follow in descending order into ever greater density all the way down to the tenth sephiroth, Malkuth (Kingdom), which, according to Phillips, denotes equally the outer organic form of the Cosmic Logos, the entire universe, this solar system, a human body, or a single evanescent subatomic particle.

Mathematically, says Williams-Heller, the fundamental realities of existence are represented by the Tree of Life through the numbers from zero to ten, with zero as the Absolute, one as the Manifesting Logos, and the other numbers representing the spiritual entities down to man in the material world at number ten. Every other number is alternately taken as corresponding to a particular level of reality, related to both the number above and the one below. And what every tree branch has in common with all the others is that it is primarily and unambiguously a number, alternately "affected" by the preceding and "cause" to the succeeding, each number being considered at all times either masculine or feminine in its relationship to the others, with a constant polarity shift going hand-in-hand with a gradual increase in value and increasing density. Through this step-by-step change from zero to ten, the infinite light from the first tree branch "materializes" into finite life in the last.

In an even more sophisticated mathematical analysis of the arrangement of the sephiroth, Phillips goes further: far enough to find the superstring space-time theory structured into the patterns laid down in the Tree of Life, a correspondence that Phillips says was already sensed by Annie Besant and Charles Leadbeater a hundred years ago, though the state-of-the-art of physics was not then up to describing the correspondence.

In Phillips's analogy, the three dimensions of ordinary Euclidean space correspond to the supernal triad of Kether, Chokmah, and Binah. Next come the six "sephiroth of construction" to represent the six hidden dimensions of compactified space. Last, Malkuth, the tenth sephirah, corresponds—aptly says Phillips, because one of the kabbalistic meanings of *Malkuth* is the temporal physical world—to the time dimension.

All of this, says Phillips, gives strong mathematical support to the notion that the building blocks of matter—subatomic particles studied by physicists—are created in the image of the Cosmic Logos.

Phillips's analysis, in no way arbitrary, is based on the numerical value attributed by kabbalists to each letter of the Hebrew alphabet. Applying gematria, number mysticism, to its twenty-two letters, kabbalists were able to assign a Jewish "God-name" to each sephirah to express in numbers the essence of its metaphysical meaning in relation to the Tree of Life structure of creation. Thus Chokmah (Wisdom), the second sephirah, was given the God-name Jehovah, with a numerical value of twenty-six; Binah (Understanding), the third sephirah, was given the name Elohim, with a numerical value of fifty, and so on.

Key to unlocking what Philips calls "the powerful, beautiful mathematics of the Tree of Life" is the Pythagorean triangle, or tetractys, an equilateral triangle containing ten points arranged in four rows, symbolizing the numbers one, two, three, four as they add up to ten.

Pythagoras, the seventh-century B.C. Greek philosopher and mathematician, known as a widely traveled initiate into the secrets of the most varied mysteries, is considered the world's first theoretical physicist. He taught that mathematics was the key unlocking the mysteries of the universe and that the number ten is perfect and sacred, the source and root of eternal nature. Hence his representation of the number ten in the tetractys, a symbolic glyph at the heart of the number mysticism Pythagoras taught his students at Crotona in southern Italy. The tetractys had an esoteric meaning that was revealed in secret only to his privileged followers dealing with the universal mystical gnosis that lies at the heart of ancient religion. It also symbolized a tenfold nature for God. Why this triangle should have been treated with such religious reverence—students had to swear an oath not to reveal what they knew of it—remained a mystery to historians of Greek mathematics, though its relevance is now made clear by Phillips.

Madame Blavatsky, hinting that she knew more than she was prepared to say, claimed that "the ten points inscribed within the Pythagorean Triangle are worth all the theogonies and angelologies ever emanated from the theological brain."

When Phillips realized that the Pythagoreans had discovered that the religious God-names attributed to the sephiroth of the Tree of Life—such as Jehovah and Elohim—were not mere inventions of the pious but express powerful mathematical archetypal principles determining the laws of nature, he saw that these had been encoded in both the tetractys and the Tree of Life. One of the remarkable properties of the tetractys is that through gematria it turns certain polygons, such as the pentagon and the octagon, into geometrical representations of the God-names.

In Plato's Timaeus a kinship is shown to exist between his five sacred volumes and the five elements, with the hexahedron, or cube, for earth, icosahedron for water, octahedron for air, tetrahedron for fire, and the dodecahedron for ether. Interestingly, this last solid contains five hexahedrons, one for each element. These essential forms have in themselves, and through their analogues with the elements, the power to shape the material world. All four volumes appear in differing combinations in the chemical elements described by Leadbeater and Besant. "In this sequence of five essential geometric volumes," says Leviton, "we have evidence of the mathematics of the cosmic mind. Precise geometrical equations and mathematical laws describe the relationships among the five, and the lawful progression of their generation, one to the next, to form a nest (or maze) of polyhedra which is the underlying geometric matrix of the physical world."

As Phillips began his mathematical analysis with the tree's infrastructure, its "trunk," he realized that the alignment of sephiroth in this central axis depicts—as it starts from a mathematical point and develops into line and triangle—the generation of a tetrahedron, nature's simplest regular polyhedron, or four-sided triangular pyramid. Counting the total number of points, lines, triangles, and tetrahedrons in this infrastructure of the tree, Phillips came up with a total of twenty-six, the number of *Jehovah*, God-name of Chokmah, symbol of the creative or generative powers of nature.

Next, viewing the tree as a three-dimensional object, he saw that it is composed of ten points, twenty-two edges of triangles, sixteen triangles, and two tetrahedra, for a total of fifty. Thus, fifty pieces of information are needed to define its form in space. And fifty is the number of *Elohim*, God-name for Binah. To Phillips it was clear that these Hebrew God-names quantify the number of bits of information needed to construct the trunk of the Tree of Life. But that was only the beginning.

Phillips soon found that the tetractys has an even more fundamental function, one that he suspects made it into the figure so highly esteemed by the Pythagoreans. Stacking a series of tetractys triangles one on top of another to represent a series of overlapping Trees of Life,

Phillips was able to construct a sort of Jacob's Ladder, or what he calls a Cosmic Tree of Life, consisting of ninety-one interconnected tetractyses, much like the scaffolding for a skyscraper. From this Cosmic Tree he was able to generate numbers that to him clearly define the mathematical laws of nature and the cosmos, including numbers that occur regularly in quantum physics. Not only did he find the twenty-six dimensions of space-time predicted by quantum mechanics clearly encoded in the geometry of the trees by Jehovah, God-name of Chokmah, whose numerical number is twenty-six, but he also found a correspondence between the seven sephiroth of Construction (which manifest in the creation world) and the ten dimensions of space-time predicted by superstring theory. From all of this Phillips concluded that superstring space-time is structured according to the pattern laid down in the Tree of Life.

One of the remarkable properties of the basic Tree of Life is that just as the DNA molecule encodes the biological information needed to grow a human body from a single cell, so, too, the geometry of a single tree, when encoded by the tetractys, contains the complete structure of a Cosmic Tree of Life. Encoded in the geometry, the part contains the whole.

As discovered by physicists Green and Schwartz in 1984, the number 248 characterizes the mathematics of those forces of nature that create stable, material forms such as atomic nuclei and atoms. And the number 248 and its double, 496, characterize the mathematical symmetry of the forces, other than gravity, that act between superstrings. Phillips found both numbers clearly encoded in the pentagram or five-pointed star.

The followers of Pythagoras, says Phillips, wore the pentagram to recognize one another as members of a fraternity. Traditionally the pentagram symbolizes the five elements: earth, water, fire, air, and ether. If its edges are divided into four points to symbolize the Pythagorean tetrad of one, two, three, four, and if a point is added for the center, the number thirty-one is obtained, which, says Phillips, has remarkable properties: as the number of the God-name *El* of El-Chesed, the first sephirah of Construction and the fourth sephirah in the Tree of Life, it represents the formulation of the archetypal ideas in the Divine Mind, the first stage of their expression in creation. And $1+2+3+4+ \ldots +31 = 496$; not only is this the number of Malkuth, it is also Green and Schwartz's number characterizing superstring physics.

Malkuth, as explained by Phillips, has the number 496 "because the number specifies the highest point in the Cosmic Tree of Life below which subquark superstrings with nine spatial dimensions become the building blocks of physical matter."

Malkuth's Jewish God-name is *Adonai Melekh,* which gives the number value of 65 for the first word and 155 for the whole name. And it can hardly be a coincidence, Phillips points out, that the ten lowest trees in the Cosmic Tree of Life have sixty-five sephiroth levels and the twenty-five lowest trees have 155. It indicates, says Phillips, that the physical level of the Cosmic Tree of Life spans twenty-five spatial dimensions—the number of spatial dimensions of bosonic strings.

Thus, while Adonai specifies the ten lowest trees in the Cosmic Tree of Life, which denote the ten-dimension space-time of superstrings, Malkuth encodes the dimensionality of space-time of both string and superstring levels.

The number 248, with its key role in subatomic physics, as identified by Green and Schwartz, is deducible again from the nineteen triangles of the lowest tree in the Cosmic Tree of Life. Transforming these triangles into three tetractyses, one discovers that there are 248 points below Kether, apex of the Tree of Life.

If this process is repeated for every one of the ten lower trees in the Cosmic Tree of Life—which to Phillips represent the ten dimension of superstrings—one makes the even more amazing discovery that there are exactly 1,680 points below the apex of the tenth tree—precisely the number of first-order spirillae in the whorl of a Leadbeater UPA, identified by Phillips as the subquark state of a superstring, each of its ten whorls being a closed twenty-six-dimension bosonic string. Of these, the lowest six tornoidally compactified dimensions manifested to Leadbeater as the six higher orders of helices making up each of the 1,680 turns of a whorl. Amazing, says Phillips, that the number 1,680, so painstakingly counted by Leadbeater, should reappear in the Tree of

Life representation of superstring space-time. This inescapable coincidence led Phillips to conclude that "the Theosophists' UPA, as a 10-d superstring, is the vibrational pattern of the ten-fold Logos, or Divine Word, impressed upon the geometry of space-time."

Stephen Phillips and Martin Gardner should have a great time confronting each other on live TV, and if C. S. Lewis is right, confrontation may eventually engender friendship.

16

The Mysteries

Most amazing is the subtle role of nature spirits or elementals in the rites of modern Freemasonry. Much of the lore about the hierarchies and their elementals has been available through what are known as the ancient mysteries on which the rites of Masonry are based. Such rites, according to Steiner, go back to Antlantean times and were revived in what he calls the second post-Atlantean epoch by Zarathustra, a highly evolved initiate reborn about 6400 B.C.E. when the sun moved from Cancer to Gemini, a sage who claimed to have received his wisdom directly from the Lord Ahura Mazdao, the great sun being known in India as Vishvakarma, in Egypt as Osiris, and in the modern world as the Christ.

Steiner describes how the great Atlantean initiate Manu established the post-Atlantean cultures in Asia by weaving into the physical bodies of seven sufficiently advanced Indians the etheric bodies of seven former Atlantean sages whose bodies "had been preserved and permeated by Angels." In India these sages became the Holy Rishis. "Wearing within their sheaths the etheric bodies of the great Atlantean leaders, who in turn had received them from Archangelic beings, these Holy Rishis were able to look back into their former incarnations and pass on, in a new form, their recollection of the ancient Atlantean civilization." In still earlier Lemurian times, according to Steiner, archai spoke through human beings; in Atlantean times it was archangels. In post-Atlantean times it was angels. Beings ensouled down to their physical body by an archai were known as dhyani-buddhas; beings ensouled down to the etheric body by an archangel as bodhisattvas; beings ensouled by an angel down to their astral bodies were known as human buddhas.

Theosophists maintain that Zarathustra, able to control his astral body, passed it on to Hermes, founder of the Egyptian cultural epoch, a real person, according to Steiner, who appeared about 4200 B.C.E. as the sun moved into Taurus, walked again as Orpheus among the Greeks, and finally took birth in the north of India as Gautama Buddha. In Leadbeater's time it was his belief and that of his theosophical friends that when the Lord Gautama laid down the office of bodhisattva to become a buddha, his mantle passed to the Lord Maitreya, a teacher several times reincarnated, most recently as a mahatma adept of the Great White Brotherhood, destined to become a future buddha, so they say, some two thousand years from now.

According to Steiner, Hermes bore within him the astral body of Zarathustra so that his master's knowledge might be manifest again. Moses, by acquiring Zarathustra's etheric body, was able to describe the happenings in Genesis. Meanwhile, Zarathustra's ego went on to incarnate in other personalities, including that of Nazarathos, teacher of the Chaldean mystery schools, and teacher of Pythagoras, though this was neither his last nor his most impressive incarnation.

Thus the primeval wisdom of humanity passed from Persia to Chaldea to Egypt, and so on down. By his Egyptian master, Polidorus Isurenus, Hodson was told that the throne of the pharaohs was one of the stages on the way to adeptship, passed through by many adepts, a notion made clearer by the Egyptian records, which indicate that the early pharaohs were guided by inspiration, an inspiration explained by Steiner as being due to overshadowing, as in Atlantean times, by higher beings. "For thousands of years adepts and initiates were incarnated in an Egypt where the whole work of training, initiating, passing, and raising and perfecting went on without interruption." As explained by Annie Besant, who, along with Leadbeater, by their own reckoning, had passed their fifth initiation and had become adepts: "Those who were purest and noblest participated as a means of destroying all fear of death, giving them the certainty of immortality, and gaining for them wisdom that others did not possess."

Yet the outer religion of ancient Egypt—the official religion in which everyone took part, from king to slave—was nevertheless described by Leadbeater, on the basis of his own clairvoyant vision of the past, as the most splendid known to humanity, a religion occupied not with thoughts of personal salvation but with the desire to be a useful agent of divine power. At the same time the mysteries—of which Leadbeater considers Freemasonry to be the direct descendant—were devoted to the hidden work of pouring out spiritual force upon all the people, a feat accomplished through a few Grand Lodges in the principal cities, whose aim was to flood the kingdom with "the Hidden Light."

Then, by 3100 B.C.E., the world entered what the Hindus call the age of Kali Yuga, or dark age, computed by Steiner to have lasted until the turn of the twentieth century C.E., dark because direct perception of the spiritual worlds had become almost wholly extinct, surviving only in a very small number of initiates. By the end of the Old Kingdom even the pharaohs appear to have lost this inspiration. Spiritual knowledge remained locked up within the Egyptian mysteries, but even they, says Steiner, could no longer be fully understood, even by the priests and the initiates.

Moses, a Hebrew, brought up in the household of the Egyptian pharaoh, born about 1400 B.C.E. as the sun moved into Aries, could still be initiated into the mysteries. But by Moses' time the ancient Egyptian clairvoyance, says Steiner, had disappeared. This was considered an essential step in the development of human freedom. So long as people had actual perception of the spiritual world and knew they were guided by higher beings, they could not be truly free. The spiritual worlds were required to be darkened. "Clairvoyance could still be acquired by initiation into the mysteries, but by the middle of the second millennium B.C.E. decadence had set in, with corruption giving rise to all kinds of magical rites and practices. While ordinary people were given the truths of their religion in the form of myths, what lay behind these myths was revealed only to initiates who kept them secret."

Throughout Greek history two different forms of religion coexisted: the mysteries, with their secret teachings imparted only to the initiate, and the popular religion with its myths, which did not contradict the mystery teachings but did not reveal their true content. Via

Rome and its second king, Numa Pompilius, the Egyptian mysteries made their way to western Europe, overlaying the original Christianity. By the fourth century C.E., with the establishment of the Roman Church, the basic idea of the mysteries—that human beings could become like unto God out of their own inner strivings without the intercession of the Church—was regarded as heretical, a notion to be combated by a murderous Inquisition. Masons teaching facts about the nature and inner life of humanity could be—and were—burned alive. Hence the great need for secrecy. Had one person betrayed, it could place the rest of a lodge in danger of being what Leadbeater calls "judicially murdered," a method of politico-religious control that has seldom flourished so exuberantly on this planet as in our days.

Looking back into very ancient times, Steiner sees the mysteries as institutions of people still possessed of the faculty of instinctive clairvoyance. "Ancient humanity could still gaze into the spiritual world whence the human being descends into his physical body on earth." By the thirteenth century almost no one in the West had any direct clairvoyance capable of perceiving and distinguishing among the spiritual beings. Some of the early Christians, says Steiner, had personal knowledge of the spiritual worlds, but popular religion became ever more superstitious and corrupted by magic. "Even such a great thinker as Thomas Aquinas had no clairvoyance, and no personal knowledge of the hierarchies."

Throughout the dangerous Middle Ages the mystery tradition survived in mystical currents such as the Grail, the School of Chartres, the Cathars, the Templars, or other such secret societies, surfacing again only when persecution became less fierce. Rosicrucian successors to the Templars kept the secret wisdom alive in small groups of powerful but self-effacing initiates. Steiner, himself an initiated Rosicrucian, tells an extraordinary story about the thirteenth-century origins of this remarkable brotherhood, attributing its creation to a dozen reincarnated sages of post-Atlantean times, the seven Holy Rishis, joined this time by five later sages deliberately chosen to revive the wisdom of the Indian, Chaldean, Egyptian, Greco-Roman, and Christian epochs. This hermetic council of twelve, aware that external Christianity had degenerated through the Church into a caricature, determined—as Steiner reconstructs the events, presumably from the Akashic Record—to revive the world's great religions into a healthier synthesis, using as their avatar a young man they considered the reincarnation of either the apostle Paul or one of his close associates. Again the method was to pass on the highly developed etheric body of this prodigy, endowed with all its accumulated wisdom, to another sensitive in the next century, a young German, Christian Rosenkreutz, who was to originate the succeeding line of Rosicrucian masters. In this strange manner the same powerful etheric body could be used to reincarnate from century to century until it reached the Comte de St. Germain in the eighteenth.

In the nineteenth, what Steiner calls "the soul forces" developed by Christian Rosenkreutz in the thirteenth century served, he says, to found the theosophic movement. According to Easton, it was not until just before the end of the Kali Yuga dark age, at the beginning of the twentieth century, that any reliable knowledge of the primeval wisdom could once more be made available to man, motivating Blavatsky and Steiner to begin to reveal some of the teachings in an appropriate form.

And it was "the strength radiating from the etheric body of Christian Rosenkreutz" that is credited by Steiner with providing the inspiration for Blavatsky's *Isis Unveiled*. The stanzas of Dzyan that she included in *The Secret Doctrine* contain, says Steiner, "some of the deepest and most significant pieces of wisdom, much of which originated with the teachings of the Holy Rishis and flooded into the sacred lore of the East." To which he adds more soberly that much of what is to be found in the stanzas will only gradually be understood in all its depths by the majority of people.

In ancient times two forms of initiation led to the mysteries, called by Steiner the Jonah and Solomon initiations. In the former the candidate was put to sleep so that his soul could leave his body to travel three days in the supersensible world. In the Solomon form the candidate received revelations in a "sublimated trance condition."

One of the clearest expositions of the mysteries practiced in modern times comes, as might be expected, from Geoffrey Hodson, to whom Freemasonry was clearly a survival and symbolic portrayal of the great mysteries. To Hodson, Masonry was "a gateway leading towards the Mysteries themselves and the power, wisdom, knowledge,, and faculties revealed progressively to initiates in their more advanced grades."

But unlike a Rosicrucian initiation, whose basic aim is the revelation of Christ, the original mystery initiation, as reconstructed by occultists, consisted in a the simpler process of rekindling clairvoyance in the aspirant by separating his etheric and astral bodies from his physical body, usually by the administration of a powerful drug. As his physical body lay in a trance lasting three and a half days, his finer bodies were freed to travel in the supersensible worlds. Wakened from this trance, the initiate found himself in possession—because memory inheres in the etheric body—of the accumulated wisdom imparted to him by priest or hierophant. Convinced of the immortality of the ego, the neophyte was considered "twice-born." In the Christian mysteries, baptism, in the form of a near drowning, could loosen the etheric body, enabling the initiate to review his current life out of body and so recover certainty of his essential spirituality—as anyone may do in any near-death experience.

Nowadays, before being initiated into the lowest grade of Masonry, the modern aspirant, or Entered Apprentice, is expected to have conquered the physical passions of his body and be "engaged in making his astral body into an instrument for the expression of high emotion"—presumably more spiritual than sexual. At the same time, the aspirant is supposed to be learning to gain control of his mind, for "what man sees and knows by means of the senses and the intellect, however refined and developed, is but the smallest and outermost aspect of universal solar and planetary existence. Man, submerged in matter, must be reawakened. The veil of Maya must be penetrated by the initiate."

To achieve this breakthrough via Masonic initiation the aspirant initiate was given, as in the ancient mysteries, a draught of forgetfulness along with a powerful shock. The object was to make him forget all of his life since birth so that he could be led into the spiritual form of his life before birth. According to R. Gordon Wasson in his books *Soma* and

Persephone's Quest, the draught used in the mysteries was *Amanita muscaria*, a species of psychotropic mushroom known in India as the sacred fungus Soma and in England as fly-agaric. Drinking such a potion as part of the Eleusis mysteries was intended to give visions of spiritual presences. Dr. Albert Hoffmann, discoverer of LSD, says that ergot, a common fungal parasite on grain used in the mysteries to demonstrate the continuity between life and death, also gives experiences comparable to LSD. In today's initiations such drugs, says Steiner, are no longer needed.

During a candidate's first initiation in a Masonic lodge, as described by Hodson, the candidate is subjected—as was the case in the original mysteries—to a series of experiences on the astral plane, real experiences unlike any sense experience he could have on the physical plane. Passing out of the physical world into the lowest part of the astral plane, the candidate is "led sightless into that more rarefied world, but feels the touch of a friend who takes his hand and guides him on his journey." All this so that the candidate's vision may be opened to what lies behind the veil of the senses, like a man born blind recovering his eyesight.

As part of the initiation the aspirant must first experience through his own body what lives in the lower kingdoms of nature: both mineral and plant. Next he must experience the passions and desires of the animal kingdom. Third, and most important, he is led to a vision of the elemental forces in nature. In considerable detail Hodson elucidates the paramount role of nature spirits in the Masonic initiation of a candidate who must reacquire enough clairvoyance to be able to see the nature spirits and, through their intercession, to gain access to the hierarchy of angelic beings.

In the Christian religion a similar recourse, says Leadbeater, is made to angels, but there is a difference between the methods adopted in Christianity and in the old Egyptian mystery religion from which Masonry derived: in Christianity great angels are invoked, far above humans in spiritual unfoldment. "In Freemasonry, angelic aid is invoked, but those called are nearer to the human level of development and intelligence. Each of them brings with him a number of subordinates who carry out his directions."

As Leadbeater puts it: "In Freemasonry we invoke the aid of non-human entities—the inhabitants of the subtler planes, who are thoroughly accustomed to deal with and control the forces belonging to their respective levels. We call rather upon beings at our own state or slightly above it, and they bring with them assistants from the kingdom of the nature spirits and even of the elementals." (To Leadbeater, elementals differ from nature spirits in that they are "half-conscious creatures" often merely the transient thought-forms of devas.)

As soon as the lodge is declared open—the Master Mason and his officers having marched in a circular procession to lay out the thought-form of a temple, mocking up the lower part of the "cella" or interior chamber, shutting in the whole of the lodge's mosaic pavement and charging it with magnetism—a call is issued to summon the nature spirits and with them their angelic superiors.

Specific questions addressed to each of the Masonic officers act, says Leadbeater, as a call to a deva of the particular type required, who immediately presents itself and acts as a captain of the nature spirits and elementals, who next gather round. Not only the nature spirits but also the elementals apparently respond to the invocation employed in this closely condensed formula or opening. "As the call reverberates throughout the different kingdoms of nature, it lets devas, nature spirits, and elementals know that an opportunity is about to be offered them . . . and they greatly rejoice to respond."

That much of what transpires in a modern Masonic initiation is solely ritual and symbolic appears not to diminish its effect, according to Leadbeater: "The fact that thousands of Masons have asked the appointed question without the faintest idea of producing an effect in unseen worlds has not deprived them of angelic assistance, which, if they had known of it, would have astounded them beyond expression, and probably even terrified them."

Yet it is through these deva representatives of the various officers that the building of the thought-form and the outpouring of the force is meant to be accomplished. As the ceremony proceeds, various nature spirits are described as manifesting "to make the walls of the temple both thicker and higher while greater Beings reinforce its magnetism by filling it with the power of their respective levels." An etheric ceiling is spread over the whole of the lodge, and from that ceiling supporting columns are described as developing downward "like the roots of a banyan tree." The thought-form thus created is supposed to be the close reproduction of a Greek temple, the rows of columns that support its heavy roof standing outside the central chamber, the only part of the temple fully enclosed. Soon, says Leadbeater, the whole lodge is pulsating with elemental life, "all of which is filled with the most intense eagerness to launch itself upon the work at hand."

The elementals and nature spirits of different levels are described as varying greatly in development and intelligence, some being well defined and active while others are vague and cloudlike. Each group shows its distinctive colors, floating over the official who is its physical-plane representative. In the case of the lower officers, it requires, says Leadbeater, but a slight development of clairvoyance to see them floating overhead. "And if an officer reaches up to his Deva and allows its force to flow freely through him, his higher principles will become one with that Deva. He will then be an excellent channel for the divine force."

It is now, says Hodson, that the candidate is presented to the nature spirit representative of four orders of the invisible forces and the intelligences associated with them—those of earth, water, air, and fire. This is to introduce the candidate to the intelligences that both build the universe and help forward the evolution of the human soul. A second reason is that the candidate is about to be made a Mason, and a Mason is considered a builder and a builder a creator.

The candidate, in Hodson's description, makes offerings, which establish an operative link between him and the nature spirits of earth, water, air, and fire, so that through them he may be linked with their angelic and archangelic seniors. "As the offerings fall to the ground, the nature spirits step onto them and absorb what they can of their magnetism, happily accepting them."

Each of the nature spirits, in its order and at its station, having acknowledged the candidate, admits him to the brotherhood. "In future they will be his men and he a member of each of their four 'guilds.'

Their four seals will be imprinted upon his finer bodies and he can call upon them and their immediate seniors for work and for aid."

From either side of the royal arch the earth elementals are invoked. If the candidate can command them, says Hodson, either by willpower through his voice or by an inherent quality of his nature, they will bow and, as the candidate turns, will make way for him to pass. "The gnomes are amused by most of the ceremony, except at those times when its force arrests them. Then they become serious for the time being. The gnomes play about the temple floor, march with grotesque and absurd mimicry behind the procession, thoroughly enjoying themselves all the time and really getting much fun out of the ceremony. But if the officiating Master Mason does not command their respect, they will laugh and mimic him and the candidate."

Hodson considers these to be a superior kind of gnome, not always so dark as the gnomes found in natural surroundings and lacking their unpleasant or hostile appearance. He calls them "ceremonial" gnomes, dressed in imitation of human clothes, generally of bright colors. Some even attempt evening dress for a few moments, "though the result could not be said to be very successful; the same being true of apron, collar, and jewels [Masonic emblems] which they assume on occasion."

As the ceremony progresses, a sylph is described by Hodson as appearing from the upper air to hover just under the ceiling, "a fierce and powerful creature of about human size and shape, with a face of great beauty and strength, but no particular sex differentiation."

Hodson's sylph accepts the candidate's offering and, stretching out a hand, touches the forehead of the candidate, pouring in its radiant vitality and giving the key by which the doors to its kingdom can be unlocked.

His undine appears as a nude female figure, of singular beauty, with a glistening aura and a body that shines as if wet. His salamander is very tall and thin, a creature of flame, with arms and legs like tongues of fire and a fiery body with the suggestion of a human shape, two fiery eyes and a flaming center in the middle of the head. Momentary contact with the salamander is described as setting the candidate's aura on fire in a "wonderfully stimulating and purifactory way."

More sylphs appear, "lovely creatures, moving about the lodge, radiant, charged with joy and vitality, their virile power liberated into the candidate: this has the effect of making his astral body more susceptible to the forces of the ceremony. Streams of force are poured into his aura which is made to glow with a white radiance and to expand in size. His astral body is purified, refined, and raised in tone and vibratory rate."

The effect of the elementals upon him, with their vibrations, helps to prepare the candidate for the great experience of consecration. Hodson says it sometimes appears that the devas throw a film across the portal so that as the candidate passes through it his aura is combed out and cleansed.

The candidate is then presented to the angelic hosts, at first through the medium of their lower orders, the nature spirits. Later he meets the higher intelligences. By this time certain parts of the lodge have been heavily charged with magnetic force.

However little the brothers may know about what is actually happening, says Leadbeater, every Masonic lodge is in charge of a highly developed angel. Such an angel, representing the Master Mason, arrives with a cohort of assistant angels to take charge of the proceedings.

This central point of the ceremony, its climax, has now been reached and consists of the definite admission of the candidate into the order—the point at which a certain center or chakra is opened, a certain potential power given. Forces are sent through the candidate's body in a definite manner during this ceremony. Basic to the process is arousal by the hierophant or Master Mason of the kundalini "serpent power" in the candidate. To bring this God-power down into the candidate and to raise the serpent or kundalini, says Hodson, is one part of the office of the hierophant of the Great Mysteries. In ancient Egypt— as Leadbeater claims to have witnessed clairvoyantly—a weak current of physical electricity was sent through the candidate by means of a rod or sword with which he was touched at certain points.

Theosophists enumerate and locate three sources for the basic and universal energy of kundalini: for the macrocosm, the sun; for nature, the center of the earth; for the microcosm, or physical human body, the sacrum at the base of the spine. Solar and planetary kundalini are said to be in constant activity, there being a perpetual interplay between the sun and all its globes. In the humanity of the preinitiation stage, kundalini is described as being but partially active and in two forms: as the creative force, the flow of which is experienced as the impelling urge of sex, and as a nerve fluid to animate the nerves. Below these outer levels, occultists count, in all, seven deeper layers or "coils" of the serpent fire, stored and, before initiation, "sleeping" in the actual sacral centers of the human spinal cord.

Kundalini, or kundalini shakti, meaning the power that moves in a serpentine path, is described as a triple force: feminine, masculine, and neuter. The central or neutral force, known as sushumna, is designed to flow vertically along a canal in the spinal cord, while the winding feminine and male forces, ida and pingala, flow together on either side of sushumna, crossing and intertwining at certain important force centers, the chakras. Ida then goes into the pituitary body, pingala into the pineal; sushumna travels straight up the spinal cord along the medulla oblongata to flow out of the anterior fontanelle. "When the shaft of Atmic fire which forms the core of the Sushumna is brought down to the densest physical level," says Hodson, "the relatively dormant positive-negative creative Life-force resident in the sacrum is awakened into activity."

Symbolically stated, the rod becomes the serpent. In a human "the rod" refers both to the spinal cord and to a canal or etheric and superphysical channel in its center, passing from the root of the cord in the sacrum along its whole length and into the medulla oblongata of the brain. This canal is considered the vehicle for the creative life-force, a measure of which plays down from above in the generative act. This current, says Hodson, is unipolar, or even of neutral polarity, since it plays and produces its effects in both the male and female organism: by occult means the same neutral force is made to play not downward but upward along the spinal cord. Before the reversal of the flow of creative energy can be achieved, the positive and negative currents must be aroused to flow upward. Entering the brain, says Hodson, this triple power so illumines the mind that a person becomes, as it were, a god, possessed of theurgic powers. "The intensely heightened vibrations of the brain, glands, cells, and aerial substance in the ventricles cause the brain and cranium to be responsive to egoic and Monadic life and consciousness."

Hodson explains that when Moses sublimated this creative force, forcing it to flow upward from the pelvis, it became the magician's wand of power in his hand. "Then the genie of the four elements, earth, water, air, and fire, become obedient to the will of the holder of such a rod."[1]

In the Great Mysteries, culmination of the demonstration of readiness to be made a Master Mason or an initiate of the first degree consists, says Leadbeater, not only in departure from the physical body in full consciousness, returning with full remembrance of all that has occurred in the superphysical worlds, but also in realizing there is no longer a "you" and an "I"; both are one—facets of something that transcends and includes them both. "It is one thing to talk about this down here and to grasp it intellectually. Quite another to enter into the marvelous world and know it with a certainly that can never be shaken."

The initiate is then required to pass into this cosmic aloneness to discover his identity with all. "He realizes at last, and forever, that he is the Eternal and the Eternal is himself, and then he is beyond the possibility of submergence into the illusion of separated self."

And so ends the initiation. With the closing of the lodge, the elemental hosts that have been gathered together are described by Hodson as scattering outward to all points of the compass. Only their captains, the representative angels of the officers, still remain. When the

---

1. Far-fetched as the notion may appear, C. Janarajadasa tells in his book *Occult Investigations* how in India Leadbeater made use of nature spirits to help him investigate various chemical elements. Some, such as scandium, being rare and difficult to obtain, were located by Leadbeater with the help of a nature spirit of the sea. He got in touch with a triton he knew to be living in the ocean near the Adyar beach and asked if it could find something like scandium in the sea. In no time, says Janarajadasa, the nature spirit produced some erbium, whose atoms were described as being "like spiculae, or a handful of tiny pencils held in the hand." Curious to know why Leadbeater should want to see them, the triton said he could not understand the reason for being asked to produce what to him were merely toys.

Master Mason utters the formula of closing, the angels of the assistant officers fade away, leaving only the august thought-form of the Comte de St. Germain. As perennial Grand Master of Masonry, St. Germain is linked by means of the thirty-third degree—the highest of the sacramental powers conferred in the mysteries of ancient Egypt—"to the Spiritual King of the World, that Mightiest of Adepts who stands at the head of the Great White Lodge, in whose hands lie the destinies of the earth."

17

Great White Brothers

The wisdom of the mysteries has been kept alive on the planet, according to Hodson, by an active brotherhood of adepts, guardians of the spiritual heritage of humankind, keepers throughout the ages of what he calls "the sacred light of spiritual and occult knowledge and wisdom." Major centers of this "Great White Brotherhood"—as described by Hodson and other theosophists—range from Luxor to Yucatán, from Hungary to Tibet, its members "the shepherds of souls, not far away but very near to mankind."

This "very near to mankind" has engendered no little controversy, as the adepts are reputed to be able to appear to their followers either alive in the flesh, disembodied in the astral, or spookily materialized in the apparently physical. Volumes have been written on how St. Germain kept his body from aging so that his presence could be recorded in widely separate historical periods. It was adepts such as these, according to Leadbeater, who deliberately devised the Theosophical Society as an instrument by means of which to reintroduce occult wisdom to the world and thus pave the way for reestablishment of the ancient mysteries. Two in particular are credited with the job: the Indian Rajput prince Mahatma Morya and the Kashmiri Brahmin Koot Hoomi, so familiar to Blavatsky. After careful consideration, says Leadbeater, "the Masters Morya and Koot Hoomi undertook the responsibility of the step and chose that noble worker Madame Blavatsky to help them on the physical plane. In due course the Brotherhood sent her to America to search for Colonel Olcott." In Blavatsky's words: "The Himalayan masters are behind our movement and we founded our Theosophical Society at their direct suggestion. They showed us that by combining science with religion, the existence of God and the immortality of man's spirit may be demonstrated like a problem in Euclid."

From the beginning, says Hodson, the theosophical movement was, under the supervision of certain adepts and initiates belonging to that branch of the Great White Brotherhood known as the Brotherhood of Luxor. Among its members were Serapis Bey, who gave instructions to Blavatsky, and Polidorus Isurenus, recorder of the Luxor Brotherhood, who instructed Hodson, as did another master known as Tutuit Bey. Leadbeater says that he and other cofounders of the Theosophical Society such as Blavatsky, Besant, and Colonel Olcott, had all "seen" some of the masters and that many other members of the society had seen one or more of them.

In the early days of the society, when Blavatsky first developed higher faculties, the masters, say theosophists, frequently materialized so that all could see them, though they were not in their physical bodies. Only in a few cases would both the adept and the person who saw him be in a physical body. Blavatsky often recounted how she met the Master Morya in London's Hyde Park in 1851 when she was sixteen and he had come over with a number of other Indian princes to attend the first great international exhibition. Later, when she lived for some time in a monastery in Nepal, she claims to have seen three of the masters constantly in their physical vehicles and to have been initiated by them into the mysteries.

According to Leadbeater, some of the masters have more than once come down in their physical bodies from their mountain retreats in India: Colonel Olcott spoke of having seen two of them on such occasions, Master Morya and Master Koot Hoomi. Leadbeater also reports two such encounters. One was with the master the Comte de St. Germain, also known as Prince Rakoczy, whom he tells of meeting walking down the Corso in Rome, dressed as an Italian gentleman. "He took me up into the gardens on the Pincian Hill, and we sat for more than an hour talking about the Society and its work."

St. Germain is described by Leadbeater as not especially tall but very upright and military in his bearing. "He has the exquisite courtesy and dignity of a grand seigneur of the eighteenth century, member of a very old and noble family. His eyes are large and brown, filled with tenderness and humor, though with a glint of power. The splendor of his presence impels one to make obeisance. His face is olive-tanned, his close-cut brown hair parted in the center and brushed back from the forehead. He wears a short pointed beard and is often seen in a magnificent red military cloak or in a dark uniform with facings of gold lace. Usually he resides in an ancient castle in Eastern Europe that has belonged to his family for many centuries."

In her autobiography Annie Besant recounts how, visiting Madame Blavatsky in Fontainebleau in 1890, she woke suddenly to find "the air of the room thrown into pulsating waves, and then appeared the radiant astral figure of the Master [Morya] visible to my physical eyes."

As an explanation for the comings and goings of the Masters Rakoczy, Morya, and Koot Hoomi in and out of physical bodies, Leadbeater says that when withdrawn "they are aware and active on the Buddhic and Atmic levels." When asked how they had attained such an exalted level, the masters told him that not so long ago they, too, had stood where we now stand but had risen out of the ranks of ordinary humanity. In due time, they said, the rest of humanity would become as they are now, the whole system being a graded evolution of life extending up and up, to the Godhead itself.

In his book *The Masters Revealed*, K. Paul Johnson goes to some length to try to show that Morya and Koot Hoomi were not disembodied spirits but well-known historical characters, the former a Kashmiri maharaja, Ranbir Singh, the latter a Punjabi Sikh, Thakar Singh. However, Johnson clouds his industrious scholarship by revealing his prejudice in the subtitle, *Madame Blavatsky and the Myth of the Great White Lodge*. If not quite denying, he at least strongly suspects, the reality of the Great White Brotherhood. On the other hand, Richard Leviton, who spent several years in England undergoing a lengthy initiation under the auspices of what he calls "several familiar angels, and a variety of disincarnate former friends and inner plane spiritual teachers," is more convincing. In the course of his probing analysis of Steiner's philosophy, he asserts that Steiner never disputed the reality of the hierarchy of mahatma adepts but "had direct contact with members of the White Brotherhood both in and out of human incarnation." The mahatmas, says Leviton, though rarefied human beings for whom being alive or dead was spiritually inconsequential, were certainly physically on earth at the end of the nineteenth century.

Adepts are universally described as distinctly fine-looking men, their physical bodies practically perfect because of their living in complete obedience to the laws of health and, above all, never worrying. Master Morya was described by Hodson as appearing to be in the prime of life, thirty-five to forty years old. "I was able to observe the texture of His skin, the hairs of His head, and the wonderful 'light' of His eyes." Yet when Madame Blavatsky met him in her childhood in the 1850s, he appeared exactly as in the early 1900s.

Master Koot Hoomi appeared to be about the same age as Morya, though he was known to have taken a university degree in Europe before the middle of the nineteenth century. Though a Kashmiri Brahmin, he was as fair complexioned as the average Englishman, with flowing brown hair, "ruddy with glints of gold as the sunlight catches it, nose finely chiseled, eyes large and of a wonderful liquid blue, full of love and joy, his expression ever changing as he smiles." In a remotely former life he is reputed to have been the great teacher Pythagoras.

Master Morya explained to Hodson that the masters lived not only in real houses with rooms, tables, and chairs, but also in what might be called "placelessness," beyond the limitations of space. "In fact this planet, earth, is only our bodily abiding place. We have bodies; so we must have homes, and do so; but our real lives are relatively bodiless and so virtually, if not wholly at first, limitless."

When Hodson asked how the adepts preserved the privacy of their homes and of themselves, even against aerial photography, he received the answer: "By the deflection of light, just as when a qualified Yogi makes himself or herself invisible, as did H. P. Blavatsky."

Hodson's master, Tutuit Bey, said his headquarters was near where Hodson thought it to be but was totally and occultly concealed from the eyes of the world. The master said they were able to conceal their centers by means of a maya veil drawn over them. "No one can see,

find, visit either ourselves or our retreats against Our will. Similarly. no
one flying over, traveling, or wandering on the Gobi Desert can see the
remains of the buildings of what was once the Great White Island in
the Gobi Sea. Intruding into our personal privacy and that of the
Government of the Brotherhood as a whole is forbidden and with
such potency that the greatest of the inventions of scientists today and
tomorrow cannot enable one single person to enter our realm against
our wishes."

Yet Koot Hoomi taught Hodson the way to visit him in the valley
where he and other members of the Great White Brotherhood reside
in their physical bodies. And Leadbeater says that over a period of forty
years he visited the masters regularly "during the sleep of the body." He
further points out that in Krishnamurti's book, *At the Foot of the Master,*
its titular author blandly admits in the preface that the words are almost
entirely those of the Master Koot Hoomi. As Leadbeater explains the
phenomenon: "Every night I had to take this boy in his astral body to
the house of the Master, that instruction might be given him. The
Master devoted perhaps fifteen minutes each night to talk to him, at
the end gathering up the main points. The boy remembered the summary in the morning and wrote it down." An edition of one million
copies was sold in the United States. Another well-known psychic author, Alice Bailey, compiler of endless books on theosophy, claims to
have channeled nineteen whole texts from the Tibetan mahatma Djwal
Khul through wide-awake dictation.

As to the precise location of these masters' residences, Leadbeater
describes a certain valley in Tibet or rather "a ravine with slopes covered in pine trees," where, in the 1930s—whether in fact or fantasy—
lived two of the masters, Morya and Koot Hoomi, occupying houses
on opposite sides of the narrow ravine. Master Koot Hoomi's house is
described as divided into two parts by a passage running through it and
surrounded by a large garden of its own with flowering shrubs and a
stretch of land cultivated by laborers. Master Morya's two-storied
house with glassed-in verandas was said to face the road, where a path
ran down the ravine to a small bridge at the bottom. Master Koot

Hoomi was described as riding a large bay horse, occasionally accompanied by Master Morya when both went together to visit monasteries, the latter on a magnificent white stallion.

Paul Jackson maintains that all these descriptions were invented in order to disguise the physical identity of the actual masters and guarantee their privacy. But either one believes in magic or one doesn't, and though Leadbeater is inclined to stretch his magic, it is reasonable to assume that both he and his fellow theosophists, including Madame Blavatsky, may have subtly prevaricated on certain aspects of their occult doings just to keep within the limits of what a highly closed-minded Victorian society might have been capable of accepting.

More fantastic is Leadbeater's description of a narrow aperture in the rock by the bridge at the bottom of the ravine leading into a vast system of subterranean halls "containing an occult museum of which the Master Koot Hoomi is guardian on behalf of the Great White Brotherhood." There are said to be stored original manuscripts of incredible antiquity and priceless value, "manuscripts written by the hand of the Lord Buddha in his final life as Prince Siddartha and another written by the Lord Christ during his life in Palestine." That Jesus of Nazareth, an Essene, could have left writings may seem far-fetched, yet the discovered Dead Sea Scrolls can hardly have been the sole product of that intensely religious period. Here, says Leadbeater, continuing his description of the caves, is kept the marvelous original of the Book of Dzyan described by Madame Blavatsky in *The Secret Doctrine*. "And there are stored models of all the kinds of machinery which the different civilizations evolved, and elaborate illustrations of the types of magic in use in various periods of history."

To Steiner, whose concepts can be stunning, none of this appeared to be far-fetched; his own readings from the Akashic Record often sound more fabulous. Yet Steiner broke with the theosophists, to some extent on the very question of their limiting human freedom by blind reliance on the tutelage of the mahatmas. Although, according to Leviton, Steiner had direct access to the hierarchy of mahatmas, incarnate and disembodied, he claimed that the occult lodges and the mahatmas had schemed to compromise nineteenth-century theosophy deliberately to obfuscate Blavatsky's accurate perception and comprehension of the Christ, "manipulating her like a puppet, pulling her in contrary ways according to their aims." Anthroposophy was therefore developed to redress the one-sided pro-Indian bias of theosophy.

Steiner, explains Leviton, may have looked into Rosicrucian, Goethean, and theosophical methods and he may have taken scientific degrees and he may have had respect for historical legacies, but at heart he was a rebel, uncomfortable with a supposedly spiritual movement founded on the autocratic guidance of remote, often disembodied, mahatmas. "He went his own individual way, breaking with the materialists, the Spiritualists, the Theosophists, and the lodges, following his own way, following the indications of the supersensible hierarchy as best he could, and presented the results within the established context of Western Philosophy, initiation occultism, and esoteric Christian spirituality." Theosophy, Leviton concludes, might be content with received authority; it would have no place in anthroposophy. Yet, carefully considered, every basic tenet of anthroposophy comes directly from the mouth, or pen, of Steiner.

Hodson, on the other hand, remained faithful to the lodges all his life. Lamenting that much of the ancient wisdom has been allowed to slip into oblivion, he reassured his followers that initiation into the higher levels of the mysteries was still being constantly performed by the occult lodges and that "among the hierophants of the Great White Brotherhood, the true secrets have been preserved, and they will always reward the search of the earnest Mason."

Leadbeater describes adepts of the Great White Brotherhood continually working out new schemes by which evolution can be quickened and by which the race may climb, some taking as pupils and disciples those willing to tread the path, "so that the ranks of the hierarchy may never be depleted." He describes how Master Morya or Koot Hoomi continued to perform the rites of initiation of a candidate to the brotherhood, usually in their ancient cave temple near the bridge across the river between their houses, where the candidate was required, as at a witches' sabbath, to appear in the astral body. As part of the first initiation by these masters, many astral objects were shown the candidate, and he was to tell the initiator what they were. He also had to distinguish between the astral bodies of a living man and a dead man, as well as between a real person and the thought-image of a master or an exact imitation of him. Up to the first initiation the candidate is described as working at night in his astral body. Then, to show himself on the physical plane, while still functioning in his astral body, he had to materialize a physical body, "a performance requiring a considerable expenditure of force."

Everything, says Leadbeater, that takes place in the second initiation is done on the mental plane, and all those involved are working in their mental bodies, not in the one used on the astral plane. Operating in one's mental body, one would have to materialize a temporary astral body.

If the initiator is the Lord Maitreya—the bodhisattva or world-teacher, leader of the Great White Brotherhood—the ceremony is described as taking place in his garden or the great room in his house, where he presides in his physical body, all others, with the exception of the candidate, being present in their astral vehicle for a first initiation and in their mental body for the second.

"The Great Ones present," says Leadbeater, can focus their consciousness with ease at whatever level is required, but on the astral and mental planes there is a perfect counterpart of everything physical; "so the accounts given are perfectly correct. The positions taken up in relation to physical objects are as described."

All the true and higher initiations are described as taking place out of the physical body. During the stages following the first, second, and third initiations, the candidate is gradually developing his buddhic consciousness; at the fourth initiation he enters the nirvanic plane.

European Orientalists have translated *nirvana* as annihilation, because, says Leadbeater, the word means "blown out," as the light of a candle is extinguished by breath. Nothing, according to Leadbeater, could be more antithetical to the truth, except that the annihilation is of man down here. "There, he is no longer man but God in man, a God among other Gods, though less than they."

For those who attain to adeptship and choose as their future career to remain upon this earth and help directly in the evolution of humanity toward the same goal, it is convenient, says Leadbeater, to retain physical bodies. "To be suitable for such purposes these bodies must be of no ordinary kind. Not only must they be absolutely sound in health, but they must also be perfect expressions of as much of the ego as can be manifested on the physical plane. The body must be fit for work and be capable of endurance immeasurably beyond those of ordinary men."

Communication between the masters or adepts and their theosophical pupils is described as taking place in such unusual ways as letters dropping suddenly from the ceiling or manifesting out of the void, with the result that much disbelief and discredit was showered on the society. But some extraordinary psychic manifestations were clearly involved. As described by Hodson, communication from adepts was invariably heralded to him by an electric current sweeping down the side of his face. Then, while Hodson resided on Belvedere Street, his attention was routinely attracted to the presence of a master ready to communicate with him when a series of very noticeable taps like a metallic rattle would come from within a wooden shrine containing portraits of the masters. With yoga exercises, Hodson would then place himself in a mentally receptive yogic condition, "and the knowledge within the master's mind would awaken within my mind." It was not, says Hodson, a process of clairaudience, for no sound was heard, only interiorly transferred active understanding. It was a transference from one conscious mind to another fully conscious mind of ideas, first into reasoned thoughts and then into verbal statements, all instantaneously and continuously. "During reception, ideas are caused to arise and to become established within my own mind in full self-consciousness— hyper-self-consciousness—as if it were my own knowledge."

Hodson explained that when he ventured to approach the process it in no way resembled mediumship because he thought out every single contribution received from the mind of the adept teacher, "fully understanding it, being mentally illumined by it before and during the process of its communication."

Master Morya corroborated—as reported by Hodson in his lifelong diary—saying that Hodson, in all his clairvoyant work and researches and in receiving from the masters and members of the angelic hosts, did so always in full physical and mental consciousness, by "hyper-mental awareness."

In this way, says Hodson, the master could readily cause him to know the inner meaning of the scriptures or of other literary texts, a gift that enabled Hodson to interpret and explain them to a wider audience. As Easton points out, numerous biblical passages, if interpreted literally, not only contradict one another but also do not conform at all to what the human mind regards as reasonable, something even more true of the supposedly revealed and authoritative teachings of many of early church fathers. Steiner warns that the Gospels are incomprehensible unless clarified by spiritual science.

For many years, as recorded in his diary, Hodson claimed to be in daily communication with Master Polidorus, receiving from him information on some of his, Hodson's, past lives, moving backward in time: England in the seventeenth century, a life that ended tragically in middle age; another English life in Tudor times as a landed gentleman. In the tenth century in India, Hodson appeared as a doctor of Ayurvedic law, studying herbs and minerals in their occult and physical properties. In an earlier Jewish life, as Aristobolus, son of Alexander Janneus, a prince in Judea at the time of Jesus, he first met Polidorus, who was then playing the role of Philo Judaeus. Before that he had been a sibyl at Cumae, clairvoyant, with fully conscious powers of spiritual perception. Here, said the master, the seeds were sown for an occult life in three successive incarnations. Hodson had then been a Roman matron in the declining period of the Roman Empire.

Polidorus told Hodson of other past lives in which he had worked hard for the brotherhood, suffering grievously, horrifyingly, getting Hodson to vividly remember being with Master Polidorus in one of the ancient Egyptian temples, much like Karnak, passing between great pillars and turning into a secret passage and crypt. Hodson was also told that he had known Francis Bacon and had been received by him into his Rosy Cross Temple at Gorhambury.

Hodson concluded that because the mysteries in many cases had been made known to him in former lives, their awakening to consciousness in what was his current life was partly a recovery of his own

knowledge attained by study or during philosophical education in previous incarnations. More important, Hodson realized that if a person
had taken the third initiation in a former life or lives and had advanced
toward the fourth, then in his current life he was able to move faster,
and eventually the necessity for ritual itself would be outgrown.

Polidorus explained that at physical initiation the powers of past
personalities are recommunicated to the present one, that the old selves
have not vanished but are indelibly imprinted on the Akashic Record,
where they can be studied. Errors cannot be erased but can be karmi-
cally balanced.

Polidorus then gave Hodson instructions and meditations to practice steadily and daily for the purpose of arousing and drawing up the
three currents of kundalini. Some time earlier, with Master Rakoczy at
his temple, Hodson said he realized cosmic fohat (or kundalini) to be
the source of all power. "It is a white, cold fire which plays like continuous lighting in and through and around those who can tap and wield
its potency."

As a parting shot, Polidorus told Hodson his reintroduction to the
mystery tradition had been no accident but was a deliberate intrusion
into his life by the brotherhood, even including the use of his dog,
Peter, with the first showing of fairies. To which Hodson added, "The
phenomena of the successful photography of Nature Spirits by two
young girls in Yorkshire, England, early in the 1920s—with which I
was closely associated—may be regarded as an Adept-inspired action
designed to draw attention to the existence of Nature Spirits and to
the occult doctrine of the existence and functions of the Angelic
Hierarchies."

In the early morning of January 23, 1983, Hodson died peacefully
in Auckland, New Zealand, at the age of ninety-six, having given his
last public lecture at the HPB Lodge of the local Theosophical Society
on the subject "Kundalini-Shakti; Its Use in Occult Research."

What's to Be Done

What then are the messages of theosophy and anthroposophy, and how do they differ? Largely over a variant view of the Christ. In India, when Leadbeater discovered a thirteen-year-old Brahmin youth from Madras, Jiddu Krishnamurti, he saw in him such great promise that he took the boy to England for higher education, believing him to be the forthcoming Buddha. Besant, going further, believed the boy to be the reincarnation of Christ. Krishnamurti, humbler and wiser, repudiated both roles but developed himself into one of the more enlightened of Indian gurus.

At this point, in 1913, Rudolf Steiner, then general secretary of the German Theosophical Society, broke away from Besant and Leadbeater on the ground that the Christ would not reappear on earth in a physical but only in an etheric body. He then formed his own Anthroposophical Society.

Whereas the theosophists' clairvoyant approach to history and science was based on the occult practice of minutely comparing the date obtained from the Akashic Record over the centuries by different clairvoyants until the evidence could be sufficiently correlated to warrant a conclusion, Steiner chose to go a different route, claiming that the basis of all that he had to say derived directly from his own conclusions based on his own scrutiny of the record. This prodigious effort resulted in some forty books and some six thousand lectures taken down by his followers. In this monumental work he detailed "cosmic history" and the "wisdom of the world," his object being to open up the "secret" and to make what was "occult" available to the whole of humankind. He said he wished to deepen human understanding by showing how both humanity and world originated from a divine-spiritual cosmos in which everyone could acquire knowledge of higher worlds.

Basic to Steiner's philosophy, indeed to theosophy, are the laws of karma and reincarnation by which the human spirit for its ethical development must live repeated lives on earth, the deeds of earlier lives bearing fruit in later incarnations. Introduced in the Upanishads as the great secret that solves the problem of human destiny, karma was seen as expressing the inexorable law of moral causation: whatsoever a man soweth, that shall he also reap. As the unerring law of the universe, the source, origin, and font of all the other laws in nature, it was considered the unfailing redresser of human injustice. Theosophists considered the great social evils, the apparently unjust distribution of classes in both society and the sexes and the unequal distribution of capital and labor, all to be due to karma, concluding that caritas was a better remedy than kicking against the pricks. As for reincarnation, they believed the human spirit to be no more created anew when it begins its earthly life than a person is newly created every morning and that any God who would create a soul for only one brief span of life, whether to animate a happy man or a poor wretch who had done nothing to deserve such a cruel fate, could be rather a senseless fiend than a God.

Steiner taught that the highest spiritual development of humanity leads progressively to the ego's control of the astral, etheric, and physical bodies; that the spiritualization of matter was the goal of humanity. For gurus, Steiner had little use, preferring that people learn by their own efforts, considering himself no more than a brotherly teacher. His anthroposophy emphasized freedom, "freedom from the machinations of occult lodges or the Mahatma hierarchy." Unlike the Easterner's pursuit of nirvana, Steiner's spiritual science was directed at modifying this world: it aimed at developing the spirit for the upbuilding of both humanity and the world, leading to an increased, not a decreased, valuation of life in the physical now. Many former theosophists flocked to his Anthroposophical Society to absorb Steiner's "spiritual science," a philosophy they have kept alive and have widely developed since his death in 1925.

But why, one might ask, with such a genius in our midst—philosopher, author, architect, painter, sculptor, poet, dramatist, educator, inventor of the art of eurythmy—do only devoted anthroposophists appear to have access to what the "master" really taught or meant? Among the general public and among academic historians, Steiner is "generally under-appreciated as a major prophet of the twentieth century, if not of the epoch." Despite (or perhaps because of) his extraordinary contribution to humanity in lectures and books over a period of twenty-five years, he is practically unknown. A short passage from Colin Wilson's biography of Steiner gives a clue: "Of all the important thinkers of the twentieth century, Rudolf Steiner is perhaps the most difficult to come to grips with. For the unprepared reader, his work presents a series of daunting obstacles. To begin with, there is the style, which is formidably abstract, and as unappetizing as dry toast. The real problem lies in the content, which is often so outlandish and bizarre that the reader suspects either a hoax or a barefaced confidence trick. . . . The resulting sense of frustration is likely to cause even the most open-minded reader to give up in disgust."

Colin Wilson, who in the end concluded that Steiner was "one of the greatest men of the twentieth century" and that it would be impossible to exaggerate the importance of what he had to say, twice refused to write his biography and was prevailed upon to do so only when a replacement author found by his publisher committed suicide rather than finish the job.

On the more positive side, Richard Leviton, with the advantage over Colin Wilson of being an initiate clairvoyant with what he calls "a direct conjunction with Steiner's teachings," found Steiner's otherwise difficult material immediately accessible and "as gripping and spellbinding as the mysteries of Agatha Christie."

To the world of nature spirits, Steiner's contribution is in any case *sans pareil*. Lamenting that people constantly move through whole worlds of spirits without seeing them, unaware of the spiritual activity that underlies everything we do and without which there is little we can do, Steiner pleads with us to give these spirit beings the chance to manifest, assuring us they will do so readily enough. "This whole chorus can either press toward us and reveal itself to us if we willingly take in spiritual ideas, or it can remain hidden from view."

All we have to do, says Steiner, is reach toward the spiritual beings that hover behind the outer world surrounding us, for only if we accept the wave of spiritual life that wants to enter our physical world will we be able to achieve our own goals. We are urged to become acquainted with nature spirits in the same way we have become acquainted with oxygen, hydrogen, calcium, and so forth. We must meet the spirit world at least halfway if we do not wish to degenerate along with our culture. We are further warned that if we fail to learn about this spiritual world, we run the risk of having the whole chorus of spirits fall into the hands of opposing spiritual powers. "Unless man draws near to spiritual reality something completely different from what ought to happen will happen to the earth."

Admitting that one needs clairvoyant skills to discover the truths of spiritual science, Steiner points out that one does not need such skills in order to live by such truths. All one needs is to look with healthy understanding at what has been laid before one. And even if one does not want to apply oneself to acquiring supersensible perception, says Steiner, one can still find life more comprehensible by accepting that which such supersensible perception indicates and by applying these indications to the world of one's experience. "If by a loving approach to nature one acquires a consciousness unspoiled by the veneer of knowledge considered authoritative today, one can gradually recover, along with knowledge acquired through initiation, the knowledge which mankind has lost."

In simple terms, Steiner advises that whoever becomes able to meet the tree spirit coming out of the tree "as did his ancient forebears" will also be able to see figures of his own previous earth lives and the development of karma that proceeds from today's human beings, a vision he says will lead to a comprehension of karma. "The more that associations are formed, and the more that feelings of fellowship are developed in complete freedom, the more will sublime beings descend to human beings, and the faster the earth will be spiritualized. Since the last third of the nineteenth century we have had to do with a pressing-in of spiritual beings from the cosmos. They are trying to gain a foothold in earthly existence—which they can only do if human beings fill themselves with thoughts about the spiritual beings in the cosmos."

Seers, adds Hodson, both ancient and modern, have all along said that we possess within ourselves all the instruments of research we can ever need. Theosophy affirms—on the basis of actual experience—that there are inactive senses in every human being, which, when stimulated to activity, make possible the investigation of a normally unseen world of nonphysical matter all around us. This sixth sense, now latent, will one day be used as a natural means of cognition and investigation. It is this sense, says Leadbeater, developed by means of expanding consciousness through meditation and sensitizing the vehicles of consciousness, "which will open up to the observer the living denizens of the vast hosts of astral beings, protean forms of the ceaseless tide of elemental essence."

In his major works Steiner lists the systematic exercises and training that may be undertaken by anyone with assured results if faithfully followed. According to Steiner, the body used at the first stage of clairvoyance is the astral body: "As clairvoyant consciousness lights up within us we get a living view of the beings of the Third Hierarchy and of their offspring the nature spirits." For the second stage, the etheric body is used; "and if one learns to use one's etheric body as an instrument of clairvoyance one can gradually perceive everything in the spiritual world belonging to beings of the Second Hierarchy."

These worlds all around us are described as freely interpenetrating, not as distinct and unconnected substance, but rather as melting one into the other. It is not, says Hodson, some new and strange kind of matter, but ordinary physical matter subdivided more finely and vibrating more rapidly on the etheric, astral, and mental planes. But only for those developed individuals who can extend their own etheric body as tentacles is it possible, according to Steiner, to know the beings of the Second Hierarchy and also the group souls (or devas) that control the various kingdoms of nature. On attaining this second stage of clairvoyance, Steiner describes a very definite experience: "One seems to go out of oneself, no longer feeling enclosed within one's skin. And when one encounters say a plant or an animal or even a human being one feels as if a part of oneself were actually within that other being. In normal consciousness, and even in the first stage of clairvoyance, one can still say: I am here and that being I see is there. In the second stage one can only say: where that being is—whom I perceive—there am I."

Steiner describes the sensation as if one's etheric body were stretching out tentacles on all sides with which to draw one to other beings into whom one plunges with the actual sensation of immersion. Thereafter, clairvoyants learn to plunge into everything conscious, into everything that can suffer and rejoice in a human way, into everything alive, but not yet into what is without life or appears lifeless, which is seen as the mineral kingdom. "At this stage of clairvoyance we only learn to live with plants, animals, and with other human beings. We also learn to recognize behind all living things a higher spiritual world—beings of the second hierarchy [exusiai, dynamis, and kyriotetes, spirits of form, motion, and wisdom]. Yet at this second stage, where we feel ourselves one with other beings, we realize that we are still there, beside the other being."

To ascend to the highest stage of clairvoyance, to the world of thrones, cherubim, and seraphim, sublime spirits of will, harmony, and love, even this last remnant of egoistic experience must be abandoned. "We must completely lose the feeling that we exist as a separate being. We must feel the foreign being as ourself. We can then look at ourselves as if seen from another being. We look out from within the foreign being and see ourselves as the foreign being. Only then, when this third state is reached do we succeed in perceiving beings other than those of the Second and Third hierarchies. We begin to see Thrones, spirits of the First hierarchy, whose lowest substance is will."

On the mental plane, "vision," as described by Leadbeater, is totally different. "One can no longer speak of separate senses such as sight and hearing, but only of a general sense which responds fully to the vibrations reaching it; so that when any object comes within its cognition it at once comprehends it fully, sees, hears, feels and knows all there is to know about it, in one instantaneous operation."

One of the tasks of anthroposophy is to make the reality of heavenly beings and the meditative practices leading to actual experience of them available to anyone wishing to tread this path in full consciousness.

Only now, says Steiner, can and should the truth be fully revealed. Easton explains why man had to lose his atavistic clairvoyance and cease to be able to see into the spiritual world. "As long as he could perceive spiritual beings, he was unable to disbelieve in them, and the possibility of such disbelief was an essential part of man's freedom." We would never have known we were human beings, says Steiner, unless we had lost awareness of the spiritual world in exchange for I-consciousness. The purpose of the physical world is to provide a context in which the free activity of the human self-consciousness can occur. Otherwise, we would have been "perpetually tied to the apron strings of the celestial hierarchy, perceiving the supersensible in only a diffused, entranced, dream-like state." To attain ego-consciousness, human beings had to be able to distinguish themselves from their surroundings. That's what makes for an "I" and an "I am." Now we must acquire consciousness of spiritual worlds by our own efforts, retaining earthly consciousness. We must learn to see the world through other beings, and in full consciousness view both the physical and the supersensible world, awake and discriminatory, as clairvoyant scientists. Our eventual goal is to spiritualize our astral, etheric, and physical bodies until they are controlled by our immortal spiritual ego, making of each of us an adept or master. Nowadays, says Steiner, thinking itself, when properly developed, is capable of grasping equally well both the sensible and supersensible worlds. "Thus there are no necessary limits to knowledge, and we do not, in order to increase our knowledge, have to await a revelation given to us by God." To Steiner, every step that leads into our inner being leads ipso facto into the spiritual world, the deeper the penetration, the higher the ascent into the world of spiritual beings.

Ideally, the clairvoyant consciousness of a human being on earth must be able to go back and forth continually between the physical and the elemental worlds, observing the spiritual world beyond the threshold while outside the physical body, "exercising in a healthy way the faculties which lead it to the right observation of the physical sense world."

But if you do not have the time or the conviction to follow Steiner's careful recipe for becoming clairvoyant, for traveling on the astral plane, or for communing with the spirit world—carefully spelled out as it is in *Knowledge of Higher Worlds and How to Achieve It*—there may be a shortcut, similar to the one taken in the ancient mysteries by imbibing *Amanita muscaria*. This alternate route is via a vine native to the Amazonian rainforest, the ayahuasca vine, whose derivative brew is known as yaje, caapi, or natema. It may not be as solid a route as is outlined by Steiner, but it may be convincing enough of the reality of Steiner's supersensible world to make the longer route worth traveling.

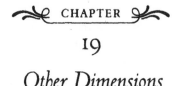

Other Dimensions

A few doses of the liquor distilled from segments of *Banisteriopsis caapi*, mixed with leaves from the bushy plant *Pychotria viridis*, quickly open inner vision to the world of Steiner's "very useful elemental beings" and beyond. But one needs a certain fortitude to go this route because it opens at first almost invariably onto a landscape of huge anacondas, fierce jaguars, and all manner of spidery and creepy beings.

This strange world is not, however, the world classified by ethnobiologists and chemists as hallucinogenic—meaning one that produces visions that have nothing to do with reality. The ayahuasca-induced reality is, if anything, even more real. From the descriptions of those who have imbibed the liquor it is, to all intents and purposes, a window into the astral world of theosophist and anthroposophist. It may indeed be close to the drug employed by hierophants of the ancient mysteries.

For thousands of years Indian shamans in Colombia, Peru, and Brazil have been drinking the ayahuasca brew as a tool to diagnose illness or to ward off impending disaster, to guess the wiles of the enemy, and to prophesy the future. They believe the vine to be both an ally that can guide people to light and truth and a teacher that can provide new guidelines for relating to nature.

The brew, as explained in more or less orthodox terms, adjusts and reorients the nerves, meridians, and internal energies that regulate the connections among mind, body, soul, and spirit. It is professed to have a natural relationship to the brain, one that turns a key and opens the door into a wider consciousness. "On the one hand it produces certain neurochemical actions based on its molecular properties—its alkaloids; on the other hand, divinities inherent in the component plants help us reintegrate with a system of knowledge that goes back to man's origins."

Taken ritually, the ayahuasca or yaje tea is described as opening the doors of communication between the mind and the astral, "a parallel dimension that is inside of us and, at the same time, in the cosmos." In this environment, thoughts are immediately perceived as real, and each figure in the ayahuasca world is able to transform its character and shape at will, just as theosophist and anthroposophist describe the astral world. Participants in the yaje rituals can have visions of far away or deceased friends or relatives, and they can experience visual insights into their own past lives and psyches. Descriptions of shamanic voyages include "ascending to heaven to mingle with heavenly people, or conversely of celestial beings descending to the place of the ceremony."

Peter Gorman, a New York writer who hacked his way through the Peruvian jungle for days to find the Matses Indians, has several times taken the yaje. In an article for the magazine *Shaman's Drum* (Fall 1992) he describes imbibing the substance in a hut in the Amazon forest to experience two of its effects: astral vision and astral travel.

"The visions began soon after my stomach settled; my mind filled with pictures of demons, skulls and hellish faces. Red serpents and hordes of insects crawled across the sea of white corpses and body parts. It was as though my mind was taking a tour of hell; a modern Dante's *Inferno* filled with images of famine and pestilence, Indian massacres, the Vietnamese war, and New York City suffering."

Gorman explained that although he had learned from taking acid and magic mushrooms during the 1960s "that there is a spirit in everything—that ours is a mystical world," his drinking ayahuasca took him several steps further, allowing him to become "viscerally involved with these spirits."

The first such encounter was with a snake, the second with a large bird. The snake was black, ringed with yellow, long and strong, and as thick as his leg. "I watched it glide though the reeds. A drop of water hit the river's surface, and I felt the ripples against my body—I realized I was swimming with the snake. My body moved with powerful contractions."

Viewing from the snake's point of view, Gorman says he saw a bright green tree frog sitting on a branch near the water's surface. "We—the snake and I—moved silently toward it and in a flash had swallowed it. It felt strange in my throat, and stranger still when it jumped in an effort to escape. I was so surprised by the feeling, I separated from the snake for a moment. Merging again I felt the muscles in my mid-section contract to kill it, and I felt it slide easily into my belly."

Gorman wondered if his ego boundaries had momentarily dissolved enough to allow him to interplay with another form. His next involvement was with a great white bird.

"At first I watched the bird from a great distance, then I felt myself merging with it. Soon, I was looking down from the bird's perspective, my sharp eyesight picking out minute details of the landscape below. I flew over a mountain range and peered into a stream. I saw fish moving about, and watched rich hues of blue and green sparkling from their scales. Unexpectedly, I tilted off the horizon and plummeted toward them. I felt no fear, only hunger; I wanted a fish. I split the water with hardly a splash and in an instant was racing skyward again with a fish in my beak. A piece of it slipped into my stomach unchewed. I remember thinking I didn't eat food that way."

The instant Gorman thought of himself apart from the bird, he found himself back in the hut in the rainforest, though both the experience and the bird remained very real to him.

Recovering his vision of the bird, he asked it to take him on a voyage to visit his wife in California, from whom he had recently been separated. "Instantly, I was in her room, hovering close to the ceiling. For a moment I saw her making love with someone, and I got jealous. A wave of nausea washed over me, and the image disappeared."

Such adventures with yajé reflect very closely Steiner's description of traveling in the elemental world. "We can learn nothing at all in that world unless we have . . . the capacity for transforming our own being into other beings outside ourselves. We must have the faculty of metamorphosis. We must be able to immerse ourselves in and become the other being. In the elemental world we get to know another being only when in a way we inwardly have 'become' the other."

Equally riveting visions produced by yajé were experienced by another journalist, New York–born Jimmy Wieskopf, a graduate of

Columbia College, New York, and Cambridge University, England, resident of Colombia, and contributor to various journals. In the magazine *Shaman's Drum* (Spring 1993) Wieskopf reported that the river communities along the lower Putamayo of eastern Colombia were producing extraordinary stories of magical events and miraculous healings experienced under the influence of yaje. Many, says Wieskopf, are so fantastic they are almost beyond the imagination of outsiders like himself, products of secular materialistic cultures, but that "after one drinks yaje, sees its magical visions, and feels its curative powers, the stories suddenly become more plausible."

During his first visit to the Putamayo, Wieskopf was introduced to yaje's healing gifts by a Siona *curandero*, Don Pacho, heir to a thousand-year-old tradition of working with the vine. The experience convinced Wieskopf that using the product under the guidance of a skilled *curandero* such as Pacho can be highly therapeutic, particularly in dealing with psychological disorders.

To prepare the ayahuasca drink, Pacho collected sections of vine from the jungle, which he cut into pieces about twenty centimeters long. These were smashed to ribbons with a stone and placed in a pot in alternate layers with leaves of chacruna, "the two plants that fit." Various plant additives called "misha" can be used, depending on the purpose of the ayahuasca session, there being a distinction between substances that "make you travel," that "make you see," and that "teach you to heal." Water is added and the brew boiled down until only 10 percent of the liquid remains.

When the time comes to drink the mixture, almost invariably at night, potions are ritually distributed in small cupfuls. Wieskopf took his in the jungle in a square hut roofed with palm fronds, its bare earthen floor and no walls making it easier to deal with the vomiting and diarrhea that come with drinking yaje, part of the cleansing process. At the beginning of his previous yaje trips, Wieskopf had experienced an onrush of nausea, dizziness, and oxygen deficiency. So he breathed deeply as he paced the clearing, preparing himself for what would come.

"As the wooziness came over me, I wondered whether this time I would have the courage—once I had survived the initial, purgative stages of the experience—to accept the additional cups which Pacho and others said would bring on the visions."

Soon he noted that without losing their familiar natural quality, the extraordinarily sharp details of the jungle landscape were being transformed into geometric clusters of color and light that shifted and coalesced kaleidoscopically. "My movie screen filled with such beautiful imagery—star-bursts, diamond facets, fireworks, mandalas, stained-glass windows, Disney Munchkins, and yellow submarines—that I became dumbfounded. For the first time, I came to know the full meaning of the word ecstasy. Despite the way the images rushed by, each one was actual and examinable. They were more real than anything I'd ever seen in dreams or under the effects of the acid and mushrooms I had tried many years before. So, far from being an hallucination, it was nothing less than a vision. As an experiment, I opened my eyes and focused on my surroundings. Then I turned back to the visions; they were as potent as ever."

After midnight, as Wieskopf thought he was getting used to the vine, he says he foolishly began to feel proud of having resisted vomiting and diarrhea. "I should have known better, for yaje has a tendency to challenge inflated egos, and it now chastised me with a characteristic flick of its tail. A transcendental nausea drove me out of my hammock, onto my knees. I managed to crawl just outside the hut, where I spent a long time with my forehead pressed against the soil, trying to throw up and nearly blanking out."

Wieskopf was then compelled to a trip to the *cagadero,* or toilet, a log placed across a small stream twenty meters away. "I have noticed more than once," writes Wieskopf, "that some of the most forceful yaje illuminations occur in the moment just before shitting or vomiting, when the gut's inner turmoil reaches a peak and you feel about as bad as you can ever feel. This happened now."

Amazingly, Wieskopf's ordeal brought to light a host of Steiner's "very useful elementals," denizens that evidently throng the Amazon rainforest. "The swarms of mosquitoes that buzzed around my bare ass and the sinister weeds lurking in the foul-smelling stream joined my trip, and a host of tiny devas, genies, and gnomes winked and cavorted round the squatting gringo, mocking his queasiness until they evaporated with the squirts of shit."

Less scatological and more inspiring are the nature spirits seen and described by Pablo Amaringo, Brazilian shaman and painter of extraordinary rainforest scenes, some sixty of which appear in *Ayahuaska Visions*, a luxurious volume· published by North Atlantic Books of Berkeley, California, accompanied by an illuminating text by Louis Eduardo Luna.

Amaringo's complex and beautiful paintings contain a cumulative amalgam of his shamanic visions, depicting not only the boas and anacondas of the jungle but also its fairies, sylphs, gnomes, and fire spirits. Amaringo's spirits of stone and metal, gnomelike guardians of subterranean treasures, are colored to represent diamonds, gold, copper, bronze, silver, garnet, and quartz, their weird elongated bodikins accordingly white, yellow, red, green, light blue, purple, or lilac.

Fairies in this Latino shaman's vision are blond and oddly reminiscent of Margaret Murray's description of spirits in the British Isles, where ranking fairies appear in long, flowing dresses, cover their hair with veils or hoods, and sport small coronets. To these familiar spirits are added mermaids and pink dolphins, the latter normal in the many rivers of the Amazon delta. Amaringo's mermaids are beautiful women with hypnotic eyes who live in caves at the bottom of lakes and rivers, particularly where the water is agitated by great whirlpools, playing musical instruments and singing in melodious voices.

Every tree, every plant, says Amaringo, has a spirit, alive and conscious, that sees everything around it; and if one takes ayahuasca one can hear the trees cry out when they are about to be cut down. His plant spirits adopt many different forms, usually anthropomorphic but also theriomorphic. In an article entitled "Sociopsychotherapeutic Functions of Ayahuasca Healing," Dr. Walter Andritzky points out that during the ayahuasca intoxication "all of nature seems converted into an anthropomorphic drama, and the myths sung by the shaman are experienced multisensorially as absolute reality. Legends are not only heard, but seen in their full vitality and experienced with their emotional impact."

Surprisingly, some of Amaringo's canvases contain spaceships with beings whose bodies appear more subtle than those of humans; he claims they belong to advanced extraterrestrial civilizations who live in perfect harmony and once contacted Mayans, Tiahuanacanos, and Incas.

Today in Brazil, Amaringo is just one of thousands of yajé-drinking followers of a new shamanic religion known as the Santo Daime Doctrine. This nationwide fellowship of spiritual leaders, led by a thousand initiates known as *fardados*, believes the vine to be a vehicle for a divine being present in the rainforest and in all creation and that the vine's juice imbibed sacramentally as a Eucharist of nature allows humankind to partake of the nature of God. This doctrine, evolved directly out of communion with the living sacramental substance, has as its central axis the teachings of Christ along with veneration of the Virgin Mary, who is seen as the rainforest's "Virgin of Conception." In Portuguese *daime* means "give me," and in the ritual it has the added overtones of "give me love, give me light, give me strength."

Founded in the Amazon forest in the 1920s by a seven-foot-tall black rubber tapper, Raimundi Irineu Serra, the sect has grown into a nationwide fellowship of spiritual seekers. Working and studying with Peruvian Indian shamans, Irineu was taught to make the ayahuasca tea and to journey through its ecstatic states, learning to understand and integrate the visions into daily life.

In one of his visions, Irineu claims to have seen "Our Lady of Conception, the Forest Queen," who told him to found a spiritual doctrine in which the drinking of ayahuasca tea would be the central ritual. At the same time, Irineu says he began to receive from the astral plane a series of hymns, running into the hundreds, hymns that in toto are considered by Irineu's followers to be a new and enlarged version of the gospel of Christ—a Third Testament.

Because of its search for "love, harmony, truth, justice and a way to save the Amazonian forest," the Santo Daime Doctrine quickly drew followers not only from among simple people of all walks of life and different spiritual traditions, but also from among city-living intellectuals, artists, musicians, psychologists, and medical professionals. Followers of this new shamanic religion now believe that the rainforest itself sent out the Daime at this time in history because humankind has destroyed a large part of the forest and threatens to destroy the rest. According to Brazilian writer Alex Polari de Alverga, a principal leader of Santo Daime Doctrine, its followers believe the Daime to be both an ally that can guide people to the light and truth and a teacher that can provide new guidelines for relating to nature.

In an interview with Polari, the American writer and photographer Gary Dale Richman, who has lived in Brazil for almost twenty years, has shot many hours of film in the rainforest, and has authored a book on the Daime, reports that this small but articulate group of Brazilians believes the best solutions for saving the rainforest may "lie within the magic of her strongest medicine and purest essence—Santo Daime."

By championing ways of living in harmony with the rainforest and encouraging an appreciation for the ecological and ethnobotanical knowledge of the Amazon's ancient shamanic traditions, the Santo Daime Doctrine, says Polari, may help preserve both the rainforest and her inhabitants.

In these times when drug abuse has become rampant in most societies, undermining community morals, ethics, and health, the Santo Daime Doctrine, says Alex Polari, also offers a message that certain natural sacraments or psychoactive substances—when properly used, as in the shamanic traditions—are not only nontoxic and nonaddictive, unlike tobacco, liquor, and crack, but also encourage high moral standards and help addicts end their dependence on drugs.

Tripping in Holland

For those who cannot afford a five-thousand-dollar trip to Brazil to be indoctrinated into the mysteries of ayahuasca, a quicker and easier way is to travel to permissive Amsterdam, where a group of devotees have formed a branch of Santo Daime. There, thanks to liberal laws governing what are known as hallucinogenic drugs, this Daime community flourishes, giving hospitable access to their rituals for about a hundred dollars a session. The proceeds go mostly to maintain the mother church in the "Heaven of Mapia" deep in the Amazon forest, a two-day canoe ride up tropical rivers into a million-acre preserve made safe by the Brazilian government.

One of the Dutch Daime sessions conducted by a master shaman from Brazil took place in an abandoned Catholic church, now refurbished in a rural area just west of Amsterdam, once an island. Arbitrarily rejoined to the mainland by an industrial project that did not materialize, its abandoned buildings have been left free to squatters.

At sunset on a warm August evening I was taken there by an illumined group of Buddhists, Dutch proponents of the Santo Daime Doctrine who have a Zen center between Amsterdam and the Hague, where they have been promoting the Daime in Holland since the beginning of 1994. The church stands in a copse of tall chestnuts and lindens—a Gothic affair of gray-brown brick with a spire surmounted by a cross. Built a hundred years ago by Flemish refugee workers who had settled in the area, its heavily worn oak doors were now open to about a hundred middle-class men and women, mostly Dutch, with a scattering of Germans and Belgians, all dressed in various outfits of white. By their looks and manner, with their regular shaves and haircuts, the men appeared to be lawyers, psychologists, artists, businessmen. Only a few of the younger ones wore their hair Jesus-length, and one skinhead, who seemed both Germanic and gay, sported a gold earring with a blue pendant. The women, in their thirties and forties, either wives or professionals, with sheer white dresses often transparently revealing, nevertheless seemed sexless, as if sex had no place in the ritual about to begin.

As the moment of truth approached, I trembled a little inwardly, worried about the visions of snakes and jaguars and because I do not like losing clarity under the influence of alcohol or drugs. Of these I have tried, and instantly abandoned, marijuana, hash, and cocaine. My only real trip, some thirty years ago, was occasioned by a bout with mescaline as an essential premise (or so I considered it) for producing a review of Aldous Huxley's *The Doors of Perception*. A magical experience, I have kept the details of it fresh in my mind all these years, though at the time I decided not to repeat it—unless I could find a way do so without benefit of drug.

Inside, the nave was roughly whitewashed, with rows of narrow stained-glass windows about ten feet up; charmingly they depicted St. John baptizing Jesus or St. Gertrude, the church's patron, staring trancelike up to heaven. The shell-shaped apse, colored blue, appeared to be of faience. Before the altar stood a long white table with candles, stacks of glistening plastic glasses, and two wartime jerry-cans, painted blue, containing the magic potions ritually produced in Brazil.

People milled around, mostly familiar with one another, the atmosphere tense but restrained. In the center of the nave stood another long table covered by a white cloth, more candles, a wooden Croix de Lorraine, and a colored photograph of Irineu, tall, dark, handsome originator of the Santo Daime ritual. Ten chairs were ready to receive the leaders of the ceremony. Along each main wall more chairs were lined up to receive half a hundred men on the right and as many women on the left.

Along the floor, ominous gallon-sized plastic buckets stood everywhere available for vomit, accompanied by rolls of paper towels. Uniformed attendants, themselves initiates—identifiable by blue skirts, blue trousers, and blue bow ties—stood ready with a score of sheeted mattresses to receive the purged and ailing trippers.

My worst fear was to restimulate a nightmare that had occurred when I was nine years old. Overdosed with nitrous oxide by an overzealous Helvetian dentist, I either died or suffered a near-death experience during which I viewed my body from the ceiling, reviewed my life up until that moment like a film run backward, then found myself in a whirling void in which an inner voice informed me that nothing else existed in the universe: that I was it, and it was I, with no relief and no way out. *Huis clos!* To avoid this nightmare I had ever since foregone ether and chloroform, opting for local or spinal anesthetics. Only many years later did I discover from Steiner that this was an elementary form of initiation, that the baptisms performed by John the Baptist in the Jordan amounted to near-death drownings and were actually initiations into the Christian mysteries.

What had me now perturbed, afraid the yaje might precipitate me back into that void, was the reminiscence of the description in a book written by Allen Ginsberg with William Burroughs in the 1950s of the "awful solitude of the universe." Then there was Steiner's dictum: "There are two poles between which lie all vicissitudes: fear of the void and the collapse into egotism."

I nevertheless perdured in my intent to drink the stuff. I had talked with a member of the Daime community who had been taking the drug regularly for seven months, and I had tried to understand from him the mechanics of its spiritual overtones. He explained that ayahuasca acts as a key into the spirit world and that the visions can enable one to see the spiritual causes of one's own problems or physical illness and that catharsis frequently accompanies these visions.

What came next is recorded in the first person.

The time is now! At a signal we all take our places. The masters of ceremonies are two Brazilian men and one woman. She is dark haired, in her forties, slim, intense, with a tiny diamond embedded in the left side of her nose. She speaks English as the lingua franca.

The Brazilian shaman, a solid fellow who could have been in the lumber trade, dressed in gray slacks and a green windbreaker, leads the congregation in a recital of the Lord's Prayer in Portuguese, followed by an Ave Maria. Only the words are subtly different. Then the Brazilian woman intones a hymn to the Daime, singing loudly in a high rasping but not unpleasant voice as everyone joins in to the rhythm of mariachis and a drum.

> The Daime is the Daime,
> I affirm it.
> He is the Divine Eternal Father
> She the Sovereign Queen.
> The Daime is the Daime
> Teacher of all Teachers,
> The Divine Eternal Father
> Of all eternal beings.

Each couplet is repeated with increasing gusto, the melody carried by two guitars, and a hypnotic effect is created by mariachis and drumming, until at last comes the time for action. All turn toward the altar, forming five long lines of men and five of women. As one by one we approach the Brazilians, they pour out jiggers of Santo Daime—dark like tea but with more consistency—into small plastic cups. I watch those ahead of me stoically drink it down in two or three gulps.

Approaching the altar, all dressed in white, as if for tennis, I am reminded of my first communion, aged nine, the main difference being that my devotion then has turned to slight anxiety now. Am I becoming involved in a ritual of the devil? Are these shamans Luciferic? Or were the priests of my childhood devils? I seem to be sensing the foretaste of a nightmare I might be about to suffer under yaje, that everexcruciating search for truth.

I drink my potion in three gulps; it tastes like Fernet Branca, only more astringent.

The effects of the Daime are supposed to be felt within minutes of taking the first dose and to last an average of two hours. Subsequent doses renew the effects with the same or greater intensity.

Back in my seat, I wonder at all the warnings I've received from friends and family not to take the stuff, that it could be dangerous.

From reading Alex Polari, I remember that before seeing visions the apprentice will pass through a craziness stage, the principal characteristic of which is fear. The first visions are pervaded by death and destruction as a test to see if the novice is strong enough to travel in the spirit world, much as occurs in an initiation into Freemasonry. And because what happens on this side of reality is but a pale reflection of what is to be seen on the other, the dangers of a journey to the other side require the presence at every ritual of a master shaman with mental stability and strength of character. Typical of the opening moments are nausea, vomiting, diarrhea, intense depression, and anxiety.

The chanting resumes, mostly in Portuguese, occasionally in English. A woman with red hair, in her thirties, almost across from me, reaches for a pail and starts to vomit. Her retching sounds like a wild beast in the jungle. She vomits and vomits while one of the female attendants holds back strands of her red hair to keep it from being filthied.

Vomiting, I have been told, is a key point in the Ꭰaime learning process, helping to release the past. As Alex Polari puts it, "Only you can cast away your old identity—the crusts of ego, personality, psychic imbalance, and spiritual obstacles—that once served as a protective shell for differentiating yourself from the spiritual world. . . . Daime accelerates the process in the psyche and dissolves even the most chronic emotional shells that hinder an individual's capacity to see, feel, and be his or her true self."

The Daime obliges one to look at oneself, especially at aspects one doesn't want to see. Seeing ourselves as we really are can be painful, and the pain, as Polari points out, "is usually proportional to our resistance to the Master who wants to show us ourselves."

The concept of healing in the Daime faith is holistic—body, mind, and spirit are treated as a unified organism. Walter Andritzky comments that whereas orthodox analytical therapy offers only fragmentary and partial insight into particular aspects of the self, the holistic vision and confrontation with the true self that is obtained through Daime constitutes "the quintessence of hallucinogenic therapy." The Daime opens the door to seeing our former incarnations and to understanding them in the context of our present one: in other words, to understand our karma.

A beefy man of almost fifty pushes past me to fall on his knees and vomit into one of the waiting buckets with even more bestial retching. The woman with the red hair moans and groans, her face chalk white, a mask. Another woman, young, with dark hair and a gossamer white dress, in trouble, is escorted by the attendants toward a mattress, on which she is laid out and covered with a sheet.

Now all the chairs are removed for dancing: one-two-three steps to the right, one-two-three to the left, the chanting rhythmic and loud, the singers, both men and women, partaking with increasing passion.

According to Gary Dale Richman, a Daime aficionado, the hymns play an important role during the difficult psychological "passages" undergone by the novices, keeping them on track as each hymn refers to principles and teachings of the doctrine. "The hymns help translate the most mysterious or unknown visions into familiar language and thus permit us to witness another type of knowledge that normally can't pass through the guards of reason."

According to E. J. M. Langdon, a professor at the Universidade Federal de Santa Catarina, in Florianopolis, Brazil, author of many articles on the ritual use of yaje, the spirits have their own designs and songs, which they teach to the yaje drinker once he can see them, and each apprentice tries to have as many visions and learn as many songs as possible. "As he enlarges his repertoire, so he increases his power with the spirits he already knows and can deal with."

The dancing, they say, plays an important role in forming a strong spiritual current among the participants. It has been described as almost like preparing bread dough, with the energy, stretched and kneaded, becoming almost visible as it condenses and expands around the congregation.

I begin to feel a pain in my heart and seem to be losing a bit of the sensation in my hands—usually a sign of stress that seems to affect my heart. Worrying about it only increases the stress.

Almost three hours have passed. Half a dozen men and women have either vomited or been stretched out on mattresses at the entrance to the church.

It is time for the second dose. I look for my mentor to tell him of my symptoms and to ask if he thinks it wise for me to continue with more yaje.

He says he will consult the Brazilians. Almost everyone has had a second dose by the time my mentor takes me to the head Brazilian. The woman interprets. When she hears my problem she laughs out loud. Not to worry! She has had three heart attacks and a tumor on her heart. The Daime, she assures me, is good, very good, for the heart.

Heartened, I approach the altar and consume my second dose. More chanting. Back in my place, I begin to feel odd. If I close my eyes and rest them in my hands, I see against a deep dark palpable void very fine corkscrew lines, bright scarlet, spinning in patterns that fill the screen. It is not unpleasant, actually rather attractive, indicative of some sort of spiral movement on a very small scale, a sort of rendition of the subatomic world.

But now I am worried that I may lose control and that the unpleasant visions may start. As I look down at my hands they turn into jaguar paws, and I feel the great energy in them as I unfurl the claws. My mouth opens into a fanged snarl.

Better keep lucid, I reflect, and invoke my guardian angel to keep me sane and sober.

By now the vomiting is continuous all around me, and one after the other more mattresses are spread before the entrance to receive more women, moaning and groaning, or making strange gestures, flexing arms and legs, rubbing their distended stomachs. The men, though fewer of them, also on mattresses, have mostly passed out cold.

A man in front of me, about forty, with a strongly lined face—I'm not sure whether German or Dutch—appears to be drunk, moving his arms and legs haphazardly to the music, as if not quite in control. Others, their eyes closed, appear lost in reverie, moving rhythmically to the chanting or making strange movements with their heads.

I worry that my visions may be starting. So I keep my eyes open and thank heaven, as I close them briefly, that I still have my safe familiar screen of black to fall back on. I am determined not to vomit.

We have been at it for almost four hours. Now comes a break as marijuana cigarettes are passed around. Soon over a hundred devotees are puffing pot in great deep breaths. Slowly the nave is awash with light blue smoke that drifts up toward the arc lamps, filling the church to the rafters with eerie clouds, almost alive.

I take only one short puff. I hate the taste and the way it scratches my throat, and I don't like feeling stoned. This, however, is part of the spiritual ritual. Followers of Daime believe that the weed acts as a key to unlock quicker access in their minds to communion with the Virgin Mary, "Queen of the Rainforest." Hence their name for the magical leaf: Santa Maria. Devotees claim that smoking it increases communion, directly through her, with the spirit of the Daime, a spirit much like Steiner's Christlike spirit of the earth.

Surfeited with inhalation, the devotees chant on.

> *Quem nao conhece Santa Maria*
> *E faz uso dela todo dia*
> *Vive sempre em agonia*
> *Mas agora chegou como eu queria.*
> He who knows not Santa Maria
> Or does not use it daily
> Forever lives in agony.

The last line in English escapes me as I try to visualize how the real Madonna might appear. Medieval and Renaissance art somehow

---

1. As Easton elucidates Steiner's concept, the Christ, after his incarnation, death, and resurrection, became the spirit of the earth: "The bread and wine, fruits of the earth, are indeed his body and blood." This truth, according to Easton, is not symbolic but a fact of complete actuality, "and if we are to have a conscious relationship with the earth, we should know that in building this relationship we are performing what in the highest sense of the word may be called a Christian duty."

misses the mark. Is what appears at Lourdes or Madjougorgie "real." or mass suggestion? Does she really have to assume the garb of a Nazarene? I see Isis, naked, smiling tenderly, pointing to her mons veneris and its radiantly creative orifice, entrance and exit to the eternal void.

All around me men are in various stages of intoxication, and I try to imagine them as brothers, to see through their eyes. It is difficult. I feel alienated and alone. Somehow I wish to retain my individuality, not merge in the common view, not become an automaton in an other-directed hypnotic daze. I conclude that if I am to become clairvoyant, see the spirit world, it will have to be through assiduously following Steiner's careful indications, retaining as much as possible of my lucidity, waiting for the spirit world to manifest whenever it will. This shortcut does not appeal to me. But then I realize that I am armored against change and may be fighting precisely what is best for me.

Suddenly I get another view of my nitrous oxide nightmare. The idea that the entire universe communicates with the interior of our bodies and minds has been part of esoteric religious tradition for thousands of years. As I remember that my only recourse against the horror of the nitrous oxide was to give in to it and let it do its worst, I conclude that my fear of losing consciousness is vain. All I can ever do is move from one level of consciousness to another, that indeed there is no exit, whether through drug or accident or death. All is here and now forever. As Steiner says of consciousness: that's all there is. The universe is consciousness, and each of us is part of it, holographically, perhaps. So, as Polari puts it, "Once we experience the irrefutable sensation of the universe within us, the only possible path is to surrender pleasurably to the knowledge that we are the universe—both the whole and the part."

Not an easy concept for a child of nine, nor perhaps for a sage of ninety, leaving but a single choice: to do unto others as one would have others do unto one: love and admire. As the apostle Paul phrased it after his bout with the light on the road to Damascus, "All of the law is fulfilled in one word: thou shalt love thy neighbor as thyself."

Walking out into the cool Dutch night, I approach a great linden tree, majestic in the moonlight. With my hand I can feel the etheric life within its trunk, but I realize that before I can truly see and communicate with its spirit I will have to purge myself of a lot of darkness—whether by Daime, by Steiner, or by some other path remains to be seen.

One thing is certain: I will not be the same again in this life.

Epilogue

Clearly the cure for both the planet and our individual souls is one and the same: initiation to clairvoyance, eventually for one and all. In the ancient mysteries the job was easier for the hierophant, who could separate the upper part of the candidate's etheric body. He could take it traveling, along with his astral body, for three and half days into the spiritual world, leaving the candidate's ego in its physical body in a deathlike state devoid of physical consciousness, a state different from ordinary sleep. Steiner, reading from the Akashic Record, describes this process in Atlantean times when a looser connection between etheric and physical bodies allowed the initiator more easily to withdraw the candidate's etheric body. This gave the candidate access, through the initiator's own ego, to the hierophant's wisdom and clairvoyant vision, revealing to the candidate the world of spirit. It was a vision, imprinted by the candidate's astral body onto his etheric body, that became available to the candidate's awakened ego along with the realization that he was not a body but a spirit actually inhabiting the spiritual world, at one with the Spirit that underlies all creation.

Over the centuries, as the etheric body became more closely molded to the physical, a near-death experience was required to separate the two; hence John the Baptist's initiation by prolonged submersion in water. Nowadays, says Steiner, by means of a Rosicrucian or Christian initiation, it is possible to become clairvoyant without withdrawing the etheric body. Instead, the candidate retains full consciousness as he or she obtains access to the higher spiritual worlds, a condition hopefully to become available to all humankind, giving access to the entire hierarchy of spiritual beings.

Were one to subscribe to Steiner's notion that the workings of these beings are actually what scientists call "the laws of nature," it might be possible, says he, to integrate one's efforts with theirs and to lead this planet back to its proper state as a Garden of Eden, thriving and healthy. But time is running out.

When fifteen hundred of the world's most distinguished and senior scientists, including a hundred Nobel laureates, issue an urgent warning (as they did in Atlanta in 1992) that we are approaching a crisis situation, that the loss of natural ecosystems around the world promises to approach catastrophic levels with the extinction of 20 percent or more of the planet's plant and animal species, and that this could soon render the globe unable to sustain life, it would seem to be time for action. Yet the establishment continues to drag its filthied feet: especially the chemical, drug, tobacco, and arms establishments.

The idea that a few moguls could deliberately set about destroying the planet for mere lucre would seem preposterous were it not for Steiner's warning that Ahriman (whom he equates with Mammon and Mephistopheles) resides in gold. If nothing is done to stem this tide, the result, Steiner prophesied, will be the "War of All Against All" from which but a few will escape—by means unspecified—to repopulate a reincarnated and redeveloped planet.

What we should be doing, says Steiner, is learning to transform nature by developing our innate talents, cooperating with the world of spirits. Human beings, says Steiner, need no longer be dependent on what Nature freely gives us; as creative artists we can shape and transform Nature by first becoming master crafters of the inanimate—*vide* the transformation of minerals into Rolls Royces and stones into a *Pietà* or a Taj Mahal—on our way to becoming master crafters of all that is living—plant, animal, and human—which, as they appear today, "are but germs of what they are to be."

For anthroposophists the world is not woven out of the atoms of the scientist but out of "such stuff as dreams are made on," out of conscious imagination. The very being of the world, says Steiner, springs not from dead matter but out of living thought. "Just as ice is frozen water, the material world is frozen thought. What you think today, that you will be tomorrow."

Humans, as artistic creators, can learn to build with atoms through the power of thinking. "When man has learned to think right into the mineral atom, when he has an understanding of how to make use of what lives in the atom and place it at the service of the whole, then will man be able to transform nature through his own spirituality." And this must not be forgotten: "Spiritual beings originally had the imaginations, inspirations, and intuitions—the ideas and the thoughts—according to which the world surrounding us was created." That is how it was. Now it is up to us.

The very purpose of the unfoldment of the cosmos, in anthroposophic eyes, is to facilitate the manifestation of humanity, for humanity to develop its I-consciousness. Human beings, we are assured, are being given the opportunity by divine worlds to achieve our spiritual freedom. Thereafter we can ourselves direct our own future evolution.

To follow this highway solely on the basis of Steiner's clairvoyant views, with no greater light than the candle of his spiritual science, does require a leap in the dark. But then so does death. Only death to Steiner is a mere interlude between lives in which to prepare for the following round. When Steiner speaks of death, he warns specifically about finding oneself in that state without benefit of his prophetic description of its scenery, its inhabitants, and what behavior is expected from new arrivals. He likens the situation to trying to find an address in an unknown city without benefit of road map. But it is not a city in which one finds oneself; it is the universe—a locale that Keppler, Newton, and Einstein have left as much a puzzle as before they applied their science.

As Hodson pointed out, there is little or no scientific knowledge about either the universe or humanity as far as their origin, purpose, goal, and mutual relationship is concerned. From acceptable scientific sources, humans have no idea why the universe exists with all its contents, where it came from, who created it, whither it is tending, and whether it is guided or just continues in a haphazard way.

A right attitude toward science, says Steiner, will recognize that its knowledge is illusion. "More knowledge, more wisdom, and more truth are to be found in genuinely old myths, fairy tales and legends than in the abstract erudition and science of the present day."

Hence the importance of Leadbeater and Besant for having validated, with their siddhi powers, the scientific basis of the ancient wisdom. But to solve the dichotomy between modern science and the ancient wisdom, or gnosis, one must clearly become clairvoyant, whether through exercise in meditation or through a sudden leap.

And there's the rub: the void. To become a true initiate one must learn to deal with the void. Of this "most terrible trial before initiation," the initiate Ouspensky, Russian devotee of Gurdjieff, is explicit: "Nothing exists. A little miserable soul feels itself suspended in an infinite void. Then even this void disappears! There is only infinity." Already in his *Tertium Organum* Ouspensky noted that nitrous oxide stimulates the mystical consciousness in an extraordinary way. "Depth beyond depth of truth seems revealed to the inhaler." And he quotes one inhaler: "No words may express the surpassing certainty that one is realizing the primordial Adamic surprise of life."

ı Steiner, writing before Ouspensky, premises his solution to the void by remarking that one does not find much recorded in philosophical literature about people either experiencing this terror facing an infinite abyss or overcoming the fear. He then gives his remedy: one must be able to face the terror, the fear of the fathomless void, the endless emptiness: one must be capable of experiencing an environment completely saturated with fear and terror yet at the same time be able to overcome these feelings through the inner firmness and certainly of one's own being.

Steiner posits two helpful ways: either through an understanding of the Gospels or by penetrating the spiritual worlds "with true, authentic anthroposophy," the latter, in his lexicon, leading to the former.

A person, says Steiner, who truly understands the Gospels—not in the way modern theologians speak about them but rather through absorbing the very deepest of what can be experienced inwardly of the Gospels—"takes something with him or her into the abyss that expands as if from a single point and completely fills the void with a feeling of courage. . . . If when we must face the terrifying void we take either the Gospels or anthroposophy with us we cannot get lost or plunge into the infinite abyss."

To enter higher worlds, Steiner's advice is simple: "Only through an intensified sense of self-surrender can a human being work towards the higher worlds. The soul must be empty and quietly able to wait for what it can receive out of the spaceless, timeless, objectless, eventless, secret, hidden world."

For those who survive the trial and recover their clairvoyant sight, their reward will be to recognize, in the etheric body of the planet, not Ahriman or Lucifer, but the Sun Spirit, the Christ, just as described by the ayahuasca followers of Irineu. To Steiner, the second coming is not the Sun Spirit's reappearance in the flesh but a gradual awakening in the human being of clairvoyant vision with which to see, with spiritually opened eyes, the etheric Christ in spiritual possession of the globe.

Index